Written Off

Written Off

Paul Carroll

Matador
9 Priory Business Park,
Wistow Road, Kibworth Beauchamp,
Leicestershire. LE8 0RX
Tel: 0116 279 2299
Email: books@troubador.co.uk
Web: www.troubador.co.uk/matador
Twitter: @matadorbooks

ISBN 978 1785890 284

British Library Cataloguing in Publication Data.
A catalogue record for this book is available from the British Library.

Printed and bound in the UK by TJ International, Padstow, Cornwall
Typeset in 11pt Minion Pro by Troubador Publishing Ltd, Leicester, UK

Matador is an imprint of Troubador Publishing Ltd

For Sophie

The rain had long stopped and the air was cool. Large puddles from the storm still dotted the piazza and he took care to step around them. As he neared the rotunda he caught sight of a dark shape floating in the water on the edge of the ornamental lake. The flickering overhead sodium light made it difficult to pick out the silhouette and he stepped closer for a better look. As he peered at the unmoving form the buzzing of the damaged light fitting seemed to get louder, as if he was being attacked by a swarm of hornets. Finally, his focus adjusted sufficiently to discern a naked corpse floating face-down in the water.

CHAPTER ONE

Would Charles Dickens have been as successful an author if another writer with the same moniker had already troubled the bestsellers list? The same could be asked of Enid Blyton, Agatha Christie or Virginia Woolf as unlikely, in their cases, a literary namesake might have been. Surely these writers would have felt compelled to adopt a *nom de plume* in such a case, if only to avoid comparison, never mind confusion? That this question should pop into the mind of aspirant novelist Eric Blair at this very moment was understandable. A door lay ready to open before him; a fork in the road awaited a footstep either side of the signpost marked 'success' and 'failure'.

While another writer, untroubled by fear of odious comparison due to the name on his birth certificate, opined that a rose by any other name would smell as sweet, Eric's conviction about using his formal appellation for his incipient career as an author was once more beginning to falter. His initial thoughts on the matter had been far from hesitant. First off, it was his name, so why change it? Secondly, he'd adroitly promoted his middle initial, P for Peter, to preclude any mistaken identity, so where was the problem? Thirdly, the handle Eric Blair hadn't been deemed good enough for the original owner to write under so the way was clear for him. This Eric, for one, wasn't ashamed of his real name. In any event, in the name game lottery it could have been worse. What if he'd been christened Anthony and was right now being mistaken for the PM who had sent troops into Iraq and Afghanistan, glad-handed Gadaffi and cosied up rather too intimately to the Fourth Estate? Yes, that would have been far more disconcerting.

Eric had long held the belief that his name was an invitation to put pen to paper and to continue a literary lineage of sorts. He was proud of his name and confident in his writing ability. He derived great pleasure from the fact that his first novel had been crafted, chiselled and honed over many years of dedicated endeavour, application and toil (he tended to overlook his abandonment of family duties in this assessment). But to what end? Writing and finishing his opus had been challenging enough. Trying to get it published was an altogether more demanding and difficult proposition. He hadn't expected it to be this hard. Of course, he told anyone who would listen that it was a very competitive market, that you needed a bit of luck to get an initial break, but deep down Eric truly believed that the call would come his way, sooner rather than later. After all, there couldn't be that many manuscripts knocking around that matched the genius contained in his. But all he'd received so far was studied indifference. Rejections from literary agents hurt. At first, he affected nonchalance as if he accepted that this was all part of his 'journey'. His wife Victoria, knowing him better, purchased a sign for his desk reading, 'Shoot for the moon. Even if you miss, you'll land among the stars'. Eric, not normally given to twee sentimentality and enduring its presence so as not to offend, was lately beginning to tend towards Isaac Asimov's rather more downbeat observation that 'Rejection slips… are lacerations of the soul, if not quite inventions of the devil'.

Of the twelve submissions (the very term denotes capitulation) made to literary agents, so far he'd received back six rejections, all of which, he knew, were standard templates. However, subsequent to these responses ('response' in the same sense that a brick thrown through a window constitutes correspondence) Eric was to discover that there was an ignominy far worse than receiving these clipped and cheerless missives; that was not receiving a reply at all. For literary agencies were quite clear in their 'don't call us, we'll call you' rules of engagement – 'if you haven't heard from us in ten to twelve weeks, assume that your submission doesn't match out needs'.

So, sixteen weeks on from the joyous animation and the giddy ceremony of hitting 'send' a dozen times it's fair to say that Eric's literary aspirations had received somewhat of a battering. Not that he ever questioned whether his work was good enough – such a heresy never entered his head. Instead he began to ruminate whether the name he'd always considered a blessing was in fact a curse – were these agents laughing at him from behind the crenellated battlements that passed for offices?

There was a reason this thought was uppermost in his mind at this moment. An unexpected event – a ping on his laptop heralding the arrival of fresh tidings, an announcement of note, a vital 'life or death' message. Idly, Eric had checked the sender – no doubt urgent advice on how to replace his toners at discount, enlarge his wedding tackle or get laid locally. But no – he could see it was from the Motif Literary Agency. The agency he'd blustered that if he could pick one literary specialist from the modest dozen he'd courted, he'd sign up with them like a shot (subject to terms, of course). And that's why Eric was hesitating or, more accurately, locked in a temporary state of paralysis. If he opened the email, what would it portend? As he contemplated the bold type at the top of his in-box he realised that it emanated from *submissions@motiflit.co.uk* – this response was not being sent to him personally by Motif's celebrated Hugo Lockwood, the agent Eric had identified at the outset of his quest as being his Svengali-in-waiting. Still, Hugo couldn't be expected to answer all of his own mail – perhaps he shouldn't read too much into the sender. It was a reply after all. Still petrified at the point midway between fear of disappointment and entitled expectation, Eric willed himself to click 'open'.

From the age of four he knew that to read anything he should start at the top, scan from left to right and make his way down to the bottom of the page. This, he understood, would be the most effective method of absorbing the substance of the words now expanding to fill the screen before him. But there's a curious phenomenon that grips the anxious. Rather like eying one's dinner plate and deciding to eat everything on it in a single gulp, Eric tried to take in the text before him in one go, to understand its meaning all the quicker. This had the unfortunate effect of trying to read a fruit machine in mid-tumble with the icons reeling and falling in a blur. As the cylinders subsided Eric could finally work out what he'd won. A cherry: 'Sorry'. A banana: 'disappoint'. A lemon: 'not for us'. He was going to have to play again. And all without the aid of a nudge function.

Hugo Lockwood was late for his lunch appointment and cursing under his breath as he burst through the door of the Lamb and Flag in Covent Garden. There, sitting awaiting him in the corner, was Emily Chatterton who at least appeared to be preoccupied as she deftly tapped away at her mobile phone. Hugo immediately suspected that she was announcing his tardiness to the rest of the planet. In the pecking order of the literary world an agent being late for an appointment with the Editorial Director of a leading publisher wasn't normally a brilliant career move so he was relieved to see Emily's smile on spotting him, immediately removing any fear of recrimination for his lack of punctuality. In any event, it was Emily who had called for this 'quick get-together' at short notice so formality wasn't the priority here. Hugo and Emily went back a long way and considered themselves friends – not unusual in an industry where constantly letting your friends down was par for the course.

Kisses on cheeks, apology, acceptance of apology and condemnations of London traffic out of the way, the two relaxed. Hugo didn't yet know the purpose of the meeting. When Emily emailed the previous afternoon to enquire if he was around this lunchtime his Pavlovian response was a straightforward 'yes'. As a senior player at Franklin

& Pope, one of the biggest publishers he dealt with, she wouldn't want to see him for anything trivial so it would be impolite to enquire as to her agenda. Despite the hierarchy at play there was a tacit understanding of their mutual dependence – he sold his authors and their books to her, so she was the client; she'd buy from him but still shop elsewhere while making sure she didn't get pipped by a competing publisher when he had a real gem to offer. It was complicated in the same way a professional gambler courts a racehorse trainer – the inside info increased the odds of cleaning up but you could still spill your guts on 'guaranteed' tips.

The choice of this 'quick-lunch' rendezvous was also of interest. Not a restaurant which might denote a deal celebration, a fervid planning session or a softening up exercise ahead of a pre-emptive bid. A pub, where he'd have a quick chicken, bacon and guacamole sandwich and a single pint of Frontier and she'd order the feta, hummus, tomato and watercress sandwich with a small bottle of Perrier. Practical, utilitarian, businesslike. While they awaited their order there was no attempt to tackle the reason they were there – protocol dictated that this would wait until napkins were discharged. Instead they talked about the brave, possibly northern, patrons who were availing themselves of the outside tables on this sunny but chill Spring day, and of the latest amusing cat video on Vine. When the food arrived Hugo moved the discussion back towards publishing by describing, in comic detail, the attire and antics of several of Emily's competitors he had encountered at a party hosted by Orion the previous evening. Emily was all ears. Hugo then raised next month's London Book Fair – his way of inviting Emily to tell him what Franklin & Pope were planning to do for his authors.

Finally, Emily was ready. At least she didn't beat around the bush. 'Hugo, I'm afraid I have some disappointing news. We're not going to be taking up our option on Reardon's final book.'

Hugo's expression betrayed that he'd not factored this possibility into the many equations he'd formulated since receiving Emily's lunch invitation. Reardon – Reardon Boyle – was one of Hugo's most renowned authors and had sold steadily over the years. For Christ's sake, he'd won critical praise from the broadsheets, had seen one novel turned into a TV series and currently decorated his work-study with at least two lumps of plastic that passed for awards these days. Emily was giving Reardon – and therefore him – the bullet? Hugo knew, from his days of being bullied at school, that it wasn't helpful to show pain even when one was dying inside – it tended to encourage further treatment being dished out. 'Really? I'm surprised,' he croaked as the disappointment thrust his head down the toilet bowl.

Emily, having ripped off the plaster in double quick time, could now afford to be concilatory. 'Listen, Hugo, it's been a very difficult decision for us to make. And when I say "we", I have to tell you that I personally fought tooth and nail against this.'

Hugo ignored this last comment to proffer a weak, 'But he's selling well?'

'He's selling steadily rather than "well" and steadily isn't enough these days, Hugo, you know that.

Existentialism is dead. It's not where it's at these days. We don't think taking up our option on the final book makes sound economic sense.'

Hugo suppressed his urge to argue, despite the bitterness he felt at this unexpected dousing. Not least because he had other authors with Franklin & Pope to worry about. 'That's very, very disappointing news. Reardon will be devastated.'

'We could be doing him a favour, Hugo. Think about it like that. You'll place him with another publisher who can give him the sort of support we can't at this moment. This could turn out to be a really good move for him.'

Hugo looked rueful. Adroit in the art of deflection he smiled and said, 'Well I'll tell him, of course. Can't give everybody good news all of the time.'

'Thanks, Hugo. I knew you'd understand.'

And Hugo did understand, knowing that the ripple that had just washed over him emanated from the rather large rock Emily had dropped into the Franklin & Pope pool eighteen months before.

'Spring is a time of plans and projects,' chirruped Chapman Hall, a man never far from a literary quote. The entrepreneur was in upbeat mood since he was about to start putting the flesh on the bones of his greatest achievement, his biggest love, the annual 'The Write Stuff' conference for unpublished writers. His PA, Suzie Q (an inevitable nickname given her baptismal name of Susan Quixall), sat opposite him with three bulging files – one red, one yellow, one blue – laid out neatly on his desk. Mindful of Chapman's ongoing struggle to constrain his stomach within the ever-tightening waistband of his trousers she had been out to buy calorie-counted prawn mayonnaise sandwiches and fruit pots from Marks & Spencer for their working lunch. She had also ensured that there was skimmed milk to accompany the large pot of coffee she'd prepared. The rest of the staff at The Write Stuff knew better than to disturb them over the next two hours.

Chapman, momentarily disappointed that there were no hand cooked vegetable crisps on hand to bulk out his lunch, got down to business. 'Right, Suze. This is going to be the most successful Write Stuff conference to date. You know how we're going to do that?'

Suzie thought for a second. 'By keeping to last year's prices?'

Chapman swallowed hard on his sandwich (his third already) indicating that the pegging of rates did not figure especially highly in his strategy for the upcoming conference. 'No, Suze. We're putting the prices up, but that's not it. What we're going to do this year is sell "fear". Find a way to convince all those poor buggers out there trying to get published that if they don't come to us, they're never going to make it. I want these people to fear not being in the know, to fear failure, to fear rejection, to fear that they're wasting their lives spending all those hours tap, tap, tapping away.'

Suzie looked up at the huge, framed poster on the wall created for last year's conference. Back then the theme was markedly different. Chapman's sales mantra twelve months ago had all been about creating belief, desire and expectation, the art of the possible and the wind of change.

Chapman's face, copying the iconic Shepard Fairey poster of Barack Obama, stared back down at her. Beneath it the word 'HOPE' remained unaltered. She scribbled down 'fear' on her notepad and underlined it three times.

Chapman loved authors. He positively adored them. In particular he reserved unqualified and abundant affection for writers who had yet to step up to the big time and get a publishing deal. Helping to transform these literary ugly ducklings into swans was the reason he'd set up The Write Stuff ten years ago. And what a move that was turning out to be. In contrast to the publishers and agents whose golden age was now a fond remembrance, The Write Stuff continued to make a killing on the back of the burgeoning market of wannabe writers, all desperate to get into print. For Chapman, it was like shooting fish in a barrel – no matter what new services or events he created 'to help authors find an agent' or 'to become a better writer', they would come forward in increasing numbers to seek his wisdom, happy to pay big money to do so. But the market was starting to get crowded as new competitors and national broadsheet newspapers tried to cash in on his territory with their own writing seminars, talks and workshops. Chapman knew he had to keep a step ahead and above all, keep polishing The Write Stuff's halo at every opportunity. Credibility was everything in this game.

Chapman crammed a fourth sandwich into his mouth as he contemplated his own genius. 'Yes, Suze. Get the creative team on that. Along the lines of, "without Listerine you'll have halitosis for the rest of your life" or something. How many are signed up so far, anyway?'

Despite the booking window not yet being officially

open, The Write Stuff took 'privilege' bookings the month following each annual conference where delegates could 'sign up for next year at this year's prices'. It was a gift from a cashflow point of view.

Suzie consulted the yellow folder. 'Seventy-five to date – a record.'

'Good. Excellent,' Chapman said. 'So we have 225 to go.' This year's target of 300 delegates would be a record for his writer support community. 'So, who do we have signed up so far on the experts side?' Chapman knew that to maintain the conference's appeal he needed to secure the attendance of topline names from the literary agency and publishing worlds. These names would persuade his ugly ducklings to commit to a weekend holed up in the cramped confines of the Lancaster university campus, dropping whatever they were doing to traverse the country to touch the hems of the professionals who could transform them into the next Ian Rankin, Sebastian Faulks or Gillian Flynn.

Suzie, this time referencing the blue folder, began to reel off the names of the agents and editors who had agreed to excrete their pheromones on her boss's behalf this coming September. Chapman, now on his sixth sandwich, held up his hand to stop her. 'No offence, Suze, but this is the same as last year's list. We need fresh blood; we need some big hitters. We need to stick some top writers in there as well. This lot are Championship level and we need Premier League if we're going to kick on.'

Suzie made another note on her pad, adding 'bigger hitters' below 'fear'.

Chapman shifted his bulk on his high back swivel chair, pleased they were making progress. Now he had another pressing question for his forbearing PA. 'Do you want that last sandwich, Suze?'

CHAPTER TWO

Alyson Hummer glanced at the bedside clock as she manoeuvred on to all fours. She had thirty minutes before she had to pick up the children from school. As her companion energetically thrust away behind her she made a mental note to remember three key details. One – his extraordinary bodily hair once he'd stripped off. Two – the raucous grunting that accompanied his lovemaking. Three – that he came fully equipped with his own impressive banana.

Alyson didn't know the name of the Simian seducer grinding away behind her – she had only met him an hour before and no names were to be exchanged during their short liaison. Of all the gifts the Internet had bestowed upon society the ability to arrange no-strings sex was, for Alyson at least, one of the most useful. Some people might condemn Alyson's leisure predilections, or counsel caution over the risk of exposing herself – in every sense of the word – to men she'd never met before. But Alyson didn't give a hoot what other people thought and in any event would occasionally experiment with females too. These same people sitting in silent judgement may also have been hard-pressed to pick Alyson out in an identity

13

parade convened to finger a venturesome, vascular, vamp. She certainly wasn't pretty in a conventional sense, or in an unconventional sense for that matter. She was short and dumpy, the wrong side of forty, bought her clothes from Matalan and sported a pair of spectacles that would have found favour with Dame Edna Everage. But beauty isn't only skin deep and in the eyes of many beholders once Alyson turned on her love lights she burned with an inner sensuousness that transcended all outward trappings of so-called glamour. It was a perfectly simple equation – she was up for it and men could tell she was up for it.

After her companion shuddered to a halt – she was slightly disappointed he didn't beat his chest in this moment of release – Alyson manoeuvred herself off the bed and started to pick up her clothes.

'Smoke?' said the hairball, reaching for a packet of cigarettes from the shirt he had jettisoned to the floor. Alyson merely pointed at the 'no smoking' sign on the bedside table and continued to get dressed. Hairball grunted again, this time not due to the throes of passion. Alyson reminded herself that conversation was rarely the priority in liaisons of this nature – they'd barely exchanged one hundred words since meeting in the car park of this budget hotel for their rapid, recreational romp. She withdrew to the bathroom for a few minutes to make herself school playground ready. When she re-emerged into the bedroom, Cornelius – she'd already decided this would be his name – was boiling the kettle and fussing over the tray of complimentary hot beverages and shortbreads. 'Tea?' he ventured.

Alyson, noting that he was getting his money's worth, shook her head and jerked her thumb back over her shoulder towards the door, indicating that she had to leave. He nodded back and focused his attention on peeling the lid off a fiddly UHT milk pot provided for the convenience of guests. As he did so, the sight of his furrowed brows and slack-jawed gaping mouth with tongue thrust out confirmed to Alyson that Cornelius as a name was definitely a good choice. Brief as their encounter was their farewell didn't exactly rival that of Trevor Howard and Celia Johnson.

Outside, in her car, Alyson dug out her iPhone and tapped some bulletpoints into the notes app: *Hairy like a gorilla. Grunt, pant, shunt. Unzip a banana. King Kong? King Dong? Cornelius/Planet of the Apes. Primal Urge? Let's go Ape.* She smiled as she put the mobile back into her handbag and switched on the car ignition. Yes, Let's go Ape would do very nicely. She couldn't believe that now she'd married her favourite pastime to writing about it she could honestly justify the afternoon's activities as researching her next book.

'Please, pretty please,' pleaded Bronte, placing her hands together in supplication and cocking her head to one side while casting a doe-eyed look in her father's direction. It was a look he knew well and one that, despite his oft-repeated protestations that this would be the last time, he was incapable of resisting. At the age of 23 it would be reasonable to expect that most children would be off their parents' hands and maybe earning a living. Embarked on a career and having a fair idea as

15

to what they wanted to do with the rest of their lives. Of course, if pressed, Bronte would argue that she had all of these staples well and truly in hand: she was temporarily earning a living working in her mum and dad's hotel and restaurant in the Malvern Hills, she had long ago decided on a future as an author, and by the time she was forty Bronte Damson books would have inspired countless TV and film adaptations. She would be known around the world.

'How much is it?' asked Adrian Damson, wearily.

'It's really good value, Dad. It's called Pathway to Publishing and it's all about getting an agent and a publishing deal. It's only one day, and…'

'I asked how much, Bronte.'

'£180, but you get a lot for that. I wouldn't ask but this is just perfect for me to find out what I need to do to get published. Won't you be able to get the VAT back anyway?'

Her father let this masterpiece of fiscal legerdemain slide past unchallenged. 'Aren't you putting the cart before the horse here? You're a long way off getting published, Bronte – you've only just started writing.'

'I know, Dad, but that's why it's so important that I find out all of this stuff now. It will really help me in my writing; stop me making mistakes. It could be the most valuable £180 ever.'

'If I lend it to you – *lend* – then you'll have to pay me back out of your wages. Agreed?' Bronte, earning a generous stipend for her occasional shifts on reception and waiting on in the restaurant, nodded enthusiastically despite knowing that any form of repayment was as likely as AA Gill dropping in to give her parents' hostelry, The

Perseverance, a five-star review. The deal struck, she then talked him up to £250 to cover her rail fare, at the same time as pointing out how much she had saved by arranging to stay at a friend's flat in London.

Negotiations concluded, Bronte retired to her room to continue work on her trilogy while Adrian sought out his wife, Diana, in the office behind reception. 'I'm afraid I gave in a bit,' he confessed before being asked.

Diana sighed. 'You need to be firmer with her, Ade, really you do. It's not just the money – Bronte not being here means I'll have to cover her shifts and pay twice for the privilege.'

'I know, darling, but she's really serious about her writing and, who knows, it could lead to something really big for her.'

Diana clearly had less faith in her stepdaughter's prospects of hitting publishing pay dirt. 'Why couldn't she be like her friends and get herself a proper job after university?'

'Not all of her friends, Diana. Some are still unemployed. Bronte's working here and she's writing a book – you should be proud of her.'

'I'll be proud of her when she's got this writing fantasy out of her system. For everyone who gets published these days there's hundreds, thousands, who are just stirring the ink.'

Adrian chuckled. Diana could be so negative at times. 'Well, I'll remind you of that when she's up for the Man Booker Prize in ten years' time and she's only got a plus-one invite.'

Con Buckley checked the word count on his manuscript. The menu bar read 75,069. He typed 'The End'. Was it now 75,071 words, or didn't the sign off figure in the tally? He pulled out his baccy tin and rolled himself a celebratory joint. Just a small one, to mark hitting land. Christ, he'd done it. It was finished. He'd only gone and written a book. In the gathering gloom of the late afternoon his computer screen blazed like the tunnel to Paradise, bathing the shabby furniture of the Kilburn flat in golden effulgence. The End? This was the beginning. Sparking his blunt he scrolled to the title page and highlighted the word count figure. He amended '00,000 words' to read '75,000 words'. That would round it off nicely, and account for the title page as well. Immediately he began to fret, not for the first time, that the book might not be long enough. He'd Googled 'typical novel length' on numerous occasions and had initially set himself a target of 100,000 words. But some sites said as long as he hit 60,000 words it would be classified as a novel. He certainly didn't want to fall into 'novella' territory but then he didn't want to run the London Marathon only to finish at Tower Bridge while all of the agents were waiting at Birdcage Walk. In the end he decided his piece of string would be as long as it needed to be. Surely 75,000 words was ample? 80,000 words would have been better though. He took a draw on his micro-joint, sucking the THC deep into his lungs. No – it was finished.

Anyway, describing his work purely in terms of its length – '75,000 words' – struck him as being inadequate and misleading. Why not 448 KB as a measure? It was equally descriptive in a factual sense. Or 426,542 characters (with spaces)? Or 297 pages? They denoted size, but what else? It was like quoting a woman's vital statistics. You say 36-24-36 and it's a combination that automatically unlocks an image of a beautiful, young, curvaceous and nubile goddess. Add your own hair colour. But that was crazy because 36-24-36 could also adequately describe a 90-year-old wizened leper with one leg. What about the *value* of what he'd produced? They didn't ask you to start giving them information on that. Never mind the quality, feel the width. And as for all that crap on presentation formats he'd had to research – how tiresome had that been? Times New Roman, 12 point, double-spaced lines, page numbers, title on every page, indentations and start a new para for each speaker. Well, tick those boxes. They wouldn't catch him out on any of that.

Now he had new tasks to address – the final polish, an overall sense check and a trawl for stray misspelled words and rogue punctuation. Then the synopsis and pitch letter, and a target list of agents to whom he could submit his work. Then... no, forget all that for now. Luxuriate in the moment. Relax. The manuscript, draft 1, was finished. He took another toke, which seemed to trigger another thought – the dedication. He had to dedicate it to Rosie of course but he shouldn't submit his manuscript to agents with a dedication in place – he'd read that sort of stuff was added at proof stage. Still, for the version he was going to print off for Rosie to start reading tonight (he'd settle for one-and-a-half line spacing and double-sided printing on that to save paper) it would be a nice touch. Yes, put 'For Rosie' on there and then print it off for when she got back from working at the delicatessen at 8pm. In the meantime, just a little bit of well-deserved chill-time. Later, given it was a special occasion, he'd make his speciality, gammon and egg, for tea. They'd toast his future success as an author with the cans of Guinness and cider he'd placed in the fridge earlier that day. Poor man's black velvet. Well, not for much longer.

CHAPTER THREE

Eric sat at his computer, furiously typing away. He had a deadline to meet. The Chancellor's annual budget statement was yet to conclude but Eric had to cut through the blubber to get to the bones – how the measures would affect the commercial heartbeat of Greater Manchester. Despite this set-piece news opportunity the editorial floor of the Manchester Evening Chronicle was quiet – it always was nowadays. Twenty years ago, when Eric had started on the business desk as a bright, young graduate, budget day was ringed in red on the calendar for weeks before and the day itself was like a cup final. Phones rang incessantly, voices competed to outshout the person making a call on the next desk, and shock, wonderment and disbelief at the unfolding announcements were met with cheers, boos and laughter – it rivalled a football terrace. They never thought they'd say it then but the one thing they had was time. Time to sit down, discuss and analyse the content before isolating the headlines and adding relevant local and human-interest angles. Nobody expected to see the paper's considered thoughts until the next morning. Today, Eric was tweeting updates at the same time as assembling his news piece on the monitor before him. In fairness, this multi-tasking responsibility was made all the easier by copying and adapting what the BBC was reporting and by keeping an eye on a number of national newspaper Twitter accounts. It was going to be a busy afternoon, especially as he only had two journalists assigned to assist him in doing a live blog, a 'key points' e-bulletin for their database, filing and updating the online version of the story and keeping the Twitter feed going. And they had to do it more quickly – not necessarily better – than the plethora of regional business news websites that continued to steal the bread from their mouths.

Eric had evaded every round of redundancies at the newspaper over the past few years. At first he thought it might be better to take the money and try something new; now he was just grateful he kept missing the cut. That was one of the reasons why his vocation to become a novelist was now an obsession. It often struck Eric that his writing ambition was akin to a busman's holiday. Tap, tap, tap all day; tap, tap, tap all night, hunched in a permanent stoop that had incrementally rounded his shoulders as the years passed – he called it his 'scrivener's slouch' and was quite proud of it if the truth was told. When he first started writing Scrub Me Till I Shine in the Dark it had been through a desire to set himself a challenge, to create something out of nothing, to earn the title of 'author' – it was an end in itself. These days, as his daily routine rivalled that of Sisyphus in its back-breaking, repetitive and futile endeavour, he set his sights slightly higher – nothing short of becoming a 'proper' author would satisfy him. That's why yesterday's latest rejection was all the harder to bear. Sisyphus? Make that

Tantalus, the fruit of the lower branches ever eluding his grasp.

Five minutes after the Chancellor wrapped up, Eric posted his first run at the budget story on the newspaper's website and then immediately checked their rivals' sites to see if they'd been beaten to it. No – they were all still running their preview pieces. Another win. Bloody hell, would he still be sitting here doing this when next year's book balancing beano came around?

Reardon Boyle sat at the kitchen table of his charming end-terrace in Islington, eating his lunch of tomato soup (a carton, not a tin) and a granary roll. He always took lunch between 1pm and 2pm, a break decreed by his strict writing regime. Normally he would do the Guardian crossword and listen to World at One but today, due to the budget, he'd turned on the television to learn what new privations the government was planning to visit upon the hard-pressed populace. As the Chancellor repositioned the deckchairs on the deck of the Titanic, Reardon found himself cursing aloud, unable to contain his anger at the cold-blooded indifference exhibited by the leadership of the country towards the rump of its citizenry. Reardon realised that he was talking to himself or, more accurately, to the television – neither of which was a good sign. Belinda, his wife, had become increasingly concerned at his behaviour of late when he would rail and rant at the slightest provocation. God forbid Reardon having to make a telephone call to his bank, local council or utility providers. Negotiating more numerical permutations than Alan Turing he'd eventually break through the different levels of the game to gain the right to speak to an armour-plated call centre operative; he or she would then decline to address his query until the small matter of his postcode, the third and fifth characters of his password, his account number and the answer to his 'memorable question' had been furnished. Drained by this point even a man of such unimpeachable liberal views as Reardon's would find himself harbouring less than charitable thoughts towards the economic foot soldiers of our former colonies, not to mention the lilt-tongued natives of Tyneside. Belinda tried to discuss his outbursts with him, to discover what was turning him into a 22-carat curmudgeon, but his refusal to acknowledge that there was a problem only made him more agitated still. Deep down he knew that things were getting to him in a way that they never had in the past. He told himself it was simply the pressures of being a successful author – people to see and engagements to attend, never mind actually having to write. But his phone wasn't ringing as much as it used to and there were great swathes of blank pages in his diary. It was like his light was fading; he was turning into the Invisible Man. Well, just wait until he delivered the new novel he was working on – then it would all start again and he'd be moaning about how busy he was on the promo trail, doing press, signings and readings. Fits and starts – that was a writer's life.

As the leader of the opposition stood to give some stick to the honourable member opposite, Reardon's distemper increased. 'Don't let them off the hook, you twat. Is that all you…' His mobile rang. His agent calling him at lunchtime? No doubt trying to impress him. He turned the TV volume down and answered the call.

'Hello, Hugo. Thought you'd normally be studying the wine list at The Ivy about now?'

'Very good, Reardon. If only.'

'You're not watching the budget are you? These bloody cretins need stringing up.'

Grimacing at his bad timing in continuing the cutback theme, Hugo went for it. 'Listen, Reardon. Bad news I'm afraid. No easy way of saying this, but Franklin & Pope have dropped their option on Original Motion. We're going to have to take it elsewhere.'

The members of the Cabinet rocked with merriment on the front benches and slapped each other on the back as if they'd just heard the best joke ever in the history of the whole wide world, delivered by the love child of Dawn French and Max Miller. No sound was needed, because Reardon was receiving their message loud and clear – he knew they were laughing at him. The bastards.

Suzie was armed with just the one folder today – the red one. She and Chapman were discussing budgets too. The diligent PA was an expert at managing costs and knocking suppliers down on price – without her, Chapman's cash cow wouldn't fill quite as many pails. Chapman's financial outlook tended to focus on the yield – he was mainly interested in the figure at the base of the columns, the one that indicated the net profit.

'No biscuits?' Chapman was feeling peckish. Suzie gave him a maternal look – odd, as he was five years older than her – to signify that not only were there no biscuits, there would be none forthcoming either. A slightly disappointed Chapman began the meeting. 'Give me the headlines, then.'

'It's looking very good. The best news is that I've got a fifteen per cent discount on conference facilities and rooms at Lancaster – double last year.'

'You're a marvel – how did you do that?'

'I told them you were thinking of moving the conference to Coventry this year – they were so desperate not to lose us they were throwing offers at me.'

'And we'd budgeted for a ten per cent discount so that should make the bottom line look very sweet,' Chapman laughed, impressed at his right-hand woman's resourcefulness.

'Plus, in the original budget, I'd worked on last year's fee levels, so with the increases you want I've adjusted those figure upwards as well, and that's only based on matching last year's attendance, not beating it.'

'Which we will do.'

'Even in this recession?'

'Listen, Suze. Forget recession and austerity. I've not met one unpublished writer who wouldn't trade their soul to get a publishing deal. What's that collective noun I came up with for wannabe writers? A "despondency", that's it. They'd renounce God, serve up their first born on toast at a vegetarian banquet and tell the Gestapo Anne Frank was upstairs in the attic to get a deal. And that's what we can get them.'

Suzie looked a little uncomfortable. 'We've not had that many people, you know, actually go on and publish a book from the conferences. We do keep getting asked.'

'You worry too much, Suze. I've been there and done it – that's a strong message.' Suzie's eyes widened at this particular sales point. 'And, we connect people – that's the key. We lead the horses to water – it's up to them if they drink.'

Suzie coughed and moved the conversation back to the budget. 'I've managed to squeeze the sponsorship rates up too. I created a few additional categories for new partners to stick their names on. It all helps ring the changes for the delegates too.'

'You're a genius.'

'And I've also agreed expenses for our pros, still at last year's rates.'

'Loving it. Second class rail?'

'I've changed it this year. Do you know it's cheaper to give them first class tickets? Crazy, but it is. It's only the ones travelling on the Friday that cost more, but they'll be off-peak and I'll be doing advance bookings in any case. Obviously, they don't know that, so it's a very nice touch.'

This was all music to Chapman's ears. 'Prudent men woo thrifty women,' he said gleefully, an acclamatory tribute to her economy and coordination. A blush suffused Suzie's neck and rose to her face as she silently cast her gaze downwards to the file on her lap. Her reaction made the unpublished writer's champion realise that he might have selected a better quote to praise his PA. 'Money pads the edges of things' for example.

In the Franklin & Pope meeting room the biscuits were being passed around the table. They always had biscuits at budget planning meetings. Emily Chatterton passed the plate to her left, resisting the temptation to help herself to a bourbon cream. Twelve editors, including four from the publisher's associated imprints, chatted idly while awaiting the arrival of Group Sales Director, Malcolm Sollitt, or 'Rocket' Sollitt according to a much-vaunted reputation for action. Rocket had been brought over from New York following the absorption of Franklin & Pope into the larger Colophon Publishing group six months earlier. The culture clash emanating from the union had resulted in the hard-pressed UK team referring to their new bosses as 'The Bottom Inspectors' – a symbol of resistance not entirely on a par with Tiananmen Square or the Poll Tax Riots.

Emily had completed her twelve-month projections earlier in the month and had forwarded the figures to be collated alongside the other eleven. This was the first opportunity they'd get to see how they stacked up together. A year of expansion or a year of decline. Margin growth or shrinkage. More importantly for the editors, what it would mean for their budgets in the year ahead.

Rocket burst into the room like he was trying to escape the forces of gravity. Such was his normal orbit it was only the second time they'd actually seen him. 'Hi, you guys. Let's do this,' he boomed.

A dozen faces around the table remained blank. Do what?

Rocket declined to sit and addressed them while pacing the floor like a demented tiger. 'First off, budgets. They don't add up,' he snarled. 'Looks like you've taken last year's and added ten percent to everything. That's not going to wash anymore. Blank piece of paper, bottom up is our way.'

Emily let go of the budget she'd prepared as if it had just been taken out of the oven.

Rocket threw a pile of documents on to the table, gesturing for them to be passed around. 'Here's this year's budgets. This is what we're going to be working to.'

Rocket saved the editors the bother of absorbing the figures. 'Read them in detail later, but let me summarise. The author cull – it carries on; we've another forest of dead wood to chop before we're done. Marketing costs – we're going to get smarter and stop throwing cash down the drain, especially in this digital age. New authors – advances are being slashed by seventy-five per cent. Saves enough to keep most of you in a job for another year. Questions?'

The look on the editors' faces didn't reflect how grateful they were feeling for this continuity of employment. Faced with the vacuum of silence Rocket had achieved, Emily bit her lip and, as elder statesperson, moved to initiate dialogue. 'I think we all appreciate the need for cost controls, Malcolm, but I'm a little concerned – I think I speak for others around the table – that cuts on this scale may render us ineffective.'

'Emily, right?' said Rocket. She nodded, already regretting opening her mouth. He fixed her in his sights. '"Ineffective" is an interesting word to use. Because that word has been on my lips this past week as I've been looking at the figures. Are we *effective* at talent spotting? No. Are we *effective* at building sales? Nope. Are we *effective* at making profits? Seven out of ten books don't even pay their way, so that's a big fat round "no" there as well.'

Nobody came to her aid.

'Now, Emily, let me give you an example of what I mean. From last year's figures I see we signed a new author who got a £250,000 advance. To spearhead our new category – "Guilty pleasure for the thinking woman", yeah? We injected another £100,000 into the marketing. How many did we sell?' Rocket wasn't expecting an answer and didn't wait for one. 'Jack Shit, that's what we sold. That single book alone wins every prize going for what's been going wrong in this place, and what I need to fix.'

The blood drained from Emily's face. Would she ever be able to forget she signed Demons Paint Their Lips or would she be forced to carry the shame to her grave?

CHAPTER FOUR

Victoria Blair was taking the weight off her feet at The Art of Tea, a Didsbury bookshop incorporating a café bar (or maybe it was the other way around).

'My treat today, Vic,' said Geraldine, her best friend from when they'd worked together in PR. Now they were both freelancing they'd made it a rule to have lunch together at least once a month.

'I wish I'd known – I'd have suggested going to San Carlo,' said Victoria. She was teasing, but only slightly as she recalled that she'd picked up the tab last month at Harvey Nicks.

They were so busy talking it took the waitress three attempts to take their order. Geraldine was much taken with the bookish setting of their lunch spot. 'Isn't this a lovely idea, Vic? You don't get this at Costa. Maybe they'll have Eric's book in here this time next year.'

Victoria shifted in her chair. 'Not at the rate things are going. I hope not anyway – they're all second hand, aren't they?'

'Oh, yes. I think you're right. He's finished it though, hasn't he?'

'Yes. Last October. It's out with agents now, seeing

if someone will take it on. But nobody's bitten yet.'

'Poor Eric. Still, it took JK Rowling years to get published, and look at her now.'

'I know, Gez, but honestly, it's breaking my heart to see how disappointed he is. He puts a brave face on but it's killing him that no one is interested. Especially after it took nearly three years to write – he thought that was going to be the hard part.'

Geraldine, who thought Eric was a bit up himself anyway, declined to offer any sympathy. 'What's it called? Have you actually read it, Vic?'

'It's called Shine in the Dark – no, Scrub Me Till I Shine in the Dark. Yes, I've read it. It's very good.'

'That's an odd title. Do you think that's the problem? What's it about anyway?'

'Well, you'd have to read it to understand the title. I don't think that's the issue. It's just very competitive to get published these days, that's all. And I don't think there's much call for gritty northern social realism nowadays.'

'What, like Kes or A Kind of Loving? I'd have thought they'd be crying out for something like that these days.'

'Geraldine – they're years old – you're showing your age.'

'Maybe, but isn't it time for the kitchen sink to have a bit of revival? Eric could be at the forefront.'

'I don't see it somehow. No, Gez, it's very dispiriting. Eric reckons Charles Dickens would get Great Expectations turned down these days unless it incorporated Ye Olde Victorian Cooke Book. I don't know where Eric turns to next.'

'Write another?'

'He's not mentioned doing that. All his hopes are pinned on this one.'

'Can't he self-publish? He could have it on Kindle by the weekend. It's easy these days,' suggested Geraldine.

Victoria looked dubious. 'Well, I mentioned that to him, but I may as well have suggested he ran stark-bollock naked down Canal Street. He really bit my head off at the idea.'

'But why? He's spent all that time on it – surely he wants to see it in print one way or another?'

'That's what I thought but he thinks it would be an admission of failure – he reckons self-publishing is an artistic sell-out, pure vanity.'

'Well, everybody else is doing it. No point in doing all that work and then hiding it away. He wants people to read it, doesn't he?'

'Yes, of course, Gez. It's just that his heart is set on a proper agent and a proper publisher – it's that or nothing for him.'

Geraldine thought this attitude typical of Eric. 'Can I have a read of it, Vic, or is it still "for your eyes only"?'

'Eric doesn't want anybody to read it yet, not until it's published.'

Geraldine thought that, too, a matter-of-course for Eric. She stopped herself from voicing what was going through her mind: *I won't hold my breath, then.*

Diana Damson was not best pleased at Bronte's latest no-show for her restaurant duties. 'Short-staffed again this lunchtime. I'm telling you, Ade, she's taking the mick.'

'Did she give you any notice? Maybe something came up?' asked Adrian, not wanting to be too quick to rush to judgement.

'A text, five minutes before service. But you could say it was an emergency – she was buying a wall chart and post-its to help her plan her novel.'

Adrian remained stoic in the face of this latest report of his daughter's dereliction of duty. 'Oh,' he said.

Christine Marks, the founder of online erotica publishing empire, ViXen, was getting turned on at the sight of her sales figures. 'You've got to hand it to Alyson Hummer – top seller again this month.' Since starting ViXen five years previously to cater for women's erotic romance she'd been amazed at how the site had taken off. It was a gift that kept on giving – on one hand she had a growing army of readers whose appetite appeared to be unquenchable; on the other hand she also had an endless supply of new material flowing in from indefatigable authors.

Christine's editor, Robyn Knott, shared her enthusiasm for their top author. 'Yes, impressive. It's her range, I think. Never covers the same ground twice. Very inventive.'

'And her productivity – she can really crank them out. You know she told me she only ever writes about her own experiences? I have to say I find that hard to believe.'

'Really?' said Robyn. 'How does she find the time to write?'

'Exactly. Whether she does or not doesn't matter – Backlash Love Affair has gone straight to number one this month, and A Love You Can't Survive and No Price on Love are still both in the top twenty.'

Robyn was studying the monthly figures. 'She's the only author we have to appear in three categories too. Range again,' she said. To help readers navigate their preferences the ViXen site was helpfully broken down into four classifications: romance, raunch, explicit and hardcore (Alyson still had to feature in romance). As if these choices weren't helpful enough readers could also search and cross-refer by topic – hetero, BDSM, lesbian, ménage and historical being the five most popular. Alyson could tick all of those boxes in her work to date.

ViXen owed its success not only to its means of distribution but also to the discretion of its readers. Word of mouth, particularly on the material that Amazon wouldn't list, had never been as powerful and at an average price of between 99p and £1.99 per download nobody was ever going to complain about value. Where Christine's business model really scored was that, from the outset, she actually paid authors a fair percentage on sales whereas most erotica sites rewarded contributors with a big fat zero. Consequently, ViXen attracted better submissions and could claim the highest editorial standards – a reassuring guarantee of quality for its growing legion of followers. Christine herself formulated the editorial policy pre-launch and it still pertained five years on – all listings had to be passed by the editorial department according to a well-established set of guidelines, the exceptions to the 'anything goes' rule being non-consensual, underage, incest, necrophilia and bestial. Over the past twenty-four months Christine had added audio books, movies and a sex toys retail section to the offer and now Vixen claimed, with some justification, to be the UK's most sophisticated erotica site for women (allowing for the fact that forty per cent of its sales were overseas).

This was a source of great pride to the founder of the business but so too was the democratic and empowering ethos she promoted among the young team she had built up. She encouraged them to have ideas and to make suggestions, which is why Robyn now felt at ease pointing out a potential pitfall that had just struck her regarding their star author. 'You know, we should really look at tying Alyson in, maybe on a three-book deal,' Robyn said, conscious that under their current contractual arrangement Alyson was free to publish her future books anywhere she chose. 'We don't want to lose her – she's a real money-spinner.'

Christine had never extended such a deal to a writer before but could see the logic of Robyn's suggestion. 'You're right. It would be a blow to lose her.'

'She may ask for a bigger percentage – I know I would.'

'Looking at what she shifts, it would be worth it. Yes, I like it – stitch her in before she gets a better offer elsewhere. Smart thinking, Robyn.'

'She's not said "yes" yet, but go for it.'

Yes, Christine thought, *I will.*

Grace Beaumont had a face of stone. 'Honestly, Rosie, I don't know how you put up with it.'

Rosie, not for the first time, regretted mentioning anything to do with Con to her sister but she'd let the cat out of the bag as they shared an after-work drink. 'He was just a bit over-excited, that's all. It's not every day you finish writing a book.'

'Not in his case, no. How long has it taken him? Two years? Longer?'

Rosie ducked the question and took another sip of her Carlsberg. She knew Grace had a point, only she wished she wouldn't labour it quite so hard. Rosie had been upset though as, even by Con's standards, he'd really let her down. She'd not told the whole story to Grace, just the bit about arriving home and finding Con blind drunk with empty cans of Guinness and Magners all over the floor. She'd not mentioned that it was supposed to be a celebration night, that Con was to present her with a print out of his first novel, that the volume of the CD player was turned up to eleven (Paperback Writer no less), that the acrid odour of burnt gammon hung over the cramped flat or that, in addition to the booze, Con was as high as a kite.

In the absence of an answer, Grace continued. 'So now he's "finished his novel" is he going back to work?'

'He will, yes,' Rosie said, trying to cut her sister off at the pass. After a millisecond pause she added, 'Just as soon as he's edited it, and got it out to agents.'

'Oh, Christ, Rosie. And how long is that going to take? If procrastination was an Olympic sport he'd be Sir Steve Redgrave.'

'Just a few more months now, that's all. Then, he's promised if he doesn't get a deal, he'll definitely go back to work.'

Grace knew that speaking to her sister about her boyfriend of four years was a delicate subject but she couldn't help herself. 'It's not that I don't like Con, you know that, Rosie. It's just that you've worked your guts out supporting him and he's taking you for granted. It was only supposed to be for one year.'

'I know, but nobody knows how long it takes to write a book, do they? There are no set rules. It's quality, not quantity or speed, that counts.'

Grace recognised Con's sage pronunciations on creativity being replayed to her and shook her head. 'And I don't want to be negative but you know that the chances of a first-time author getting picked up are pretty slim?'

'Yes, yes, of course. But Con is really confident he's got something really different with this book. It's good to see him so positive.'

'Have you actually read it?'

'Not yet – he wanted to finish it first, but he's going to print it out for me.'

'Let's hope it's not, "All work and no play makes Jack a dull boy" a million times. Has he finally decided on a title?'

Rosie took another sip of her lager. 'It's called A Refugee From the Seraphim.'

Now it was Grace's turn to take a deep draught from her wine glass. Poor, poor Rosie.

CHAPTER FIVE

'A wise man will make more opportunities than he finds.' Chapman was mid-stride during the official launch of the upcoming Write Stuff Conference. His chosen platform for the announcement was his company's one-day 'Pathway to Publishing' seminar where fifty hot prospects already sat pumped and primed – all he had to do was push them over the dotted line. He'd carefully selected the date and the location of the seminar to gain the halo effect of London Book Week taking place in the same venue. His charges, their noses pressed up against the window, could kill two birds with one stone and dream about where in the cavernous halls they'd be next year. 'Can a three-day conference make the difference in finding an agent, securing a publishing deal, making you a better writer?' The wide-eyed audience knew what answer they wanted to hear. 'No other conference – and plenty of imitators have tried to emulate our successful formula – comes close to putting you, the writer, face to face with agents and editors. Experts who will read your work and give you direct feedback. That ten minutes could be the breakthrough moment you've been striving for, the vindication of all the months and years of blood, sweat and tears you've poured into your work.' Chapman had them now. 'I only need to point to the number of successful delegates who've picked up representation from agents after attending our courses. Every year, we get writers placed. This is our seventh annual conference and we've not failed yet. This year, it could be you.'

His stirring words conjured images of Waterstones window displays in the collective imagination of the audience. Chapman pressed on. 'Of course, you may not be at that stage yet. You may be just embarking on your writing career or have a work in progress. My message to you is that The Write Stuff conference is equally, if not more, valuable in that case. Why? Because as well as rubbing shoulders with the most influential agents and editors in the UK and finding out how the industry works, you'll also be able to attend sessions with the best – and when I say the best I mean *la crème de la crème* – literary academics and book doctors in the business who will revolutionise your craft. I guarantee you'll never write the same way again.'

There was more. 'And each year we have guest authors along to share their experiences with us. Why? Because we know writing can be a solitary occupation. When we take time to look up from our keyboards it's reassuring to discover that many people are on the same journey. Some behind us, some ahead, some who've reached their destination. Believe me, it gives one heart, and belief, and renewed determination to succeed.'

Chapman still had his joker to play. 'Above all though, what's the best thing about The Write Stuff conference? Let me tell you. It's the enjoyment and the fun that marks the three days. Do we provide that? No, we facilitate it.

It's you, the delegates, who make the weekend truly come alive. Old friends returning year after year; new friends to be made. It doesn't matter what stage you're at in your writing, or what genre you specialise in, this conference is for you.' There was a murmur of approval and a nodding of heads in front of him. He moved for his closer, shouting out, 'So, who's coming?'

A number of hands shot up, including Bronte Damson's. Chapman reckoned about half. Not bad. Not bad at all. He'd make sure nobody left that evening without having secured their deposits.

Belinda Boyle was trying to cheer her husband up and needed all her reserves of patience to do so. They were having lunch in Balthazar ahead of an afternoon excursion to the National Gallery – her treat. 'You mustn't get despondent, darling. Remember what Hugo said – this could be an opportunity for you.'

Reardon was far from convinced. 'What does that halfwit know? He's well-practised in the art of letting people down gently – I'll give you that. I should have known not to have stuck with him.'

Belinda, losing the will to live, placed the menu slowly back down on the table. 'I think that's a bit harsh. You've always spoken very highly of him in the past.'

'When he was good. When he was interested. When I was his meal ticket. Now he's got too many balls up in the air long-standing clients like me are being taken for granted.' A month had passed since Reardon had learned his option wasn't to be taken up by Franklin & Pope and his mood swings had veered wildly in the interim. His initial disappointment and disbelief at the news was short-lived, to be replaced by lengthy bouts of chagrin. Occasionally he'd surface from the ocean of self-pity to snatch at the lifebelt thrown to him by Hugo, that this might turn out to be a good thing after all. But as the drowning man broke the surface of the vast briny expanse in which he found himself, a ship on the horizon came there none. Faced with the prospect of never seeing land again, he took to railing at the pilot who had steered him into these treacherous waters. 'Complacent, that's what he's become. Bloody complacent. I mean, how much has he earned out of me in the past few years? A fortune, that's what.'

'I'm sure he's earned it,' Belinda said, before realising that the comment could be interpreted in two different ways.

'Earned it? Earned it? Christ, did he write anything? On, no – that was me. Did he even discover me? No – I discovered him. Intermediaries like Hugo are scavengers – they add nothing but still take a cut. An estate agent gives better value when I think about it.'

'Reardon, you know that's not true. If anyone can get you a new deal, it's Hugo. And he's made you money, too.'

'Made me money? Which I have to give him his commission out of as well as paying the taxman. What does that leave me with? Not a lot is the answer. If you took all of the hours I've slaved away writing, and what I've actually earned, a punkawallah with a broken arm would have been on a better day rate.'

Belinda sighed, but she knew that the worse thing she could do was to endorse Reardon's paranoia. 'You're just being impatient, darling. I know it must be hard for you but you must trust Hugo to do his job.'

'I'd trust him as far as I could fire him. Do you know why he'll fail to get me another deal?' It was clearly a rhetorical question because he ploughed on. 'I'll tell you. Because commerce has now replaced culture, that's why. If he does get me a deal it wouldn't be worth having anyway. That's the way things are going these days – advances are in retreat. I'd be better off asking for a job here, waiting on or scrubbing away in the kitchen.'

The waiter who had been hovering to take their order manfully ignored Reardon's last comment as he closed in on the unhappy pair. Belinda looked sorrowfully at her husband. How much longer was she going to have to endure this? She hoped, for the sake of her sanity never mind Reardon's, that Hugo could come up with something, and soon.

Back over at Olympia the man on whom Belinda, if not his client, was pinning all of her hopes was taking a well-earned break from his busy schedule at the London Book Fair. As he looked around for a seat in the busy cafeteria Emily Chatterton beckoned him over to her table.

'Hugo, I didn't think I'd see you in here – are you hiding from someone?'

'Just taking a well-earned breather from the mayhem. But you're here so you must be avoiding somebody too.'

Emily laughed. 'Let's just say I had the same idea as you. We should be safe for fifteen minutes.'

'Aren't you doing a seminar this afternoon?'

'Yes. Will you be coming? I'm sure you're dying to find out why "Bigger is Better" when it comes to publishing?'

'You might have to let me pass on that. Preaching to the converted, obviously. You're going to have to be careful nailing your colours to the mast, aren't you? What if it turns out that the best things come in small packages?'

'I had the same thought myself but unfortunately Rocket agreed to serve me up on this particular topic with onion rings and a side salad.'

'Is Malcolm Sollitt here?' Hugo said. 'I'd really like to meet him.'

'I bet you would, Hugo. You'll have to join the queue I'm afraid. He appears to have a lot of fans.'

'Ah, I take it you're not one of them?'

Emily looked around to check there were no colleagues in earshot before she answered. 'Well, to be honest, he's shaken things up a bit since he arrived. I can see where he gets his nickname from.'

'So I'm right in deducing that Reardon got singed in his afterburners?' Hugo wasn't going to waste this opportunity to confirm his suspicions that all wasn't well at Franklin & Pope.

Similarly, Emily knew how to be loyal and discreet while dishing the dirt. 'Him and another fifteen mid-listers. And he's not going to stop there. You didn't hear that from me, of course. How did poor Reardon take it?'

'Oh, he took it as well as can be expected. He was always a moaning old bastard, so it was hard to tell the difference.'

'Well, I'm sorry, you know that. It's a sign of the times.'

'That "Bigger is Better", you mean?'

'Very funny, Hugo. Have you had any interest for Reardon anywhere else?'

Now it was Hugo's turn to go on the defensive. 'Well, it's early days and all that, but "no" is the answer. He's absolutely plaguing me as well.'

'It will be difficult, I suspect. And if you do get anyone interested, they'll offer a tenth of what he was on before and knowing Reardon he'll tell them to shove it.'

'You've hit the nail on the head, Emily. To be honest, it's a bit embarrassing pushing him *too* hard – it sort of reflects badly on my authors who are on the way up.'

'Flogging a dead horse, literally. How far has he got with Original Motion?'

'Well, that's the irony – it's nearly finished.'

'He could be self-publishing it at this rate.'

'God forbid he'd do that. I think he'd rather take himself off on a one-way trip to Switzerland than do that.'

'Well, changing times. If he'd put some effort into communicating with his readers he might have had a ready-made audience.'

Hugo grimaced, remembering the number of times he'd urged Reardon to embrace Twitter, to build up followers and to create noise around his work. All he'd been met with was, 'Hugo, I have no desire to waste a single word on anything but my books. Talent will out.'

Emily looked at her watch, and made to leave. 'Well, looking at the amount of self-publishing and marketing companies here this week he'd have been able to get plenty of advice.'

As Hugo bade farewell, the image of Reardon haggling a deal with Dignitas jumped into his mind.

Bronte was beyond excited as she rubbed shoulders with other would-be writers enrolled on the Pathway to Publishing seminar. Over the cheapest house wine Olympia catering could muster she and a handful of fellow delegates were enthusiastically agreeing how much they'd learned and how the gems that had been revealed today would be central to propelling their writing careers in an upward trajectory. The thrill of the London Book Fair taking place under the same roof added further fuel to their determination to move up the chain, and into the main hall, in future years. As she listened intently to the middle-aged woman (genre: historical fiction) holding court within their little group, she gasped as she espied Chapman Hall bearing down on them – he was coming to speak to them.

'How did we all find it today?' he breezed genially in the manner of somebody not expecting any deviation from the party line.

Historical fiction, the self-appointed spokesperson for the group, gushed on cue. 'I think I speak for everybody when I say that our eyes have been opened today. We can't wait to put all of the tips into action.'

Chapman beamed. 'Well, that's why we're here. The more determined you are, and the more mistakes you eliminate, the easier it is to attain that dream of getting published.'

Another delegate, a male in his early thirties (genre: satire) whom Bronte noticed had kept himself to himself all day, now tagged himself on to the group.

An elderly gent (genre: autobiography) plucked up the courage to speak. 'I must say I found it all rather daunting. Very informative, yes, but to the point that I think I'll be self-publishing if I'm honest, and I'd consider that a defeat.'

Chapman shook his head slowly. 'Self-publishing a book isn't a defeat, oh no. In fact it's a wonderful opportunity for many writers to get their work out there; wonderful because it's never been easier.'

Satire chipped in. 'But isn't that a contradiction? I mean, aren't we all here today trying to find out how to get published properly?'

There's always one, thought Chapman. 'Yes, you're right, of course...' He squinted but was unable to read the name badge on the delegate's chest to address him by his Christian name. '... but to be published at all is a gift so if gaining a deal with an established publisher isn't to be, then self-publishing is a more than acceptable option. We all want to see our work reach the maximum possible audience, don't we?'

A number of heads nodded in agreement at Chapman's sage words. Satire maintained his steady stare in Chapman's direction. 'I'm afraid I don't agree. I'm here today to find out how to get a proper publishing deal and for you to suggest self-publishing seems to me to be a bit of a cop out.'

The group shifted uneasily at the tough line of questioning their host was being subjected to; however, nobody sprang to Chapman's aid as they were all keen to know the answer to the question that had just been posed.

'Well, let me give you an example,' Chapman said as he played for time. 'I myself have been fortunate enough to have gained a publishing deal in the past. You may recall A Poisoned Heart and a Twisted Memory? But if circumstances had been different, I don't think I would have had any qualms whatsoever in self-publishing my work.'

'When did that come out?' asked Satire, clearly not familiar with the tome in question.

'It was a few years ago now but that doesn't alter the fact that I was immensely proud of it, and if I hadn't secured a publishing deal I'd have made sure that it saw the light of day, one way or another.'

'Just the one book? Or did you have others?' pressed Satire.

Chapman kept his cool despite wanting to kill this snivelling creep who was ruining his sales pitch. 'I stopped at the one novel as The Write Stuff took over my life. It was then I decided it was better for me to help other writers, many of whom were better writers than me, to achieve the goal I'd already attained. Most of my published work these days is of a didactic nature.'

While the group nodded away once again in recognition of Chapman's self-sacrifice the entrepreneur decided that it was time to cut Satire off at the pass. He turned to Bronte. 'So, if I recall correctly, you are hoping to join us in Lancaster in September?'

Bronte's eyes opened wide. 'Oh, definitely, Chapman. I wouldn't miss it for the world. I realise now how much more I have to learn.'

As a not-altogether convinced Satire took himself off to get another glass of wine, Chapman relaxed. 'You know, it's natural for writers to get anxious about whether they will get published or not. Our aim is to help everybody attain their true maximum potential, that's all.'

Bronte made a mental note. Attain true maximum potential. Yes. That said it all.

CHAPTER SIX

Eric's first reaction on meeting his new intern surprised him – what a very presentable young lady she was. His previous charges, both male and female, had sported an array of tattoos, piercings and 'individual' haircuts while appearing to have acquired their workday wardrobe from the local charity shop or the Primark sale. That didn't make them any less able as journalists, of course, but Eric couldn't help feeling that standards were somehow slipping (which was ironic given that the words 'journalist' and 'dress style' were rarely found in the same sentence). Julia, on the other hand, looked like she was ready to attend a board meeting in the City. Tall, slender and attractive, Julia was already turning heads in the newsroom. Yet, Eric noticed immediately, she didn't look cocky or full of herself – quite the opposite; there was an air of humility, expectation and, dare he say it, awe at being ushered into his presence.

As the HR manager left them to it Julia handed him a packet of dark chocolate ginger biscuits. 'Do you like biscuits? I just wanted to say thank you for taking me on.'

Eric was impressed – the only thing his previous

helpers had ever given him was a big fat pain in the backside. 'You didn't have to do that, Julia – that's very kind of you. And don't worry, I love biscuits.'

Julia relaxed. It was a good start.

Eric jumped up and fussed around as he settled his new assistant at her desk and showed her how to log on to the server. This avuncular manner would have surprised his earlier interns who found Eric to be rather stiff and given to pantomime exasperation when things didn't go according to his plans (but being treated as more trouble than they were worth was the lot of most interns).

'Now, what do you know already about what the business desk does?' Eric enquired.

'I've studied the output for some weeks now. I've worked out what professional areas are covered on the different days of the week and have an idea of the average word counts for lead stories, features and NIBs. I just can't wait to get started.'

Eric was impressed. To maintain mastery of the relationship his next task was to ensure Julia knew exactly how he liked his brew, the constant supply of which she was now entrusted with. Over their first mug – he noticed she had brought her own Early Grey teabags while he drank the regulation-issue builder's tea – he continued with the ice-breaking.

'So, you've done well to get in. That's always the hardest part I think. There's a lot of competition for these intern positions.'

'Yes,' replied Julia. 'I realise how fortunate I am and I'm determined to make the most of the opportunity.' She hadn't forgotten her father's advice not to mention that her presence here was down to him being a major advertiser with the newspaper.

'So,' Eric said. 'You really want to be a journalist? Has nobody tried to talk you out of it yet?'

Julia wasn't sure if he was joking. 'Ever since I was twelve years old. I've always loved writing – it's like a vocation.'

Eric decided that he should tone down his cynical hack impression. 'Well, that approach will get you a long way. Good for you – I hope you make a name for yourself one of these days.'

Julia looked bashful, but pleased. 'Well, I'll never have a name as good as yours for a writer,' she said.

If Eric had been given a pound coin for every time he'd heard that line he wouldn't still be working at The Chronicle. He ignored her comment and, adopting the face familiar to his previous interns, asked, 'So what journalistic experience have you had to date?'

Julia, realising that her attempt at familiarity had been pitched too soon into their acquaintance, searched in her bag for her CV. 'It's all on here, Eric. Editor of the student newspaper, and I also write a blog which keeps my hand in.'

'A blog?' Eric said, hardly able to contain his scorn. 'A blog on what?'

'It's about all things Japanese – you know, Anime, Manga, general Japanese culture and food. I'm a bit of a geek on the side.'

Anime? Manga? So this is what became of the Pokemon generation thought Eric. 'You know, I read a statistic recently that said most blogs are only read by one person – the person who wrote it.'

Julia looked wounded. 'I know what you're saying, but I have built my followers up over time. I've got five thousand now.'

Eric backtracked. 'Really? That's excellent. But one of the things you'll be learning here is the precision of journalism – the skills and discipline required to present objective facts in short order. Blogs won't equip you for that.'

Julia's impressive list of attributes also extended to diplomacy so she let Eric's comments ride, calculating that allowing his slight would neutralise his touchiness over her Eric Blair comment. 'Yes, I can see that, Eric. Completely different disciplines.'

Authority restored, Eric could afford to be the benign patron once more. 'Right, Julia, let's get you sorted with your first story.' He wheeled his chair up alongside hers to take her through the brief for her first serious piece of journalism. He hoped that she would remember this day and to whom she owed it when she hit the heights in a few years' time.

Before they could get started they were rudely interrupted by a young man whose piercing blue eyes nestled beneath the bushiest of jet-black monobrows. Ignoring Eric he stood over Julia and thrust out his hand. 'Dylan. Welcome to the madhouse.'

Julia hesitated, and looked to Eric for guidance. Her mentor's frown signified that this intrusion wasn't welcome. Not wishing to appear impolite, she held out her hand and mustered a breathy, 'Hello, I'm Julia, the new intern.'

'Clocked that already, Jules. What's someone like you

doing editing press releases? You should have got yourself fixed up in the department that keeps this ship afloat.'

Eric felt compelled to intervene on behalf of the brotherhood of journalists. 'Dylan, as you may already have deduced, is from the sales team. He has a somewhat singular view of the relationship between what we produce in editorial and what he sells.'

Dylan plonked himself down on the corner of Julia's desk. 'We basically pay for Eric's wages but he doesn't like to admit it. Now, how about I give you a tour later of what we do – complete your insight into how newspapers work these days?'

Eric stepped in quickly. 'I'm sure that would be very educational for Julia, Dylan, but as this is her first day then maybe it can wait? There'll be time enough for that, I'm sure.'

'Whatever you say, Eric, whatever you say. Just want her to know we're here to look after her, all right?'

Julia, caught between the rutting bucks vying for her attention, managed a neutral, 'That's very kind, thank you.'

'No problem. Don't get too attached to this one, though,' Dylan said, gesticulating in Eric's direction. 'He might not be here for much longer.'

Julia looked surprised at this unexpected tiding. 'I didn't know you were leaving, Eric?'

Before the beleaguered journalist could respond, Dylan delivered his punch line. 'Oh, yes. He's going to be a world famous author. Just like his namesake. Well, he will be when he finds someone to take him on.'

'All very amusing, Dylan, but we do have to get on if

that's OK with you?' said Eric, who had evidently heard all of this before.

'Laters,' Dylan said as he sauntered off, hands in pockets, pleased as punch at his own rapier-like wit.

Eric slowly shook his head. She could tell he wasn't pleased. 'That was Dylan, or to give him his full name, Dylan Dylan, head of the sales department. A man who is not shy at coming forward, but you'd probably worked that out for yourself.'

'He's rather young for that position, isn't he?' It was a fair question.

'Well, the powers that be have deemed that he's some sort of wunderkind, a super salesman who can persuade the hard-pressed advertisers of the region to continue to pour their money into our circulation-crippled craft. Personally, I don't quite see it, but then I'm not making those sort of decisions.'

'I can see he's self-assured. I suppose that must be an asset in sales?'

'Yes, I suppose the suspension of disbelief must be as beneficial in sales as it is in the theatre. Just different stages, that's all.'

'And he's really called Dylan Dylan?'

'Yes. Parents with a sense of humour, perhaps, or an unstinting dedication to Robert Zimmerman. Or maybe just lacking a scintilla of imagination. Probably the latter as it appears to run in the family.'

Dylan's brief appearance prompted a further question in Julia's mind, but she wasn't too sure how to broach it. 'What was that he said about you writing a book? Was he just teasing?'

Eric sighed. Bloody Dylan, bloody DD, bloody snake oil merchant, taking the mick out of him since he'd discovered that he'd written a book. 'Dylan has a very perverse sense of humour, but yes, that bit is true. I have written a book, and it's currently out with agents for their consideration. It's early days yet, so I won't be disappearing just yet. Probably ever, in fact.'

Julia looked admiringly at Eric. Not only an eminent business news editor, but an author as well. 'Can I read it, or is it still secret? What's it called? What genre?'

Despite feeling flattered Eric noted that he would have to teach her a little about interview techniques. 'That's a lot of questions, Julia. Best to line them up rather than launch a fusillade. But yes, let me see. It's called Scrub Me Till I Shine in the Dark, it's a coming of age novel set in the north, and I'm afraid that it's not for general consumption just at this point. No offence.'

'Oh, I understand. Sorry to be cheeky in asking. A friend of mine is writing a book and she's exactly the same.'

'Quite. It's important to be sure you've reached the point where you're ready to share it. Only my wife, Victoria, has read it to date.'

'Well, when you're ready, I'll be in the queue.'

'Very good. Now, Julia, shall we get back to this story? Deadlines to meet and all that.'

As Eric briefed her on how many words he wanted on the exciting news that a new industrial estate was to open next to Manchester Airport, Julia couldn't help but reflect how befitting it was that a man blessed with such a name as his should have also written a novel. Had he adopted a *nom de plume* for his book she wondered, but realised that now was not the time to ask. If he had, it certainly wouldn't be a name as daft as Dylan Dylan. This was quite an introduction to the world of newspapers. And as for sharing with Eric the fact that she, too, had already written a novel, well, perhaps that was best kept for another time.

CHAPTER SEVEN

'Survival of the fittest. Kill or be killed. Right?' Emily nodded – she looked as if she got Rocket's general drift. It was a different kind of language to what she was used to hearing during her rise up the Franklin & Pope ladder. Those days seemed far off now, like a memory of an idyllic summer once the harsh winter had set in, a faint echo of a carefree time now lost forever. Had those days really happened or were they a figment of her imagination? Ever since Colophon had taken over the business it had been hell for Emily and her colleagues – their new masters marched to a different beat and appeared to view the staff and ethos they'd inherited with deep disdain and distrust. There had already been a number of staff defections to other publishers but for someone like Emily, near the top of the tree, she had to be careful over her next move. She didn't want to take a salary cut by going to a smaller business yet positions at her level were thin on the ground and generally a question of 'dead man's shoes'. A year ago the most important part of her job was picking critical winners, getting them to market and burnishing the reputation of her employer. Her workmates looked up to her and sought her opinion on authors, budgets, manuscripts and marketing. She was respected, revered almost. Now, she was a profit centre. Accountancy had overtaken advocacy. She once thought of herself as having the best job in the world and gambolled into work each day. She was known for her energy, her judgement, her experience and her unerring eye. Now she woke up in the middle of the night, worry gnawing at her unconsciousness like a rat chewing on a Tommy's toes in the First World War trenches. And the first casualty of this particular war was her self-confidence. A large conglomerate like Colophon swallowing their business would have been difficult at any time but for Emily the timing couldn't have been worse coming as it did in the immediate wake of Demons Paint Their Lips. At Franklin & Pope, and within the UK publishing industry as a whole, Emily's deadeye for talent was well regarded – she could pick winners. She was the golden girl. All the more surprising then when she punted big and lost on an erotic pot-boiler with artistic pretensions – 'erogenous nonsense and insensibility' as one critic dubbed it. She wasn't the only editor in this particular boat – after the ridiculous success of 'that book' every publisher had rushed to cash in on an already aroused readership. It was just unfortunate for Emily that she took the biggest gamble of them all when she trumped all bids for Demons Paint Their Lips (or, as it was now known out of her earshot at Franklin & Pope, 250,000 Shades of Red in acknowledgement of the unprecedented deficit it had earned). If Colophon hadn't entered the picture at that juncture she would have got over the misjudgement, put it down to experience, relied on her overall record. One mistake in a hundred isn't bad. To her and Franklin &

Pope it would have been an acceptable risk, an aberration. Instead, to Colophon and the redoubtable Rocket, it was a cudgel to beat her brains out with, an albatross she was constantly forced to sport around her neck.

'So that's why we're taking a different tack, Emily. We're going to get our retaliation in first.'

What on earth is Rocket talking about? thought Emily. She was nervous in any case having been peremptorily summoned to this one-to-one without having been advised of the purpose of the meeting. 'Sorry? I don't quite follow.'

'The market is changing, right? So we're going to change too. Big advances are cutting our margins. We're spending too much on marketing. Amazon is bleeding us. E-readers have reduced our product to bargain basement pricing. So what do we do?'

A wave of panic came over Emily. He was asking her what they should do? Of course, he wasn't remotely interested in her views as he'd already made up his mind what they were going to do – he was merely testing her. 'Well, the market is going through profound change, that's true, and it's something all publishers are facing, not just us...'

'Yes, right, so here's what we're going to do. We're going to corner the market for new writers. Cut out the middleman and get directly to the talent. Everyone else is zigging, we're going to zag.'

Emily couldn't believe what she was hearing. 'Take on new writers directly, without agents?'

'Sure. That's a fifteen per cent swing right there. Plus, we can negotiate deals new writers will salivate over and make even more savings.'

'But, isn't there a quality issue here? I mean, agents have a vital role to play in terms of talent spotting, sorting the wheat from the chaff.'

'They don't do anything you guys can't do.'

'But they help to guide the writer, and edit work before it comes to us.'

'Edit? Remind me again what your title is, Emily? Editor. So edit – it's simple.'

'Agents are a filter for us. If they weren't there, we'd have writers sending work to us directly; we'd be swamped.'

'So you think a publisher shouldn't have anything to do with new writers? I thought you Brits were traditionalists? You should be pleased at this new direction.'

Emily knew she had to be careful. She had to argue her point of course, but constructively. What she couldn't afford to do was look like she was in total disagreement with Rocket's radical plan. 'How do you see it working? I mean, how will we position it?'

'We set up a new imprint. We encourage agentless writers to apply. We run new writer competitions, we put more resource into the slush pile – a couple of interns, won't cost anything – and we find some winners.'

'Yes, I can see where you're coming from, but we'll be wading through an awful lot of garbage.'

'Wrong attitude, Emily. You'll be sifting for gold is what you'll be doing. Just because a writer doesn't have an agent doesn't make him or her a bad author. All writers have to start somewhere – the only problem is we pick them up by the time they've added a few noughts to their price. We're going to grow our own with this little diversification, that's what we – or rather you – are going to do.'

'Me?'

'Yup. I'm putting you in charge of all of this.'

'But what about my writer portfolio?'

'It's a lot smaller than it was, Emily, so you can juggle both for the time being. We'll slide a few more of your authors out to other editors if the squeeze is too tight. This is a big opportunity, Emily. I'm putting all of my hopes on you to make it a success. I know you can do it.'

Like a guest at Belshazzar's feast, Emily wrestled with the meaning of the writing on the wall. Rocket was no Biblical scholar but he knew what their conversation had just foretold: '*Numbered, weighed, divided.*'

Hugo had been ducking Reardon's calls for the past week, figuring that confirmation of the lack of progress in finding a new publishing deal for him would only heap more misery on the already despondent author. Plus, Hugo could do without the hassle. Then, this morning, a miraculous occurrence had taken place. Not quite a publishing deal, but a reminder that Reardon still cast some light within the literary firmament, a distant echo of his authorial value and reputation. Hugo also reflected that he would earn a nice little commission on having fielded this one single phone call. So, a freshly brewed cup of coffee to hand and his feet casually propped up on his desk, Hugo made himself comfortable in order to break the good news to his chary client.

'Reardon. I call with good news. I hope you're sitting down.'

The author, who of late had found it increasingly difficult to raise himself from his bed before noon, was comfortably reclined. Despite his supine position, Reardon felt his body tense. Good news? What news? Who had Hugo placed him with? On what terms? He also felt a slight twinge of guilt over the names he'd called his hapless agent over the past three months. He collected himself. 'Yes, Hugo. Do tell.'

Hugo, as was his custom when selling something, was keen to build to his 'reveal'. 'Well, as you know, Reardon, I've been testing the market for some time and, if I'm being honest, I'd missed a trick.' Reardon shifted himself up on his pillows. Bloody Hugo, never getting to the point. 'It struck me that we were only chasing one fox when we could have been after more.' *Good God, what was he on about now?* thought Reardon. 'So, I broadened my sights beyond simply finding you a new publisher and explored some new areas. And you know what? I've come up with an absolute winner. You're going to be very pleased with this, Reardon, I know.'

The author resisted the temptation to berate his agent for his unwarranted prolixity. 'Perhaps you could just tell me what "this" is, Hugo?'

'I've only lined you up for a professorship in creative writing at the King Edward VIII University. Forget your next advance, Reardon, these academics are paying big.' Hugo, at last, shut up, ready to be showered with heartfelt gratitude from his grateful client. However, the agent's announcement was met with silence. Hugo, shifting his feet from the table back to the floor as if that would help the author construct a response, thought maybe the line had gone dead. 'Reardon, are you there? Reardon?'

The award-winning writer, the voice of his age, this colossus of literary fiction, did not stir as he absorbed the news imparted by Hugo. Finally, he cleared his throat and, not removing his gaze from the framed photograph of him receiving a BAFTA for best screenplay that held pride of place on his bedside cabinet, he spoke. 'Hugo, you are my agent, correct?'

Hugo was now sitting fully erect at his desk, his cup of coffee placed on a coaster sporting the Motif Literary Agency logo. 'Yes, of course I am, Reardon.'

'And under the normal terms of an agency-author relationship it would be expected that you, as my agent, find me, the writer, a publisher. Not just any old publisher, but one that will respect me as an author, promote and help my work to reach the widest possible audience?'

'Yes, of course, but...'

'Hugo. Let me continue, please. So, after three months, you call to tell me you are no closer to the accomplishment of your primary task but somehow I'm not to worry as you've found me a job as a performing seal in a travelling circus?'

'Reardon, I think you're looking at this all wrong. This is a massive opportunity. Most writers would give their right arm for an opening like this.'

'They would, would they? Do you really think I'm "most writers"? Is that how you view me?'

'Of course not, Reardon, you're exceptional. That's why the university is busting a gut to get you.'

'I'm intrigued, Hugo. Do you really think that writing can be taught? That through the serendipitous presence of an established author a shower of literary gold dust somehow settles on the young shoulders of those paying £9,000 a year for enlightenment? Is there such a thing as belletristic osmosis? I think not.'

Hugo felt his hackles rise in the face of such ingratitude. 'I've just landed you a fantastic, highly-paid post that will gain you tons of prestige and you're telling me you don't agree writing can be taught? Seriously?'

'I think that pretty much sums it up, Hugo. How can I look students in the eye and pretend to be Prospero to their ambitions?'

'Reardon. I think it's important to be objective about this. One, you don't have a publisher at the moment. Two, I'm trying, but we have to face facts that it may take a while yet to find someone who'll take you on, and the deal may not be too brilliant when I do. That means, three, this university post is a no-brainer.'

'To borrow your gauche idiomatic phrase, Hugo, it's a "no-brainer" that a sane person could believe that being subjected to lectures, cosy chats and individual critiques of their amateurish scribbles from a published author will help them to become better writers. Creative writing courses, and the positions attached to them, are symptomatic of the commoditisation of everything we once held dear. Colleges desperate to ice their particular cake in the name of competition pander to today's "quick-fix" mentality by claiming that, rather in the same way you can lose two stone in a week, you can now write War and Peace in three ten-week terms. I won't participate in this deception.'

'Reardon, if you don't do it, then somebody else will. All you have to do is turn out for a few days a year and encourage, let's say inspire, the students. Surely, that's not a deception or a sell-out?'

'The only advice I have for those who wish to write, is to read. Is that worth the king's ransom of a stipend you imply is attached to the post?'

'Yes, absolutely. That's exactly what they're after. You and this position were made for each other – you're a natural teacher. What was that line from The History Boys? "Take it, feel it and pass it on." That's all there is to it. Come on, Reardon – at least discuss it with Belinda first before making any rash decisions. Promise me that much?'

'I will discuss it, but the answer will be the same. And Hugo, now we have dealt with that, perhaps you could refocus your attention to the matter in hand? Goodbye.'

As Hugo sipped his by-now cold coffee and contemplated the commission he would lose if this gift horse remained unmounted, he told himself that this was the last straw with Reardon. He could start looking for a new agent as well as a new publisher if he buggered up this deal.

CHAPTER EIGHT

Alyson Hummer was having a day off. No research today, no writing, just a pleasant day out with her best friend, Alison. Their names could get confusing when they were out together in company so they were identified by their acquaintances as Ali – I and Ali –Y. Alyson was in an especially good mood as the two women checked in for their special treat – a day of pampering at their favourite spa in Bath. There they were planning to enjoy a massage, a facial and a relaxing soak in a hot tub before celebrating their health-promoting regimen with a glass of champagne. Aly was also keen to canvass the opinion of her chief gossip on an important decision she had to make.

The two had been friends since school days, which was a surprise as the two were poles apart both in temperament and outlook. The years hadn't narrowed those differences. Ali for example had only ever been with one man in her life, her husband, and had held down the same job as a nurse for over twenty years. Aly's antics shocked and amused Ali in equal measure but she never passed judgement; on the contrary, she derived a vicarious pleasure in being Aly's confidante. Aly, on the other hand, loved Ali for always encouraging her, never looking down on her and for consistently being able to help her to see things objectively. It was the best kind of friendship, a partnership of mutual interest and respect, a comfortable attraction of opposites.

Ali read Aly's books, of course. She claimed she was unqualified to comment but the truth was that the writer valued her friend's input more than anyone else's and made a point of always sending first drafts to her. Ali had an unerring knack of asking the 'daft' questions that made the biggest difference to the edits: *Why did she do that? When did she decide? What was it about him that made him so appealing? There was a bit missing in the story there* and so on. She never commented on the sex scenes *per se*, adopting a professional, anatomical indifference to the myriad bodily functions and interactions she found within the virginal typed-up pages she received. 'I'll take your word for it, Aly,' she'd say.

Aly knew she had the sex nailed – it was the rest of her approach she fretted over – characterisation, plot, conversation (not that there was a lot of that), grammar – which is why she felt so indebted to her oldest friend. If she felt any contrition at all over Ali's diligent work on her scripts it was that her friend would self-effacingly laugh off the value of her contribution – 'it's a good job I was paying attention in English GCSE when you were round the back of the bike sheds messing with the lads,' is all she'd say when Aly poured praise on her. Ali politely declined the offer the author extended to dedicate a book to her, or to mention her in the credits.

Now Aly needed Ali's view on another matter. As

the two women, complexions the colour of the rosé champagne they were now sipping, relaxed in the bar after their treatments, Aly broached what was preoccupying her. 'Ali, something's come up and I don't know what to do about it.'

Ali didn't rush to drag it out of her friend. 'Well, take your time, Aly, we're in no hurry.'

That was another reason why the author cherished her best friend – she always remained calm and never jumped in with two feet. 'It's not a "problem" problem, Ali, it's, well, it's a big opportunity. But I'm not sure about it.'

Reassured that the crisis wasn't health or family-threatening, Ali relaxed. 'Come on then, spit it out.'

'You know I publish with ViXen? Well, they've been on and offered me a three-book deal at a better commission rate.'

'That hardly sounds like a problem, Aly. You should be delighted, surely?'

'Yes, I am. Well, I was. It's the first time they've done it apparently and the money will be better, but it means the next three books have to be in the same vein as my others, and to be honest I've been thinking of changing my style.'

'Changing your style?' It was the first Ali had heard of a U-turn in her friend's literary approach. 'But you're successful because of your style. Why would you want to change it?'

'I know it sounds poncey, but for artistic reasons. I know I'm good at the hardcore stuff and I earn a decent enough living, but I want to go more mainstream, switch genre. I think I can do it.'

'You mean get a proper publisher?'

'Yes, that's my dream. ViXen has been great and I've enjoyed it, but I feel like I'm in a rut. Another three novels of the same old filth and it will put me off sex forever. But it's not just that – I need to prove to myself that I can be a proper writer.'

'Don't say that, Aly. You are a proper writer.'

'You know what I mean, Ali. Bookshop signings, media interviews, bestseller lists, Richard and Judy – that's what being a proper writer is all about. I don't want to be only associated with filth.'

'I think you're being a bit hard on yourself. I bet E L James doesn't think she has to apologise about writing erotica.'

'I don't kid myself that my stuff is as tame as hers – that's the whole point. That ship has sailed. I either keep grinding away – literally – with ViXen or I throw a double six and go legit.'

Ali, ever practical, had an obvious question. 'Have you written anything that's not, you know, extreme?'

'Not yet, but I know I can. I want to write romance. Say goodbye to dicks, clits and butt plugs. Sensual, yes; filthy, no. I need to find out if I can do it – that's why the ViXen offer, while it's brilliant, is also a problem because I don't want to commit.'

Ali sucked on the strawberry floating in her glass of champagne and contemplated her friend's dilemma. 'The way I see it is that it's a toss-up between a bird in the hand and two in the bush. You've got a good income from ViXen, you can do it standing on your head and you've enjoyed yourself doing it. I'm not saying you couldn't make the switch to romance but you'd be starting at the bottom and aren't millions of people trying to write romance these days? You could end up with nothing.'

'I know, but it's driving me mad. How will I know unless I try?'

Ali could see how her friend's vision was firmly fixed on the two birds frolicking in the treetops. 'Listen. Here's what I think, Aly. Say you'll decide on the three-book deal with ViXen depending on how your next one does but ask for the higher commission for that book anyway. Then, get cracking on your romance novel and see if you can get someone to publish it – find out what you're up against.'

Aly weighed her friend's suggestions. Walk before I can run. Don't scorch the earth behind me. Yes – that was sound advice. What would she do without Ali as a sounding board?

Con Buckley sat staring at the rain mingling with the dust on the windows of Kilburn Library Centre. It was fascinating how the shapes shifted, conjuring up different images as long as he kept his focus fixed on the panes. He had decided on a change of environment for the all-important task of the final edit of A Refugee From the Seraphim. In front of him was a clear plastic folder containing the 297 A4 printed pages that represented the sacrifices he – and Rosie – had made. In monetary terms a bundle of stationery costing less than £10 but in a wider context the past two years of his life. He fiddled with the red pen he'd bought especially for the task of marking up amends, rotating it through his fingers, first on the left hand, then the right. He'd yet to start on page one. He thought of going for a cup of tea before getting stuck in – the truth was he just wasn't in the right frame of mind for the task. It was all Rosie's fault. He should never have shown her his manuscript. For months, as he'd slaved away on the novel, he'd looked forward to the moment of communion when Rosie would read it and they could share in the creation together. She would heap praise on him, naturally, admire his brilliance, express surprise at his hidden depths and they would then engage in an ardent intellectual exchange on the themes, motifs and influences of this literary breakthrough. It would be a congress as deep and sacred as the first time they made love. It hadn't turned out like that. At all.

Con had purposefully avoided asking Rosie what she thought about the book as she spent the best part of a week, every evening after work and at the weekend, studiously reading his manuscript. Her face gave nothing away as she turned the pages. Then, at 7pm on the Sunday night, she placed the final sheet on the pile of inverted pages to denote she'd finished and said, 'There. Done.'

Con, who was making a show of preparing their evening meal at the time, tossed the potato peeler on to the kitchen work surface and jumped into the chair opposite her. 'You've finished it? What do you think?'

Rosie gathered her thoughts and tried to select her words carefully. 'It's not what I'd imagined.'

'Not what you'd imagined? What does that mean?'

'It's not what I thought it was going to be like, that's all. It's a bit more "out there" then I'd pictured it.'

'It's meant to be "out there" – that's the whole bloody point. But did you like it?' implored Con.

Again Rosie searched for the correct response. 'It's difficult reading something by somebody you know. It makes it harder to be objective. Yes, I liked it.'

Con knew what she really meant. 'You're just saying that. You hated it.'

'Don't be silly, Con. I did enjoy it. It's very clever and, … it's different. Different is good if you're going to get published, isn't it?'

Con felt his world shrink to the size of the potato he still held in his hand. 'So you think it's crap, basically. "If" I'm going to get published?'

Rosie tried to mollify her over-anxious partner but only seemed to fan the flames. 'It's a good book, Con. I liked it, honestly. It's intellectual, it's dense and I…'

'"Dense"?' screamed Con. '"*Dense*"?' He flung the white tuber in his hand at the wall above her head, dislodging a photograph of the two of them taken at last year's Glastonbury Festival. The glass shattered and the frame crashed to the stripped pine floorboards. 'Well, thanks a lot, Rosie, for your keen literary insight. I should have known better than to ask someone who reads Twilight for relaxation.'

A lot of women might have been intimidated by Con's needy and aggressive behaviour, but not Rosie, who now stood up to tower over her boyfriend. 'Don't you ever, ever, talk to me like that. If it wasn't for me you'd never have written a book in the first place. Two years it's taken, and you've not done a day's work in between. You've no right to kick off.'

Con's Irish temperament meant he had no concept of discretion being the better part of valour, so he ploughed on despite the long odds on winning. 'Not done a day's work? What do you think that frigging is?' he said, gesticulating wildly at the uneven pile of paper on the coffee table. 'I've slaved my guts out on that and all you can say is "it's a pile of crap".'

'Don't be so pathetic. You've written a book, you've not given birth. I think it's good. I think it's interesting. I think it's different. I suspect other people, people who don't read Twilight, will think it's good but don't start giving me grief because I don't fall at your feet and say it's going to sell a million. I don't know, that's all, and neither do you.'

Wounded, and realising that he may have gone too far, Con went for the sympathy vote. 'I just thought you'd like it more, that's all. I was relying on you liking it.'

'It doesn't matter what I think. It's what a publisher thinks.' And then, the killer. 'But I'll tell you one thing, Con. You've spent two years on that book, and that's enough. Get yourself back to work now, because I've had enough of supporting you.'

Con hadn't seen that one coming and immediately regretted having pushed his normally placid girlfriend to this ultimatum. 'But I need a few more months to polish it up and get an agent. I can't go back to work now.'

Rosie, surprised at her own resolve, decided to press her advantage home. 'You get it sorted, now. You finish the book. You start applying for jobs next month. If you don't have an agent by the end of September, you start a proper job on October 1st. Otherwise, you and me have had it.'

The rest of the evening had been spent in fraught silence. Rosie had told him to sleep on the settee, and when he awoke she'd already left for work. Now, as Con indulged in writerly procrastination, he had time to evaluate the implications of the previous evening's outburst. Rosie's explosion had taken him by surprise – she was normally so, well, yielding. He must have done something to upset her. Maybe he should have printed off the manuscript for her earlier as it had taken him seven weeks to get round to it, what with the printer being on the blink. Could that have been it? No. More likely it was that cow of a sister, Grace, who was stirring the pot against him. She'd never liked him, and the feeling was mutual. How was he supposed to cope with all this? Jack Kerouac wouldn't have got down the road very far faced with these odds. Worst of all though was that he knew Rosie meant what she said when she'd imposed the guillotine – there was no doubt in his mind that she'd drop the blade come the end of September. Well, she'd be sorry when A Refugee From the Seraphim hit the bestsellers and she'd walked out on the fame and glory at the wrong time. But what if the novel was too 'dense', as she'd called it? What then? He'd be back working at the hospital pushing codgers, cadavers and cartloads of dirty laundry around all day, or out on his ear. He couldn't face that. He had to get a publishing deal, he just had to. This was shit or bust now. He *had* to make that breakthrough. But how?

Feeling more dejected than when he'd arrived he put the red pen back in his pocket, gathered up his file and headed for the exit door. He was too bloody depressed to edit today – he'd start again tomorrow.

CHAPTER NINE

'Two hundred and twenty-four.' Suzie was updating Chapman on the number of delegates already signed up for the conference in three months' time. 'And we have around a hundred unconverted enquiries on file that we'll be chasing up.'

Chapman looked pleased, and not only because he was eating a large piece of chocolate cake brought in for one of the staff's birthday. 'Well done, Suze. At this stage that's well on track.' He brushed the crumbs from his lap on to the floor. 'How many are repeats, and how many newbies?'

'About half and half – well over a hundred first-timers.'

Chapman did some quick mental arithmetic. 'We need more writers dipping their toe into the ink for the first time.'

Suzie, who knew their prospects of hitting 300 delegates now depended on getting to people they'd not previously encountered, had this covered too. She placed the yellow folder back on the desk. 'The online campaign of pay-per-click ads starts next week. Anybody searching for literary terms like "finding an agent", "getting published", "writing a novel" or "editing your manuscript" will have the conference ad pop up.'

'Love it. That's the beauty of our market – there's fresh meat all the time. A never-ending flow.'

Suzie fingered the blue folder, anticipating Chapman's next question. She guessed correctly. 'And how are we doing on those big-hitting experts to galvanise our punters?'

This news wasn't as positive. 'We've been concentrating on the delegate recruitment to date so there's not much movement on new experts. But the list we do have doesn't seem to be deterring people from signing up, does it?'

Chapman scooped the stray crumbs clinging to his paper plate and stuffed them into his mouth before responding. 'People are signing up, that's true, Suze, but what's the story they're going to have when they go home after the conference? We have to dazzle them.'

Suzie looked downcast. 'Delegates have never complained about the calibre of our experts before.'

'Come on, Suze. Just two or three more names, but they've got to be stellar. An agent, editor or author the punters will drop everything for just to share the same postcode as them for a day.'

'Is there anyone you can suggest?' asked Suzie, not unreasonably.

Chapman raised his arms in the manner of an Italian catenaccio appealing against a yellow card. 'Suze – I don't need to give you names. You know who we need. Think A-list, that's all.'

Suzie made to scribble a note on her pad but all she could manage was a big question mark. She moved the conversation on by picking up a fourth box file from the floor, new to this meeting. It was green. 'We should really spend some time on the programme.'

Chapman stood up and strolled to the window. 'I've been thinking about that. I want to ring the changes there, too.'

Suzie looked concerned. 'I've already done an outline three-day plan,' she said, 'and there doesn't look to be an awful lot of space for too many new things.'

Chapman was now walking back and forth in front of the window, forcing Suzie to swivel her chair around to face him. 'There's always room for new revenue opportunities, Suze. I've got a new concept we should launch at Lancaster.' Suzie put down her pen. She recognised the signs that Chapman had been donning his thinking cap and when he did he usually came up trumps. Chapman could be frustrating to work for at times but he never stood still – his inventiveness was one of the main reasons she'd stayed at The Write Stuff all these years. He may only have had an audience of one but Chapman was revved up, bursting to share his new idea. 'We're only just scratching the surface, Suze. That's the reality. Our editing services and workshops do well but their main purpose is to feed the conference. But others are copying us now and we're going to lose out unless we innovate.' Suzie looked up at Chapman, her face bathed in admiration and expectation. 'So the next step for us is a radical one, but a lucrative one. It's something people are ready to spend big money on, and I want them spending it with us in future.' Chapman looked Suzie in the eye, challenging her to guess the source of all this extra income. Not wanting to break his flow, and not having the faintest idea what was on his mind anyway, she stared back, her dilated eyes urging him to admit her into his confidence.

'Self-publishing, Suze, that's what we're going to offer. A full self-publishing service with typesetting, cover design, printing, trade distribution, e-versions and marketing support services. There are more people writing books these days than are reading them. The mark-ups will dwarf what we're currently making – the time is right.' He paused to await his PA's reaction.

Suzie, aware of Chapman's less than complimentary comments in the past on self-publishing companies, was confused. 'But doesn't that contradict what we offer at the moment? We're all about getting our writers agents and publishing deals.'

'Yes, it is. Or it was. But think about it. How many people are we actually going to get properly published? Not very many. You only have to read their stuff to realise that – there's only so much we can do to polish a turd. If you think about it, what we're actually doing is getting first-time authors to a point where they recognise they're never going to get an agent or a publishing deal. The bridge of despair. And what do they do then? They go off and spend thousands of pounds with a self-publishing company so they don't feel like they've wasted their time. That's what we're missing out on.'

Suzie recalled another of Chapman's bugbears about self-publishing. 'You've always said that it would harm The Write Stuff to admit that our writers may not succeed.'

'Good point. But define "success". All I'm doing is *stretching* the parameters of success for these writers. A

78

small number will get deals; for the rest I'd rather they spent their money with us rather than someone else when they realise self-publishing is the only way their work is ever going to see the light of day.'

Suzie was still trying to get her head around this apparent *volte-face*. 'I still think it could put aspiring authors off coming to us. Some would run a mile at the idea of us being connected with self-publishing; they'd see it as a failure.'

'That's true, Suze. That's why we're going to announce a "partnership" with Wellington Self-Publishing at the conference. It's an association, a tie-up, a working arrangement between the two companies. Created so we can continue the journey with our authors to their work's final destination. And who better to assist them than us? It's the ultimate integrated offer.'

'But who is this Wellington Press? I've never heard of them.'

'I've not set it up yet, Suze. But rest assured, it will be up and running and ready for orders come September.'

The literary universe populated by agents and editors is remarkably small. In the constant criss-crossing and interchange of orbits it was therefore no major surprise that Emily and Hugo should find themselves sitting together at yet another book awards ceremony. This time it was the inaugural Great Book Awards to recognise the novel that best captured the natural and cultural beauty of the British Isles. The sponsor rolling out the red carpet and a lavish dinner at the taxpayers' expense was the National Tourism Agency, funded by the Department for Culture, Media and Sport.

Hugo was studying the menu that was predictably split into Scottish, English, Welsh and Irish courses. 'They're pushing the boat out on this, Emily,' he said. 'At least we'll get a good meal out of it if nothing else.' Emily smiled, but didn't bother to look at the menu. Her appetite had been somewhat diminished of late. Hugo knocked back his welcome glass of Nyetimber sparkling wine and then helped himself to one of the bottles of Three Choirs Oaked Reichensteiner nestling in the ice bucket in the middle of the table. He thought he might as well make a night of it as he'd given up a day-night game at Lord's to attend. Neither Hugo nor Emily had any shortlisted candidates up for the award but that was immaterial – the organisers' aim was to put the event on the map so anybody and everybody from the literary industry was invited.

As per the convention at these dinners Hugo and Emily conversed vacuously with the other guests on the table and made positive noises about how well everything was going in their respective fields. As they drifted towards the Blue Rathgore cheese course Emily and Hugo turned their heads inward to each other. Emily by this time was matching Hugo on the wine consumption front and as they poured themselves another glass of the Sharpham Pinot Noir Precoce both felt highly relaxed. Hugo was bursting to tell Emily about her former charge. 'Get this, Emily. I land Reardon a professorship in creative writing at the King Edward VIII University and you know what? He's "thinking about it", the twat.'

Emily giggled. 'I thought you were good, Hugo, but not that good. How on earth did you wangle that? They've obviously not met him.'

'The old magic coming on strong, I suppose. But seriously, his dithering is putting me in an awkward position.'

'Silly old fool. He should bite their hand off.'

'Exactly. But "writing can't be taught" according to his lordship.'

'Well, he might have a point there,' Emily said. 'But it's not stopped a load of other authors pretending it can, especially with the sort of money that's on offer. About time Reardon relaxed his principles, otherwise he'll starve.'

Hugo saw an opportunity for some intelligence gathering. 'So, you've chopped a few more as well as Reardon, I see?'

Emily looked around as if she expected Rocket to be standing behind her posing as a waiter. 'You wouldn't believe what's been going on, Hugo, you really wouldn't.' Hugo topped up her glass and waited for her to continue. 'It's the craziest thing I've ever heard, but apparently we're – I'm – going to be setting up an imprint specifically for unagented writers. Rocket is going to open the floodgates to a tsunami of typos.'

Hugo halted the trajectory of his glass halfway to his mouth. 'Unagented?'

'Yes. Apparently you're obsolete, Hugo, and I can do your job in the fifteen minutes I have spare each day.'

Hugo bristled. 'That's the daftest thing I've ever heard. Madness. It's like going back to the dark ages.'

'Well, Hugo, I suspect it won't affect you. You'll still be the golden boy. It's me that's going to have to carry the can.'

The agent understood the implications for one of his favourite editors. 'Is it time for you to look around, Em?'

'I have, but where? I don't have that many options.'

'You'll just have to go with the flow for now. It's on Rocket's head really.'

'I doubt if it will be his head on the chopping block when it all goes wrong.'

Hugo nodded sympathetically at this last observation. 'So when are you going to tell the hungry authors you're laying on a free buffet?'

'Rocket has this idea that I should find a suitable Writers Conference and launch it there. It will be like being the only woman on an island full of sex-starved sailors.'

Despite Hugo's apparent compassion towards Emily's plight he couldn't help but let out an astonished laugh at the thought of Emily being sent off to a conference full of desperate wannabe authors. 'Oh dear, Emily, that is tough luck. Poor, poor you.'

'You won't tell anybody, will you? I shouldn't have said anything but I know I can trust you.'

'As if you need to ask,' Hugo said as he patted her on the arm.

Almost instinctively, both pulled out their mobiles – time to update the world on the important work they were carrying out in the pursuance of their respective crafts. Each made sure they added the greatbookawards hashtag to their tweets describing the glittering night in which they were playing a major role – a guest's way of thanking their host these days. However, Hugo let out an exclamation as he checked his timeline. 'Arsehole. Being bloody trolled again.'

Now it was Emily's turn to be amused. 'Another of your fans, Hugo?' It was no secret that Hugo had a tendency to court controversy within this most popular of social sites.

Agents and editors like Hugo and Emily had no trouble attracting thousands of followers on Twitter – most of them eager to have any form of contact with the literary world they were so desperate to join. Professionals like Hugo and Emily never followed back – this was strictly a one-way transaction. Since Hugo had found himself in this position of power he could be icy and sharp – pompous – when it came to expressing his views and opinions on Twitter. He tried hard to be affable and chatty – many of his numerous followers continued to be baffled by his ongoing comments on cricket – but if it's true that sentiments set down in writing can often be misconstrued then the restricted canvas of 140 characters was an amphitheatre of misinterpretation.

'Some idiot attacking me saying I singled him out to make a point. As if.'

Suzie looked at her timeline to pick up the thread. 'Did you?'

'Never bloody heard of him. I put out a tweet earlier saying that one of the things that really got my goat in submissions "was, the, over, use, of punc-tu-a-tion". This nutter thinks I was having a go at him and is accusing me of personally humiliating him. "I should use generic examples, not specific ones" etc.'

'But you don't mention anyone by name.'

'Exactly. The guy's paranoid obviously. Bollocks to that.' He took up his mobile and responded. 'Sorry, if, you, thought, I, meant, you. But, you, clearly, think, you've, got, a, problem, so, you, may, need, help.' The MC announced that the awards ceremony was about to commence. 'Just think, Emily,' beamed Hugo. 'Soon you'll be able to meet all of these stalkers and inadequates in person.'

CHAPTER TEN

All around him, there was darkness. He gingerly extended a hand in front of his face, but came into contact with... nothing. A bolt of fear shot through his frame and he clutched his arms to his chest in a gesture of self-protection. He could feel bare skin. He ran his hands downwards over his torso – he was totally naked. Straining his eyes in an effort to penetrate the gloom he could make out no discernible shapes or outlines in the pitch-black void. Where the hell was he? He tried to recall his last waking moments but his mind was as impenetrable as his surroundings. It was warm, which must be a good thing? He also realised that he was standing. He took a deep breath and achieved two slow steps forward before being met by a solid surface. He kneaded the vertical plane in front of his face to identify any giveaway features. A door surround, and after more scrambling, a doorknob. He braced himself to turn the handle. Another deep breath, a rapid twist and push, and he was suffused in a blinding fluorescent light as bright as creation. Reardon Boyle stood stark-bollock naked in a long, featureless corridor and wondered what on earth he was doing there.

As his sight adjusted to the glare he could discern

numbers arrayed on the doors to both his right and left. Another light went on – he was at the Villa Madame Hotel in Paris, taking a well-deserved city break with Belinda. But what was he doing out here? And more importantly, what was his room number? Hands cupped over his privates he advanced down the hall and contemplated the four doors surrounding him – numbers 24, 25, 26 and 27. He looked at his watch – the only thing he was still wearing – and noted it was 6.30am. Should he knock on each door? Or should he go to reception? Before he could decide on his course of action the lift mechanism started up and he instinctively knew it was heading his way. He ran back to the sanctuary of his hidey-hole. Finding the light switch he saw an assortment of mops, brushes and pails in a room barely two-metre square. He looked around for something to protect his modesty. The only thing that would serve was a newspaper left on a shelf by one of the staff. Footsteps approached and the door swung open. Without a hint of surprise, as if naked men lingering in the cleaner's cupboard was a daily occurrence at Villa Madame, the Algerian h*omme de ménage* merely looked at Reardon and said, '*Bonjour, Monsieur. Puis-je vous aider?*'

Reardon had to hand it to the French. Within two minutes of him explaining, in approximate Franglais, that he must have been *marchant en sommeil* and had *oublié le numero de mon chambre* the receptionist appeared, opened the door to number 26 and stood aside for Reardon to enter. As the door clicked behind him Belinda stirred, waking to find her husband *déshabillé et désorienté* at the base of the bed. She immediately recognised all was not well. 'Reardon. Are you alright?'

Reardon looked at his wife, then down at the newspaper still held over his midriff. It was only then that the author noticed the front page headline on the journal maintaining his dignity, a comment on last week's visit to the city by Chelsea fans: *La honte de l'Anglais*. He burst into tears.

Once Belinda had got Reardon back in his pyjamas and into bed she made him some tea. If she had been worried about him before, now she was deeply concerned. She took her time coaxing out of him what had happened. Reardon, embarrassed about his walkabout, tried to laugh it off. 'I must have mistaken the room door for the bathroom door when I got up to go to the toilet.'

'If that was the case, you would have knocked on the door to come back in. And you would have been wearing your pyjamas.'

Reardon didn't have an answer to these rather obvious points. 'Well, maybe I was hot in the night. And then I sleepwalked. It's not that implausible.'

Belinda suggested an alternative theory. 'It's stress, Reardon. Your publishing deal, this university job offer.' The crestfallen author shrugged his shoulders, knowing she was right. 'You've been miserable for months and you've no right to be. You're a brilliant writer, and well respected. You've finished your new book and the university is desperate to have you. Yet you think you're a failure.'

'Yes, but will Original Motion ever come out? And you know my views on selling out to academia.'

Belinda gave Reardon's hand a squeeze. 'You can't give up. That's fatal. The book will sort itself. You need to be active and engaged again, and out there where people can see you. You have to accept the university job.'

Reardon squirmed. He'd thought of nothing else for the past two weeks. Could he accept the thirty pieces of silver Edward VIII was tempting him with? Could he square his own views on the worth of these writing courses? Would Original Motion ever see the light of day? He squeezed Belinda's hand. Maybe it was time he went back to school.

Eric Blair had barely slept and couldn't shake a cloying feeling of guilt, shame and remorse from his mind. How could he have been so stupid as to enter into a Twitter spat with Hugo Lockwood? He knew he'd made a big mistake and exposed himself to ridicule. Worse, he'd used his real Twitter account to take exception to one of the agent's comments. People were probably looking him up now to see who he was. Should he delete his Twitter account? No, he couldn't, as it was the one followed by the region's business readers too. As he lay waiting for the alarm clock to go off he wondered what messages would be queuing up on his mobile. No doubt more opprobrium from sycophants attempting to curry favour with the oleaginous agent. What would his editor say if he saw it? He glanced over at Victoria who was still soundly asleep. Should he tell her?

Eric was rarely rash but had to admit that he'd lunged in without thinking. Bloody Hugo Lockwood. Not only did the agent appear to derive vicarious pleasure from his high-handed shattering of writers' dreams, he was also overfond of spreading his wisdom to the great unwashed with frequent smarmy observations and slights. Other agents and editors Eric followed didn't behave like Lockwood. They weren't trying to act as some sort of irreproachable guru, a sneering, know-it-all, smart-arse. Eric had noticed Lockwood's modus over the months he'd been following the agent but prior to being rejected by him had chosen to interpret the style as being direct and businesslike. Now Eric's views on Lockwood's tweeting style had changed to a point where he read his outpourings with mounting rage (not that he stopped following him). And how many novels had Hugo Lockwood written? None.

There was a reason why Eric had snapped when he read the comment from Motif's mouthpiece on the use of over-punctuation. Eric prided himself on his rigorous adherence to grammatical correctness – he worked in journalism after all. Only the afternoon before, Julia had innocently asked him why he used semicolons; surely there could be no valid reason to continue to do so? Despite Eric's patient explanation and examples, Julia remained unimpressed – in her view semicolons were outdated and she cited Kurt Vonnegut's observation that their employment only served to show the user went to college. Eric wasn't used to such grammatical sparring with his interns, but then Julia moved on to other peculiarities of written English. 'And another thing I don't understand. Why do we sprinkle commas everywhere?' she asked. 'It's like Tony Blair dictating into a computer: "She, was, the, people's, princess" – it just slows everything down.' As

Eric reflected on this conversation on his way home he put Julia's views down to the impetuosity of a generation who had learned to write by texting and tweeting. But then the thought had struck him – could an over-pedantic use of grammatical conventions have blighted his novel? Could that be a reason why he'd not had any offers yet? He resolved to take another look at the manuscript with a fresh eye at the weekend. And that's exactly what was on his mind when Lockwood's tweet hit him.

Before retiring to bed later in the evening he realised that the agent's tweet couldn't possibly have been aimed at him and he deleted his two tweets – the first one about Hugo having no right to criticise an individual's perceived grammatical failings, and the second one about how Hugo must have been bullied at school as he was such a twat.

It was no good – he was going to have to tell Victoria. He gently shook her awake and owned up to his indiscretion. Victoria, still groggy with sleep, took a moment to register what he was telling her. Then she burst out laughing.

'It's not funny,' Eric said. 'People are going to see it.'

'So what if they do? He does sound like a twat from what you're saying. Anyway, you've deleted your tweets so forget about it. You've not murdered anybody.'

'No, I haven't, but what about my submission? What if other agents see the tweets and it scuppers my chances?'

Victoria got up and put on her dressing gown. 'You've got to stop being so paranoid. You've written a really good book, it's tough to get an agent and you've got to be patient. Keep trying, and then if it's still "no", publish it yourself. How many more times?'

Here we go again, thought Eric. 'I'm not doing that.

You know I won't. I want to be published properly or not at all.'

Victoria pulled the duvet cover off her husband. 'Get the kids up for breakfast, Eric, and stop being so bloody precious about your book.'

Eric dragged himself up to meet the day. At least he hoped no one at work had seen the tweets.

Dylan Dylan greeted the business editor on his arrival into the office. 'Morning, Eric. Good night last night?' The insufferable head of sales was sitting at Eric's desk in his swivel chair. Julia, sat opposite, just nodded meekly by way of welcome.

'Planning a transfer to editorial?' Eric asked as he plonked his bag down almost in Dylan's lap.

'Just keeping your seat warm for you. And seeking the advice of a colleague.' The human monobrow got up to let Eric reclaim his chair. 'I wanted to check the punctuation on a new sales email I'm planning.' Eric didn't rise to the bait. Dylan smirked. "Tricky, is punctuation. Can alter the meaning of things if you get it wrong, like "Stop clubbing, baby seals" for example.'

'Your sales message must be very creative if it involves reference to baby seals, either as party animals or cull victims,' said Eric.

'We aim to please,' said Dylan. 'Anyway, you were the one wielding a big stick last night. Beating that agent around the head.'

Eric could have punched the swaggering, sarcastic, Salfordian shit. Julia kept her head down and said nothing. She'd obviously seen it too. 'Is that all? Can we get on with our work now, Dylan, or are you going to be hanging around here all day?'

Dylan sauntered off, resisting the urge to chalk up an imaginary score with his finger as he left. Eric was such an easy target it was embarrassing.

Eric sat down. 'I suppose you know what he was referring to?'

Julia nodded. 'I did see your exchange last night, yes, but he shouldn't be poking fun. You must have been upset.' The catalyst for his outburst at least wasn't lost on her.

'Just one of those things, Julia, and a salient lesson to look before you leap when it comes to setting down any sentiment in writing.'

Julia had been busy. 'I've done a quick analysis, and it's died already. It got a bit of comment last night but hardly any favourites or re-tweets. Think you'll be out of the woods now.' Eric wasn't really sure what Julia was telling him but at least he picked up on the supportive tone.

'Thank you, Julia. Most kind. Now let's get on, shall we?

Would you like a cup of tea first? I've got you a *pain au chocolat* too. Thought you might need cheering up.'

For the first time in his life Eric could have hugged an intern.

CHAPTER ELEVEN

Alyson and Alison sat poolside on a hard wooden bench in the local leisure centre, breathing in the chlorine and raising their voices above the din to talk. 'I wouldn't mind running a shot across his bows,' Alyson said, admiring the physique of the young lifeguard in charge of the children's Pirate Ship swimming party. A woman within earshot on the next bench tutted and moved off to the other end of the pool. 'Stuck-up cow,' ventured Alyson, before the two of them dissolved into giggles. The two friends, initially keeping half an eye on their children as they enthusiastically repelled boarders from the giant inflatable galleon, soon become engrossed in their own conversation. Thank goodness for organised activities in the half-term holiday.

Alyson had a favour to ask her friend and it was a big one.

'You want me to have the kids for a whole three days?' said Alison. She was used to looking after Alyson's kids, Saffron and Teddy, and did so regularly but three days would be the longest stayover ever.

'I can drop them off at school on the Friday, so you'd only need to pick them up at 3.30pm. Then, I'll leave early on the Sunday and be back for mid-afternoon, so it's closer to two days really.'

Alison still didn't commit. 'But are you sure it's going to be worth it?'

'It's exactly what I'm looking for. I can put my new style in front of two agents in one-to-ones as well as finding out how the real publishing world works.'

'Have you actually written in your new style yet?'

Alyson looked hurt. 'Yes, of course. I told you I would. I'm working on an idea that's completely fresh for me. And this conference will give me the right sort of incentive to get it finished.'

'Is this the best writing conference around, though? Wouldn't it be a good idea to check what else is available first, before signing up?'

'I can send you the stuff, Ali, but I doubt I'll find anything better. The testimonials are great, they've got loads of agents there, the programme looks interesting and people have been signed up for publishing deals on the spot in the past.'

Alison was still contemplating the three-day stretch with Aly's kids and wondering what her husband would say. 'Lancaster is a long way away though – isn't there one a bit closer?'

'It's only three and a half hours by train. I can write two chapters in that time. Will you, Ali? I'm so excited.'

'Can you afford it though? It sounds a lot of money.'

'I took your advice and negotiated a bigger commission on my next book with ViXen – that will pay for it. I'm thinking, can I afford *not* to go?'

Alison could see her friend had made her mind up.

She had one last question. 'How did you find out about it?'

'I was Googling the difference between "affect" and "effect" and the ad just popped up. It was like some sort of miraculous intervention.'

Alison chuckled – her friend certainly didn't lack enthusiasm or ambition. 'Go on, then. Just this once, but you'd better get a deal out of it.'

Alyson jumped up and danced a small jig of delight before giving Ali a big hug. 'You bet I will. You're a lifesaver. Talking of which...'

Alison turned to see what Aly was looking at and caught sight of the young lifeguard getting ready to deflate the SS Bluebeard. The air pipe he was holding between his legs looked like a huge phallus. Alyson's eyes widened with glee as she projected an altogether different interpretation on this innocent scene. 'Actually, Ali, that gives me an idea for two new stories. One on Pirates and one on lifeguards.'

'I thought you were going mainstream?' Ali reminded her.

'All in good time. I've still got bills to pay. Seriously though, thanks for helping me to go to this conference.'

'I get the impression you'd have gone whether I had the kids or not. But you enjoy it and get something out of it.'

'I will. And you never know, there might even be some dishy men there...' Alison had long given up wondering if Alyson ever turned her libido off – she knew she couldn't. It was like a runaway train where the deadman's handle had stuck – she was gathering speed and destined to stop only after she had careered off the track and into a ravine.

94

Victoria was really looking forward to lunch. It was Geraldine's turn to pay and she'd managed to persuade her it was about time they tried Manchester House. To offset the spike in the average lunch cost Victoria had volunteered to fund cocktails in the 12th floor bar first. Swings and roundabouts. As they sipped their Pornstar Martinis on the open sunlit terrace high above the city centre they felt very superior indeed.

Geraldine approved. 'Good choice, Vic.' Then, pointing down at the Manchester Evening Chronicle's offices off Deansgate, 'I reckon you'll be able to see Eric from up here.'

'As long as he can't see me,' Victoria replied. 'He probably wouldn't approve of such daytime decadence. I'll just pretend that we've been to Costa if he asks – not that he will.'

Seduced by the sunshine and their vertiginous vantage point they decided to have another cocktail. It was the sort of day where one would be all right, two too many and three not enough. Later, when they'd taken the lift down to the restaurant on the second floor, they were both feeling very giddy indeed.

Geraldine recounted an amusing tale about one of her clients asking her out on a date. He was twenty years older than her, blessed with a 'flexible marriage' and keen to drink champagne out of her glass slipper. As their laughter subsided Victoria decided to tell her lunch companion about Eric's cyberspace exchange with the ogre agent. 'Honestly, Gez, it's like giving Basil Fawlty a Twitter account. Touchy is not the word, and all over something where the guy didn't even mean Eric.'

Geraldine whinnied in a Sybil-like bray. She thought Victoria's description suited Eric perfectly. 'How to make a bad situation worse. Speaking of which, dare I ask how he's getting on with his book?'

'Not very well is the answer. That's obviously why he lost it on Twitter. Even the rejections have dried up now.'

'Well, I've said it before, but if I were Eric I'd self-publish in a heartbeat,' Geraldine said. 'God, it doesn't even need to be any good. At least he can call himself an author then, direct people to Amazon and give copies away as Christmas presents. Anyway, some self-published authors have done really well. He's being a bit bloody-minded if you ask me.'

'Can't disagree with you there. But he's adamant it should be published "properly". He's doing my head in with it to be honest.'

Geraldine nodded, a little too energetically. 'So what next? Does he just keep sending it out to every agent under the sun until there's none left, or what?'

Victoria hadn't really worked out the end game. 'I don't know. What else can he do? He'll give up soon but then he'll just sulk even more. He reads the bestsellers lists every week and it's "that's crap", "I bet it's not as good as mine" and "how can people read this rubbish?" all the time.'

Despite the cocktails and bottle of wine they were sharing Geraldine put her work head on. In fact, that's when she was most inventive. 'If this was a client problem, then we'd go to Plan B as Plan A hasn't worked. So what's Plan B?'

'He hasn't got one, Gez.'

'OK, so let's come up with one. How about he goes on one of these "meet the agent" conferences I've read about? The worst that could happen is they tell him his book stinks, but you never know."

Victoria was intrigued. 'He can discuss his book with an actual agent?'

'Course he can. Writing courses include that sort of offer to get the punters in. The Guardian runs pages plugging events like that all the time – there will be loads if you look. Eric would love that sort of academic approach anyway.'

Victoria could spot a small flaw in the argument though. 'What if he did go on something like that, and they told him his book did stink?'

'I'm sure they'd be a bit more diplomatic than that. Anyway, then we'd advance to Plan C – he'd *have* to self-publish then.'

The two conspirators cackled away, jubilant in their problem-solving skills and with nary a thought to Eric's sensibilities. They were so pleased with themselves they asked for the dessert menu.

Con and Rosie were having a rare night out. Normally they didn't venture much further than their local pub but Con had decided to make an effort, surprising Rosie with tickets for The Brian Jonestown Massacre at The Roundhouse. Admittedly, the neo-psych rockers weren't exactly top of Rosie's playlist but she knew how much the band meant to Con and she appreciated the gesture.

Since Rosie's ultimatum to her boyfriend she'd been surprised at how he'd bucked up his ideas. He'd finally finished his edit and shown impressive organisation in ploughing through the Writers' and Artists' Yearbook to identify likely agents. While Con's insurrectionary instinct had reared its head on reading some of the agents' pedantic and punctilious submission guidelines, he knuckled down and played it straight. Each email and – far more labour intensive – written applications for the agents still in the dark ages, were ceremoniously despatched. Could this be the one?

Con agonised over which agents would be most receptive to his work and how many submissions to send out. He'd read that six would be a good initial number and that's what he started with, only to crumble a week later and send out another six. He typed the list of agents contacted and marked up each name in blue to denote 'pending'. After the high-pitched excitement of submitting his queries he told himself he'd have to be patient, that it would take weeks to start receiving replies. Deep down he fantasised about receiving an urgent call from an agent who, having read his work, couldn't believe he was still on the market. In fact Con did receive a reply within three days of his first mail-out – a rejection. He updated his list and turned the agent's name from blue to red. After the first six weeks the colour of the list was starting to resemble a litmus test where the combined pH of vinegar, lemon juice and battery acid was in the ascendancy. He administered a Rennie in the form of another six submissions to keep the overall balance neutral.

Rosie watched all of this activity with mixed feelings. She wanted him to succeed, of course, but as Con swam against the red tide she felt that the law of probability would most likely see him running out of options. She was determined not to go back on her injunction to him to return to work after the end of September, but at the same time she knew how crushed he'd be at not having made a breakthrough.

Con was becoming increasingly desperate as his options narrowed and this was another reason why he'd arranged this special night out. As they lingered in the bar during the support act, each clutching two bottles of Beck's to save on queuing, he adjudged the timing to be right. 'I'm getting nowhere with my submissions.'

This was hardly news to Rosie; she recited what she'd said one hundred times already. 'I know, but you've got to stick at it. It could all change tomorrow.'

'I think I should try another approach.'

Above the general hubbub of pre-gig pre-loading, Rosie gave him a quizzical look. *Like what*?

'You know I've done loads of research – writing sites, blogs, Twitter, yeah?' She knew that much was true – he was never off his laptop picking up the litter of the *literati*. Rosie nodded. 'There's this massive writers conference in Lancaster in September. If I went to that I'd be able to talk directly to agents about my book.'

This was news to Rosie, on a number of fronts. 'Really?'

'Yes. You get to see two agents and they read your opening chapters before you meet them. Then you discuss it with them. People have been signed up on the spot before.'

Rosie, despite being impressed at the sound of such an opportunity, had a practical query. 'But doesn't it cost a fortune to do something like that?'

'It's not cheap, no. But there's loads of seminars and

talks as well on how to get published. It could make all the difference. It's quite good value for a weekend.'

'A weekend? Con, how are we going to be able to afford that?'

'I was hoping you'd lend it to me? I'll pay you back, I promise. If I don't get any interest in Lancaster I'll start back at the hospital on October 1st. Cross my heart. I've already asked and they said they'd take me back.'

Having established the magnitude of the conference fees and train fare for Con, Rosie worked out that it was roughly the same as the both of them going to the Number 6 Festival in Portmeirion being held the same weekend. She'd had her eye on that. However, the hash cakes they'd taken at the door to get them in the mood for the gig were now beginning to kick in, she felt mellow, and Con was right – after Lancaster there were no more lives to play with. 'Right. I'll lend you the money. Last chance saloon for a deal.'

Con felt euphoric. How brilliant his partner was, and not just because the hash cakes were starting to exert their influence on him too. 'I'll not forget this, Rosie. I'll make you proud of me.' He flamboyantly threw his arms around her, causing her to brush him off in embarrassment.

'You'd better. Come on; let's get a good spot. They'll be on soon.'

CHAPTER TWELVE

After Reardon announced to Hugo that, following considerable thought, he'd decided to take the university job, he became an even bigger pain in the backside for the agent. The author now added to his incessant mithering over the lack of a new publishing contract an endless round of questions regarding his unexpected academic role. Hugo's commission from the Edward VIII posting was scant consolation given the new role now provided Reardon with *carte blanche* to pester him on a daily basis. Would he have an office? How many days did he actually have to go in? What events and engagements would he have to attend? Did he have to mix with the other lecturers? How many students would he have to deal with? On what day of the month would he get paid? Hugo regretted not having dropped his client at the same time Franklin & Pope did. Today though, the agent was looking forward to calling him. Here was a chance to give Reardon something to worry about for a change.

Reardon was sitting in the GP's waiting room with Belinda when his mobile rang. Belinda gesticulated to him not to answer it as a dozen pairs of ears honed in on the ringtone, Every Day I Write The Book. She hated her husband's use of a novelty call alert, not so much because Elvis Costello was last year's model but because she considered it inappropriate for a man of Reardon's years to be personalising his phone like a 15-year-old. Reardon answered regardless.

'Can you be brief, Hugo? I'm tied up at the moment,' he boomed.

Ignoring the obvious question as to why he'd picked up if he was otherwise engaged, Hugo pressed on. 'You asked me to give you the heads up on events you have to attend for Edward VIII. Well, I've got the list now and I've noticed that the first one isn't that far off.'

'Can't you email it?' Reardon said, trying to ignore Belinda's dumb show to get off the phone.

'I'll send the list later,' said Hugo, who could have done that in the first place except for the fact that he wanted to convey this news personally to his esteemed client. 'I just want to make sure you get this one in your diary. It's the first weekend in September, a writers conference at the University of Lancaster campus.' He paused to let the information seep in properly.

Reardon, his eyes fixed on a poster promoting prostate screening for the over-60s, thought there must be some mistake. 'Lancaster? I think you have the wrong university, Hugo. And when you say "writers" conference, who, exactly?'

'No, it's definitely Lancaster, Reardon, and the writers are all unpublished. It's a conference on how to get published. Like your course students, the delegates will be looking to you for inspiration and guidance.'

Feeling as if a lubricated, latex-sheathed digit had just

been inserted into his anus, Reardon let out a howl. 'You can forget that, Hugo. There is no way on God's earth I'm taking myself off to the arse end of the world in order to commune with a bunch of repetitive strain injury victims.'

'I'm afraid you don't have a choice, Reardon,' said Hugo, loftily. 'Edward VIII is very keen to reach out to aspiring authors – they see conferences like these as a recruiting ground for future creative writing students. This is very important to them – you're the best billboard they have.'

Belinda, along with 12 patients, could divine the call wasn't particularly pleasing news for her husband. She pointed urgently at the exit to tell him to take his conversation outside. As he barged through the door Reardon crashed into a young mother pushing a pram on her way into the surgery. Hugo picked up the author's next comment together with the accompaniment of a baby's loud crying. 'I'll tell you now, Hugo,' shouted Reardon over the din, 'there's as much chance of me attending this conference as Salman Rushdie turning out at the Tehran Book Fair.'

Hugo continued to play with a straight bat. 'These are the commitments that come with these positions, Reardon. I'm sure it won't be that bad – you may even enjoy it. I'll send you the details.' And with that he rang off.

A red in the face Reardon made his way back into the waiting room past the accusing eye of the young mother trying to sooth her distressed child. 'You'll never believe what they want me to do,' he started, breathlessly.

Belinda glared at him. 'Not now,' she hissed. 'At least

you'll have no problem describing your symptoms to the doctor.'

Since Rocket's decision to target fresh, unagented talent Emily had been making discreet enquiries among industry colleagues concerning the lie of the land on writing festivals. The feedback surprised her. Initially, she feared that having to attend a conference for new writers would be akin to doing community service, a sentence to be endured. As she asked colleagues and peers about their experiences at these events she discovered that, far from being a chore, some of the agents and editors actually looked forward to them. Was it the prospect of discovering a new John Niven or Philippa Gregory that drove them? Not a bit of it. They'd have been quite happy to discover a writer who could shift 20,000 copies of a book detailing the author's anthropomorphic relationship with a pet cat, or anyone who could bring a new twist to the story of Henry VIII and his six wives. No, it was because in the literary world in which they operated an event like a conference provided yet another social outing. It was a works do but without the boss looking over your shoulder. And not only could agents and editors continue their clubbable chatter without scrutiny, at the same time they could be treated as gods by delegates and organisers alike. So when Emily let on to her confidantes that she was considering checking one out, they urged her to join them. The more the merrier. And without doubt, the best shindig was the Write Stuff weekender in Lancaster. It was all about *quid pro quo*. Yes, they had to read a few opening chapters and do a number of one-to-ones, and maybe even prep a seminar, but it wasn't overly taxing. On the plus side, you got expenses, got paid for sessions and seminars and got to hang out with your mates for the weekend while your bar tab was picked up by the organisers. In a corporate sense you were also underlining how your business nurtured and encouraged new talent. And for this noble flying of the company flag you also got days off in lieu.

In addition, Emily had discovered a further reason to attend a festival like this. Rocket had decided that as part of their – her – championing of unagented authors, they should set up their own novel-writing academy. His math, as he called it, was compelling. Limit it to 15 punters a time at around £2,000 a pop, and then use in-house staff and contracted authors to dispense knowledge over a few evenings and weekends. You never know, it might turn up a winner anyway. Charged with structuring such an academy as part of her new remit Emily calculated that by attending Lancaster and taking notes she'd create a painting-by-numbers outline for their venture that wouldn't need much more colouring in.

So Emily decided to anoint Lancaster with her presence, not least because the dates suited her as her boyfriend was on a lads' trip to Dublin the same weekend. Inviting herself was out of the question, not to mention necessary. She opened her junk filter and typed 'Write Stuff' in the search box. There must have been over ten emails from a Suzie Quixall there. She flicked through them, some going back to April, and felt the love and the desire coming her way. 'Could she consider/would she be free/it would delight them' and so on. Well, Suzie, she thought, today's the day persistence pays off. Emily could have emailed a reply but she had another reason to talk personally to the conference organiser. She picked up her phone and called Suzie Quixall on her direct line. 'Suzie? Emily Chatterton of Franklin & Pope. You simply won't believe this, but we've been having an issue with our email system and I've only just seen your emails...'

Chapman handed a glass of champagne to Suzie. 'You are on a par with Jane Austen when it comes to persuasion.' As a toast it was a clumsy effort, particularly from a published writer, but the founder of The Write Stuff was in exuberant mood on learning of Suzie's sterling work on the big-hitters list. Chapman had insisted on leaving the office and repairing to the wine bar opposite to celebrate. Pausing only to ask for some nibbles to go with their bottle of house champagne, Chapman wanted the whole story. 'Blow by blow, Suzie. Tell me how it all unfolded.'

Suzie, intoxicated before the glass even touched her lips, started the account of her remarkable day from the beginning. 'The Faculty of Humanities at King Edward VIII University called first. I'd contacted all of the universities with new creative writing courses to see if they'd like to put forward a speaker.'

'That was smart thinking, Suze.'

'Yes, but I didn't think we'd get such a well-known author. I thought, if we were lucky, we'd maybe get a professor or a lecturer.'

'Reardon Boyle is a big name, Suze. I can guarantee he's not done anything like this before.'

'I know, isn't it exciting? I couldn't wait to tell you but I thought I'd keep it a surprise for when you came in. And then I got the second call.' Reardon topped her glass up. 'It was only Emily Chatterton, the editors' editor – I couldn't believe it. I never expected her to reply in a million years, but, you know, nothing ventured...'

'Wonderful, wonderful. Go on.'

'It turns out that she'd not seen my earlier emails – some blip in their system – but she'd be delighted – *delighted* – to join us for the weekend as she'd heard so much about us. Chapman, you could have scraped me off the ceiling.' A flicker of a memory flashed through Chapman's mind. 'And if that wasn't fantastic enough she then suggested the third name.'

'Yes, that's curious. Another massive coup.'

'Well, you never thought we'd land Emily Chatterton either.'

'True. Anyway, what did she say?'

'Well, she asked me what agents were coming, so I told her, and then she asked if Hugo Lockwood had been invited.'

'Had he?'

'No. We daren't invite him. Thought he'd chuck it in the bin. Anyway, Emily says she's heard that Motif were casting their nets a bit wider for promising debut authors and she thought he'd be up for it.'

'Incredible. And what did he say?'

' I didn't actually speak to him. Emily suggested I call Hugo's boss and explain what we were all about and then invite Hugo because finding new talent at the conference was as easy as falling off a log.'

'You said that to him?'

'Not in those exact words. Anyway, he said

straightaway that Hugo would do it, that it fitted their current strategy wonderfully. Consider him signed up and all of that. Three in one day.'

Chapman was beside himself. This would be the most impressive line-up they'd ever mustered for a Write Stuff conference and would be sure to give last-minute bookings a boost. He congratulated himself on the merits of aiming high and never giving up. Flushed with success he now had another idea. 'Suze, what's the capacity for one-to-ones at the moment?'

Even without the blue file Suzie knew where they stood. 'It's good. Most of the experts are there for a minimum of two days so the one-to-one schedule has been the easiest to organise yet.'

'That's what I thought,' Chapman said. 'So if we were to give each delegate the opportunity to have three one-to-ones instead of two, we could just about juggle the schedule to accommodate that?'

The look on Suzie's face betrayed the amount of admin work that would be involved. 'Theoretically, yes. But it would be a lot of juggling. I'm not sure it would be worth it.'

'But it would be if we sold those extra slots at £50 a go, wouldn't it? I mean, that's what delegates value most, isn't it – the one-to-ones? What's another £50, or £100 if you can see three or four agents over the weekend instead of two? If two-thirds of the delegates opt for a third one-to-one that's another £10,000 income – think of the extra profit even after we pay the agents out.'

Despite the additional weight Chapman had just added to Suzie's already onerous list of duties she had to acknowledge that her boss didn't miss many tricks. No wonder he was buying champagne. 'That's genius, Chapman.' But she may as well have saved her breath. He knew that already.

CHAPTER THIRTEEN

It was Eric's birthday as well as a Friday and Julia had brought in two homemade chocolate chip muffins to celebrate. As the business editor was meeting Victoria for lunch he asked if they could save them for the afternoon. Julia's internship had now lasted four months and Eric was not looking forward to the end of September when she was due to leave. Without doubt she was the most able intern he'd ever worked with. Her writing was exceptional and she was so quick on the uptake he rarely had to tell her anything twice. With his previous interns the relationship had been a one-way street; he told them what to do – end of story. Julia, however, had opened his eyes and given him a fresh perspective. It wasn't only that she asked lots of questions that forced him to re-appraise whether his answers held water, she also challenged slavish adherence to old-fashioned working practices and suggested practical improvements. In addition, her knowledge of new media and how her generation consumed news shamed the newspaperman for the shallowness of his outlook. Eric began to see his job of two decades in a new light – he'd been on automatic pilot for too long. And Julia was so pleasant and considerate, always making him tea, bringing him biscuits and cake, and showing genuine interest in his literary ambitions. Eric wondered if he could fix a full-time job for her at the end of the internship but knew he'd be powerless to pull the right strings in a department where his own job could be the next to go. He'd miss her when she went, that was for sure.

Still, it was his birthday, the sun was shining and he shouldn't be worrying about what he couldn't change. As Julia went off to recharge their tea mugs Eric decided to check his personal emails – his mid-morning ritual. As the incoming emails streamed into his in-box one heading in particular stood out – 'Request for full manuscript'. Eric, who had virtually given up on his submissions by this juncture, could hardly believe his eyes. This time there was no rain dance, deep breaths or counting to ten – he clicked the message open and read: 'Dear Eric. I've had the opening chapters of your novel passed on to me and I'm interested in looking at it further. Can you please send me the full version at your earliest convenience?' Eric stared at the screen, dumbfounded at this change of fortune – this was the break he'd dreamed of for months. The disappointment and pain of the past year was swept away in an instant. He felt the urge to run down Deansgate shouting at the top of his voice that he was going to be published; he'd struck oil, received a knighthood and discovered a cure for EBOLA all at the same time.

He would send the manuscript right away. The sooner the better. He checked the identity of his saviour again. Hugh Moran. He didn't recognise the name, but then he did say he'd had the work passed on to him. Passed on by whom? Another agent presumably. What was the agency called? Golden Fleece. He didn't recall them from the Writers' and Authors' Yearbook but maybe it was a start-up, a breakaway of some description, an agency keen to swell its list of authors. Julia was approaching his desk with two mugs of tea in her hands – should he tell her before Victoria? He had to – he couldn't keep this news bottled up, even for a couple of hours.

'Julia, it's happened,' he croaked as she put down his drink. 'I've had a request for my full manuscript.'

His expression conveyed such excitement, relief and indebtedness she felt like a rescue worker unearthing a survivor from under tons of rubble six days after an earthquake. 'That's brilliant, Eric. What a lovely birthday present. I'm really pleased for you.' He stood up and gave her a clumsy high five, made even more awkward by the fact she was still holding a mug of tea. She could see he was at bursting point.

'I'd just about given up hope, to be honest, but it just goes to show. Stick in there and all that.'

Julia sat down opposite him. 'Who's it from?'

'Golden Fleece. It's a new name on me, but I don't care.'

'Look them up – see who else they handle.'

Eric entered 'Golden Fleece literary agency' into his search box. Nothing but 'Jason', 'Argonauts', and a gastro pub in Cheshire flashed up. He tried again, this time adding 'Hugh Moran' to the search term. More Greek myths and The Fleece pub in Dorset run by a Mike Moran came up.

At that moment Dylan Dylan strolled over to their workstation. He wasn't welcome at the best of times, but certainly not now. 'What's all the excitement about?'

asked the head of sales. 'I could see you jumping up and down from over there.'

'None of your business,' said Eric, tartly. He had no intention of sharing anything with this scourge of civility.

'No need to be like that,' said Dylan in a mock, injured voice. 'I just thought you must have received some good news, that's all.'

'Nothing to worry about, for me or for you,' Eric said, trying to look like he was getting on with his work.

'I just thought you should know our firewall has been compromised so you need to be on the lookout for spoof emails.'

'I think we're quite capable of resisting the urge to pass on our bank details to Ugandan solicitors,' Eric said, desperate to get back to his search.

'Well, scams like that are a bit old hat these days, Eric. They're getting more sophisticated all the time.' Dylan looked meaningfully at Eric, who didn't deign to respond. 'The latest one is some guy pretending he's from a literary agency.' Dylan again paused for effect. 'You'd have to be a real moron to fall for it, but there's one born every minute as they say.'

Eric's face turned incarnadine as the penny dropped. He was numb, unable to utter even the mildest of curses to his tormentor as the extent of his credulity, like an elephant lumbering into quicksand, sank in. Dylan turned on his heel and sashayed off, holding his sides in mirthful glee. Eric and Julia sat looking at each other in stunned silence.

Two hours later in Cicchetti, Eric still hadn't thawed out of his cryonic state. He wished he hadn't agreed to meet

Victoria for this birthday lunch. Detecting he hadn't had the best of mornings she tried to prise out of him the reason for his agitation. Given his cue he told his wife about the cruel hoax visited upon him by the Salford snake and awaited her sympathy.

She was aghast, but curious too. 'But why, Eric? Why would he play such a nasty, mean trick on you?'

'As far as I can tell his motivation appears to derive solely from being a loutish, lairy, little shit. I can only imagine he has some form of learning difficulty.'

'Are you sure? He sounds quite clever – I mean he knew which buttons to push.'

'Maybe you should have invited him out for lunch as well if you're so impressed with him?'

'Don't be ridiculous, Eric. I'm only saying that it's unusual for someone to go to such lengths to wind somebody up.'

'I dare say it's *de rigueur* where he went to school, a badge of honour. People like Dylan are symptomatic of the sick world we live in. He comes swaggering into the office like some Britpop-throwback, regaling us with his exploits and how bloody wonderful he is…'

'He must be a good salesman to keep that job down?'

'So he would have us all believe. Really, can we change the subject now?'

Victoria was only too glad to talk about something else. As she fussed over which sampling plates to opt for Eric sat looking morose with his 'you choose' face on. Victoria was now subscribing to her husband's unstated view that this lunch was a mistake. As she started on her second glass of prosecco (Eric, going back to work, declined) she rallied. It was present time. Reaching into her bag she produced a parcel, neatly gift-wrapped in a colourful collage of Penguin classics. 'Come on, Eric. Cheer up. Happy birthday.'

Bucking himself up, he took the gift and tore away at the paper. Victoria, who'd been planning on recycling such a lovely gift-wrap, suppressed a sigh. He reached inside and pulled out a copy of Stephen King's On Writing. As he turned over the book to read the blurb, Victoria explained its significance. 'They told me in Waterstones it was *the* definitive book for any author.'

'A pity you didn't buy it for me last year, then,' said Eric, a tad ungraciously.

Ignoring him, she pointed at the torn package. 'There's something else.' From the shredded wrapping he pulled out an envelope bearing his name. 'Go on, open it,' she urged.

Looking at her for clues, Eric did as he was told and slid out a sheath of papers. He read the top sheet. 'I don't believe this,' he said. 'Really?'

'I thought you needed a bit of encouragement. Are you pleased?'

Eric didn't know what to say. He didn't want to appear ungrateful. 'A conference on how to get published? Interesting. Thanks.'

'What do you think?' asked Victoria. 'You don't look too sure?'

'It's just a surprise, that's all,' he said, before adding rather too brusquely, 'It's not self-publishing, is it?'

'No – it's the best writing conference around and you get to meet two agents who read your opening chapters. I've checked it all out.'

'Isn't it a lot of money though? Can we afford it?' Victoria had removed the price list from the pack.

'It's worth every penny, Eric. It could make all the difference.'

'You don't mind me going away for a whole weekend?' Eric said, scanning the programme of events.

'That's all part of my cunning plan. Not if you come back with a publishing deal. Maybe I should have bought you this present last year but better late than never.'

'Well, it's very original of you. Thanks. I'll look at all the details tonight.'

Victoria nodded. She was used to her husband's cautious pessimism. He'd get it in good time. 'Do you want to share a pudding?' she asked.

Mindful of the chocolate chip muffin waiting for him at the office, Eric passed. 'Better get back. A lot to do.' As he got up to leave he added, 'It's been lovely, though.'

Julia was ready with tea and confectionery when Eric got back from lunch. Yes, he was going to miss her when she left, no doubt to be replaced by some unwashed, inarticulate tenderfoot whom he'd have to show the ropes from scratch.

She noticed the book he bore under his arm. 'Oh, On Writing? What a good choice. It's brilliant.'

'You've read it?' Eric didn't cease to be amazed at the breadth of his young intern's terms of reference.

'Yes. What's good about it is that it's not at all like a textbook. Half of it is about his life and really funny, and then the other half, on how to write better, is pure common sense. You'll love it.'

Eric eyed the book, and resolved to start reading it that evening. He appeared to be behind the curve on virtually everything these days. 'I've never read any Stephen King. Not my cup of tea, usually.'

'You don't need to have read any of his novels to enjoy On Writing. He knows what he's talking about, although I don't agree with his view on plot development.'

Now Eric felt really inadequate. 'What view is that?'

'He thinks that you shouldn't plan out your plot in advance, but set off on page one and see where it goes.'

'Really?' Eric didn't like the sound of that. Every chapter of Scrub Me Till I Shine in The Dark had been planned in meticulous detail before he started writing it. 'That's like jumping in a car and driving around aimlessly to see where you end up.'

'Or putting a message in a bottle and throwing it into the mid-Atlantic hoping it hits land,' said Julia. 'People say his novels all end up the same in any case – maybe that's why. Anyway, you'll love the book.'

'It's a present from my wife. In fact, she got me something else to do with my writing. A place at a weekend writing conference. It's in Lancaster in September.'

'The Write Stuff annual conference?'

Again Eric was taken aback at how well-informed Julia appeared to be. 'It is, actually. How do you know about that?'

'I've got an ex-uni friend going. She's desperate to be a writer.'

'And she thinks this will help?' Eric was keen for any form of endorsement for this amateur authors assembly.

'Bronte thinks so. She can't wait. She's been full of it for three months.'

Eric relaxed a little. Maybe he'd been a little too quick to judge. He hadn't wanted to offend Victoria by appearing ungrateful but his initial reaction on seeing the conference pack was a feeling of dread. It had conjured up an image of mixing with scores of earnest, middle-class scribblers, scraping the small talk barrel with people he didn't know and wouldn't meet again, and learning the square root of sod all. The middle-class bit was unkind, he knew. He was middle-class, but who else could afford to go on these things? Now Julia appeared to approve the concept he could see that the weekend could well hold possibilities. Thank goodness he'd not let his guard down and looked disappointed when Victoria gave him his present. 'So you think I should definitely go?'

Julia, pleased to be consulted by her mentor on such a matter, nodded enthusiastically. 'Definitely. You get to see two agents. It would be worth it for that alone.'

Eric could already envision his two agents fighting over him, like judges on The Voice each trying to convince him how they were uniquely equipped to help him on his 'journey'. 'Yes, you're right. That's quite a plus, really, isn't it?' Eric's mind was made up. 'It would be a shame to look a gift horse in the mouth.' He smiled at his own little joke. It was decided – he was going to Lancaster. Julia passed him his plate. 'No candles?' joshed Eric. After the unpleasantness of the morning things were looking up.

Eric and Julia had cast a silence over Dylan's morning wind-up, recognising it was a subject best avoided. The steely intern, however, wasn't prepared to let Dylan think his actions met with her approval. That lunchtime she'd emailed the head of sales to see if he would have a drink with her after work. Dylan simply emailed her back with, 'Alchemist, outside terrace, 6pm'.

The bar was busy when she arrived but she could see Dylan had already bagged a table on this fine summer's evening. His greeting consisted of thrusting the menu into her hand and saying, 'The cocktails here are brill.' Without perusing the list she asked for a glass of Chenin Blanc. When it arrived five minutes later it looked rather staid next to Dylan's crimson-coloured Dead Red Zombie, bubbling and smoking away in its hi-ball glass, more of a statement than an aperitif. Dylan gave the impression that he was very much at home in this most modern and opulent of Manchester watering holes. Julia realised this was his natural habitat, not the antiseptic office environment where he retained a desk.

'So you're happy with the job?' asked Dylan when the chemical reaction in his cocktail had abated.

'Yes, thanks, loving every minute of it.'

'So your dad's happy too?'

'Very grateful.'

'Music to my ears,' said Dylan, dispensing with his straw.

Julia and her father, sensitive to accusations of nepotism, had been keen to maintain an air of meritocracy over her placement. Eric still hadn't twigged exactly how Julia's internship had come about, which was surprising given that most placements at the newspaper were favours to advertisers' offspring. At least Dylan had kept his end of the bargain and not mentioned it – he wouldn't

119

do anything that could potentially compromise a client relationship.

Julia didn't tarry over her main reason for asking to see Dylan. 'Why are you so horrible to Eric?'

Dylan sniggered. 'What do you mean? It's just a bit of harmless fun.'

Julia wasn't being brushed off with such a casual denial. 'It's hardly harmless. I wasn't sure at first if your joking was banter, but this morning you were just cruel.'

Dylan was taken aback. How could anybody not find his japes amusing? 'I was having a bit of craic, that's all. Alleviating office boredom.'

'I don't think Eric saw it that way, and neither did I.'

'He's a grown man – he can take it,' said a defensive Dylan. Despite his bravura, Dylan's already busy brow congested still further. The last thing he wanted was word getting back to an advertiser that he might be anything less than wonderful.

'Eric's poured his heart and soul into his book. I don't think you realise how sensitive a writer can be trying to get their work recognised. You humiliated him.'

The normally unflappable head of sales looked puzzled. Christ, it was only a wind-up. Where was all of this arty-farty, bleeding heart stuff coming from? It was pathetic – no wonder Eric-bloody-Blair was such an easy target. So his booky-wook hadn't been published – so what? Hardly a surprise, as it would be shit anyway. But he could do without Eric bellyaching and putting him in a bad light if it got back to Julia's dad. So Dylan did what he always did when being confronted – he took the line of least resistance. 'Julia, what can I say? I'm really sorry. I hadn't realised.'

'So I see. It's not just doing the writing – that's the easy bit – it's getting an agent that gets you to square one on the board. Eric's sent his book to lots of agents and nobody's bitten yet. That's why your so-called spoof was so sadistic.'

'I just didn't think,' said Dylan, trying to adopt a hangdog look. Inside he was punching the air that his casual hoax had scored so heavily.

'He's getting to the point of desperation. He's even going on a weekend conference on how to get published in Lancaster this September – that's how much it means to him.'

'A conference away from home?' leered Dylan. 'Sounds like a good excuse for a dirty weekend to me.'

Julia's expression warned him that he was on the verge of undermining his act of contrition, however insincere it was. He held his hands up to acknowledge he was stopping his attempts at humour now.

'You need to apologise to Eric,' said Julia, enunciating each syllable for emphasis.

Good God – would he have to? Whatever. 'I will. I will. I see where you're coming from – I hit a raw nerve and that wasn't my intention,' he lied. 'You seem well up on the life of a struggling writer, anyway. How come?'

Satisfied that she had wrung this undertaking of repentance out of Dylan, Julia relaxed. 'I know how hard it is, that's all. I wrote a book the summer after I graduated.

Let's just say you get very attached; you want everybody to tell you how beautiful your baby is.'

'And not to say "would you like a banana for your

121

monkey?"' said Dylan, helpfully trying to summarise her point.

'I guess something like that,' said a bemused Julia.

'Did you try to get your book published, like Eric?'

'No. I thought about it, but I'm sitting on it for a while. Maybe I'll go back to it when I finish this internship. They say it's good to leave time between finishing a book and submitting it.'

Dylan was intrigued. 'You dark horse. What's it about?'

Julia reddened slightly. 'It's about a time–travelling detective. She goes back and forth to crack crimes.'

'Dr Who meets Shirley Holmes? Sounds like a winner to me.' That Dylan felt competent to predict Julia's future literary success was all the more remarkable as he'd read only one book since the age of 16, and that was one on football hooligans.

'That's one way of putting it,' said Julia, now laughing.

'So you're in competition with Eric to get an agent?'

'Not at all,' said the intern, looking serious again. 'I've not told Eric about my writing – I thought it would make his efforts seem, I don't know, less unique.'

Dylan was learning a lot this evening. 'You're very considerate, I'll give you that.'

'He is my boss – intern's intuition.'

Dylan felt an urge he'd not experienced in quite a while. 'Can I read your book? What's it called anyway?'

Julia looked hesitant. 'Well, it's called The Pendulum Swings but I'm not sure I'm ready to let people see my baby yet – just in case they do offer it a banana.'

Dylan wasn't to be denied. 'Only, I've got a mate who's

an actor and if it was any good, he could pass it on to his agent.'

'It's a book agent I need, not a theatrical one.'

'Yes – but they're all connected, aren't they? Won't do any harm if I read it, will it? I've got a good eye, me.'

Julia wasn't sure. Dylan didn't strike her as an authority on literary criticism. Was she being too precious? Maybe a totally objective viewpoint would actually be a good thing? And Dylan did appear to be well-connected. Maybe it was the Chenin Blanc, Dylan's persistence or his screwball charm, but she buckled. 'I'll send it to you on the condition that you don't give it to anyone without my permission, OK? Read it first and let me know what you think.'

'Deal,' said Dylan. 'Now, can I interest you in a Dead Red Zombie?'

CHAPTER FOURTEEN

Two hundred miles south another red-eyed, undead soul mired in perpetual unrest was getting under his wife's feet. Reardon was recounting to Belinda exactly how he'd laid his terms out. 'I told him they could forget an entire weekend – I'd travel up on Saturday and leave first thing Sunday. It was that or nothing.'

Belinda, preparing their evening meal, was glad Reardon had not jeopardised his new university position by refusing to go to the conference. Following his initial outburst at the news she had known better than to push him. She let him blow off steam, allowing time for the idea to settle and for the anti-depressants the doctor had prescribed to start working. Then, in an invisible pincer movement along with Hugo, the author was reminded of his duties to his wallet, if not academia. Reardon, though, still had to call the shots. 'Well,' she said. 'That sounds like a sensible trade-off.'

'I made them change the programme a bit,' he said with sombre satisfaction. 'They wanted me to do a Sunday morning keynote address, and a seminar group on the Saturday, but I wouldn't agree to that. "Keynote address", I ask you. It's not the United Nations, is it?'

'So what exactly are you doing?'

'I'm now giving the after-dinner speech on the Saturday – their so-called gala dinner. Gala is such an odd word isn't it? French origin, "to make merry". I don't think I'll be doing that.'

Such an observation was wasted on Belinda who was struggling to recall the last time Reardon had been of a gallant disposition. 'If it's only for one night, would you like me to come with you?'

'I'm quite capable of looking after myself, Bel, but thanks for the offer.'

Belinda, while relieved at the prospect of a night off from Reardon's repining, also knew that this would be the first night they'd spend apart for some months. The image of Reardon sleepwalking wasn't that distant a memory, and it certainly wasn't dim. Fortunately, he'd not repeated his somnambulistic wanderings since Paris and after starting his Citalopram prescription had actually been sleeping very well. Better than Belinda in any event. 'If you're sure?' she said.

'I don't see why we should both suffer the heady delights of Virgin Rail, student beds and a campus full of clamorous culture-climbers. I will fly solo.'

The issue settled, Belinda took the baked salmon from the oven and asked Reardon to set the table. 'Are you imbibing?' he enquired as he reached for the wine glasses.

Belinda shook her head. 'Not for me. Are you sure you should be?'

Reardon merely shrugged his shoulders as he poured himself a small compensatory Chablis. 'At least I will die happy,' he said. Again, Belinda doubted that.

'Well, overall it doesn't sound too bad, Reardon. I think that you might quite enjoy yourself if the truth be told,' ventured Belinda.

Reardon stopped sniffing the bouquet and assayed the same deadpan humour with which he no doubt hoped to win over conference. 'I admire your good cheer, Belinda, but I rather lean towards Voltaire's view that "optimism is the obstinacy of maintaining that everything is best when it is worst".'

'If you expect the worst, you'll never be disappointed.' Hugo was waxing philosophical as he sat in the Mound Stand at Lord's. Middlesex's prospects of overhauling Yorkshire in their run chase were looking increasingly forlorn. As the shadows lengthened over the outfield Hugo was keeping his followers on Twitter updated regarding the progress of the match – few would care. Notwithstanding impending defeat for the side he'd supported from boyhood he was enjoying a wonderful day out in the August sunshine. Hugo rarely missed this annual pilgrimage to the home of cricket with a group of old school friends – not least because he feared to what degree his ears would be burning if he didn't turn out. Once the date was set he'd move anything to be there. The group of eight had been drinking all day – beneath their feet lay empty magnums of Moet, plastic jugs of Pimms, cracked disposable glasses and various discarded wrappers from the Waitrose picnic range – the sort of detritus that could inform future archaeologists that Middlesex, not Yorkshire, held home advantage. Hugo had added an artistic flourish to their conspicuous consumption by thoughtfully bringing along a punnet of fresh strawberries to immerse in their polycarbonate flutes of champagne. The high-spirited coterie now faced a dilemma – they had run out of alcohol and ten overs remained on the board. A further reason for Hugo's invitation now became apparent as the cry of 'Locker's shout' went up. Knowing his place, Hugo didn't resist their petition and good naturedly set off to the bar to acquire the next round. As he gripped the stair rail on his way down the back of the stand, his mobile buzzed. *Go away* was his first thought, but curiosity compelled him to at least check who was calling. Emily Chatterton. Swaying slightly, he took a deep breath and answered.

'Emily. How the devil are you?' At the same moment a huge cheer went up from the crowd inside the ground as a tail-ender sent the ball clear of the boundary.

'Have I caught you at an awkward moment?'

'Not at all, Em, just a day out with the boys. Taking Lord's by storm.'

Emily could tell by his voice – Lord Charles on crack – that Hugo wasn't dressed for the weather. 'You sound like you're having fun. Anyway, I called because I just found out we're spending the weekend together next month.'

This was news to Hugo. 'Really, where's that?'

'Stop being coy, Hugo. As if you'd forget?' she teased.

Hugo was drawing a blank. 'Give me a clue?'

'Lancaster. The Write Stuff conference. I've just got the joining instructions and couldn't believe your name was on it. I thought you'd be the last person I'd see up there.'

Lancaster. Of course. Hugo knew she'd have to find

127

out sooner rather than later. He'd even considered a pre-emptive bid to tell her the news before she discovered it from another source. Well, she knew now. 'Oh, that. Well, I didn't want you having all of the fun, Emily. Seriously, I thought it was about time I took a look.'

Emily, relishing the mental picture of Hugo squirming as he made light of his change of heart, said sweetly, 'It's just that you were so insistent that writing conferences were full of inadequates and stalkers, that's all.'

Hugo gripped the stair rail tighter to remain in an upright position. 'I was only joking. No, we were talking about it at the agency and decided it wouldn't do us any harm dipping our toe in the water. You know, get out there in the frontline for fresh talent.'

Emily was tickled to learn that her plan to set Hugo up had worked so efficiently, but not half as amused as hearing Hugo protest it was his idea and part of Motif's new strategy. 'I see Reardon's going, too. I thought you were trying to avoid him these days, Hugo?'

'Not at all. In fact I organised his attendance.' Hugo's amusement at Reardon having to attend the conference had disintegrated at about the same time he realised he would be joining him. 'I'm looking forward to it immensely. Should be fun.'

The editor didn't break step. 'That's exactly how I see it, Hugo. We can prospect for gold together.'

Hugo finished the call and ran down to the bar – at least there was no queue at this late stage of the match. He cursed, once again, at being forced to attend this scholarly symposium in the sticks but his boss had given him no choice – 'We can't always rely on our good looks, Hugo, to pull the prettiest girls at the ball. Sometimes we have to ask for a dance first.'

As he staggered back up to his friends clutching two bottles of house champagne a large groan went up from the crowd. Middlesex had lost their last wicket. An even louder lament emanated from his friends. 'Christ, Lockers, did you go to Rheims to get those?'

Suzie Quixall took a bite of her hoisin duck wrap and tossed it back on the plate in disgust. Friday night, home alone, with a cheap bottle of Chardonnay for company. The late evening sun streamed through the window of her neat two-bedroom flat, bestowing a glorious golden hue to the grey wreck of her evening. Suzie opened her laptop and clicked on Jagged Little Pill in iTunes – a musical accompaniment for the detailed job ahead of her. The power behind the throne at The Write Stuff was no stranger to taking work home – she would often slog away evenings and weekends to finish off urgent tasks for Chapman. This Friday, however, an assignment of the most personal kind lay before her – she was working on a tribute movie clip to celebrate ten years of The Write Stuff, or rather, she was crafting a paean in honour of her boss. This was not an unwelcome chore in Suzie's eyes; in fact no one, particularly Chapman, knew she was doing it and in any event she would not have delegated such a duty to anybody else. Suzie had been with Chapman since day one of The Write Stuff and only she fully understood the workings of the business and the genius of the man. Since having the idea to do a celebratory movie clip Suzie had excitedly collated on to her laptop images and video files from across the company's history. She'd assiduously organised the images into ten files – one for each year – and tonight she was going to develop a storyboard and clipboard before briefing a professional editor to create a slick mini-movie. She could already picture the look of surprise on her boss's face and feel the warmth of his approbation when the film was revealed at the conference gala dinner on the Saturday night.

She mused over what sort of narrative frame to build the film around – this would dictate which pictures to cherry-pick. Would using the chapters of a book be an appropriate theme, or too hackneyed? If so, was it a fairytale, a fantasy or a thriller? 'Once upon a time', or 'A long time ago in a galaxy far, far away?' She turned Alanis up and recharged her glass. Folder one. The launch story picture. Gosh, didn't Chapman look young? He was certainly carrying a bit less timber back then. There was the first anniversary party – just look at her dress. At least she could still fit in it. There was only a team of three at the start – it was much more intimate back then. Year two – the cutting from The Bookseller with the headline 'Write Stuff's record growth' over a picture of Chapman with a cropped haircut. Thank goodness that style hadn't lasted long – it never suited him. Fast forward to year three – the Christmas party. She laughed as she remembered how Chapman had thrown her over his shoulder and charged across Millennium Bridge, nearly dropping her into the Thames. She was so drunk at the time she dreaded to think what would have happened if the dark waters had swallowed her up. These captured moments of yesteryear flashing before her wasn't dissimilar to drowning. The same year – and that picture of author Chapman Hall surrounded by copies of A Poisoned Heart and a Twisted Memory at the book launch. How crucial the book had been in establishing The Write Stuff's credentials. As Chapman had quoted at the time, 'Give a man a reputation as an early riser and he can sleep 'til noon.' They both knew that without A Poisoned Heart The Write Stuff would never have had the credibility to prosper. The right boost at the right time. She dragged the images she'd highlighted so far across to the master file and carried on. Now, shortly after the book launch, the first conference. She looked at the group shot of the delegates, 70 in total, with Chapman and Suzie the triumphant couple in centre front. Back then they'd held it in Roehampton. A number of these self-same delegates still came to conference. How she wished for those days again, before Chapman began to appreciate her less. Year five – the move to their new offices. New? They'd been there five years. She emptied the remains of the wine bottle into her glass just as Alanis stopped emoting. She went to the compilation folder on iTunes and scrolled down until she saw it – the track that meant so much to her, the one Chapman always insisted on playing at staff parties. Suzie Q. He liked the way she talked. He liked the way she walked. She'd remain true so he wouldn't be blue. As Creedence Clearwater Revival crawled out of the swamp with their pulsating R 'n' B take on Dale Hawkins' classic, the images already wheeling across her temporal lobe took on more vivid hues, bursting into life as if she was re-living those very moments. The voodoo was strong. The magic compelling. Then she had a blinding flash of inspiration as to what theme she could use for the film. Yes – that would work like a charm. She set to finishing off the rest of the photo files with reinvigorated zeal.

CHAPTER FIFTEEN

Dylan was in work early on the Monday morning, hoping to see Julia before Eric arrived. Much to his surprise he had read the whole of The Pendulum Swings over the weekend. After Julia had left the bar on Friday night he'd gone on a bender with his friends, arriving home at 3am. He'd surfaced, feeling like death, at 11am when he found the PDF file of the book in his email. Julia had sent it to him as soon as she'd got home the previous evening. At first he ignored it and wondered how he could pass comment without actually reading the book. Then, fortified by a solid fry-up, he determined to at least spend an hour on it before getting ready for another night out larging it in Manchester. Stretched out on his settee, with the windows of his city centre flat wide open to the traffic buzzing below, he opened the file in iBooks and began. Dylan knew he wasn't equipped to constructively critique the novel – any novel – but mindful of Julia's father as much as consideration for the author he calculated that to be seen to be making an effort would suffice. In any event, he could pass it on to his actor 'friend' (who he'd only actually met twice) so he would actually be helping. However, within five minutes, a strange phenomenon occurred – Dylan found himself fascinated by the unlikely heroine and gripped by the intriguing era-hopping plot. He read steadily all afternoon until he had to meet his friends at 6pm. Even when out that evening he couldn't quite escape the characters he'd encountered earlier in the day and was hungry to find out what happened to them next. He didn't share this beguilement with his mates in case they laughed at him but he did make sure that he didn't get uber-smashed that night. He wanted to get back to The Pendulum Swings. Awaking at 9am the next morning he was soon reclining on the settee where he stayed reading all day. At 6pm he finally found himself on the last page. His emotions at reaching the end were a mixture of exhilaration and sadness. Excitement at how the story had built to a climax, and sorrow that he had nowhere else to go now he'd finished it. He was in awe that someone like Julia, an intern, could hatch such sorcery. He'd underestimated her.

As Julia arrived at her desk he thrust a cappuccino from Café Nero towards her and smiled. She immediately wondered what was up. 'You're in a good mood for a Monday morning,' she said.

'I'm in a good mood every morning,' he replied. 'But an even better one today now I know I'm working with a budding author.'

Julia laughed. 'So you got the file, then?'

'Got it? I've read it. All of it.'

Julia couldn't be sure if he was joking – surely Dylan, of all people, hadn't managed to read a whole book over the weekend. 'What happened in the end, then?'

Dylan recounted the denouement for her, albeit in clunky, black and white terms.

Julia was taken aback. 'You did read it. Well, what did you think?'

'It's the best book I've read in years,' he said. Although factually correct as it was the *only* book he'd read in years, his summary wasn't meant to be tongue-in-cheek. 'Seriously, I just had to tell you how bloody brilliant it was. I was gobsmacked.'

Julia was uncertain as to Dylan's sincerity. 'You seriously read it all? And you really liked it?'

'Every page, I'm telling you. Dr Who meets Shirley Holmes, like I said. I could see that on television, I could.'

Julia felt like Alice in Wonderland after wolfing down the cake marked 'Eat Me' – her head was pressing the ceiling in the face of such praise. The effect, however, didn't last long. She soon checked herself – this was, after all, Dylan. She knew he didn't read books, almost certainly wasn't a reliable critic and knowing him, he was probably up to something. 'Thanks. I appreciate it. I'm glad you liked it.'

'Do you want me to give it to my mate to look at?' Dylan asked enthusiastically.

Julia tensed – things were going a little too fast. She needed time to re-evaluate the situation. She guessed Dylan meant well but it didn't mean she had to appoint him as her agent. 'Not yet, if you don't mind. It's very kind of you, but I'm going to take my time. I'm going to go back to it after I finish here.'

Dylan, tribute paid, adopted his usual swagger and ambled off. 'No sweat, Jules. You're the boss. But it's a brilliant book.'

Nevertheless, Julia was still buzzing half an hour later when Eric arrived. 'Running late,' he said as he dumped his bag on the desk.

Julia dutifully went to make him some tea, and determined to be extra – careful not to mention Dylan within earshot of her mentor. 'Good weekend?' she ventured as she passed him his mug.

'Very good, indeed. I spent quite a bit of it looking at the conference programme and activities. It's really well put together, I must say.'

Julia was genuinely interested now she knew two people who were going. 'Did you pick out which agents you want to meet?'

'That was quite a challenge, I can tell you. Some of the ones I'd have loved to have met were already booked up – I'm a bit late signing up, I suppose.'

'But there are some slots left?'

'Better than that – I've managed to bag some extra slots – I'm going to be seeing four agents in total.'

Julia was impressed that Eric had somehow negotiated double the number of allocated one-to-ones. 'How did you manage that?'

Eric paused for a second before telling her the truth. 'It wasn't that hard. You could pay for extra slots. I thought I might as well be hung for a sheep as for a lamb and took advantage. Incremental cost and all that.'

Julia didn't ask how much the extra slots cost but knew that such a luxury wouldn't be within the grasp of all the delegates. Still, good for Eric if he'd somehow doubled his chances of success. 'Well, why not? And what about the rest of the programme?'

'There are quite a lot of seminars and talks but I don't think a lot of them are that relevant to me,' he said airily. 'Looks like they're covering a lot of ground specifically for really new writers. Characterisation, plot, that sort of thing. The ones that caught my eye the most are the sessions on how to get published, writing killer query letters and scintillating synopses. They're the ones I've opted for.'

'You have to say now which ones you'll be going to?'

'Yes – it's very organised.'

Julia made a mental note to check with Bronte what plans she'd made for conference. Maybe she should get Eric and Bronte to meet up? Then again, maybe not.

Eric changed the subject. 'I don't suppose you've seen our stellar head of sales today?'

'I did see him first thing. Why?'

'I want to see his face when he realises that his brand of humour isn't going to be tolerated around here for much longer.'

Julia hadn't heard Eric sounding so bellicose before. It disquieted her. 'What are you going to do?' she asked nervously.

'It's not what I'm going to do – it's what I've done,' said Eric, the Judge Dredd of the newsroom. 'I've reported him to Human Resources for abusive behaviour.'

Julia's eyes widened. The intern was shocked that Eric had taken such a course of action but didn't want to say so in case it riled her boss. She spluttered, 'What did they say?'

'As you can imagine, they were very concerned. They told me such behaviour could constitute bullying in the workplace.'

Julia grimaced. Surely Eric didn't have to resort to HR over a few jokes? 'What are they going to do?'

'They're going to investigate, but first they'll be telling him that his number has been called. They'll want to interview you, too.'

'Me? Why would they want to interview me?' she said in alarm.

'You're a witness. You were there on Friday when he played his latest prank on me. And before that, as well.'

Julia now felt like she'd guzzled the bottle marked 'Drink Me' as she seemed to shrink into her clothes and disappear. Here was an aspect of office life she'd never thought to experience on her secondment. Was Eric really that affronted he felt justified in wielding the inflatable hammer of employee legislation to settle a squabble? Was Dylan really that iniquitous he needed to be caned in front of the whole school? Should she show some sympathy with Eric's cause? What would she say to Dylan if he raised it with her? She feared such a chain of events wouldn't end well. She turned her gaze to her keyboard and said quietly, 'I've got to finish this.'

Later that afternoon Dylan Dylan emerged from the HR manager's office and slammed the door behind him. He was not thinking kind thoughts. That bastard, Eric. That lily-livered, self-righteous, keyboard-pounding wanker. What sort of man ran to Mummy every time someone pulled his leg? How old was he? So he'd wound him up once or twice and this is how he reacted? By trying to get him disciplined or even sacked? Everybody knew Dylan liked a bit of banter. It stopped the office being a stuffy place. It provided some fun and entertainment for the team. God knows they needed it. But cowards like Eric always hid behind someone else, never having the balls to fight for themselves. He was a sneak and a creep who could only stand up for himself if he was stabbing people in the back. Eric-bloody-Blair, thinking he was so special, delicate, artistic and vulnerable to the point where he needed special protection.

Dylan's first reaction on hearing he was to be investigated over a potential breach of his employment terms and conditions was to go down to the editorial floor and have it out with the business editor right away. Man to man. He punched the lift button, but as he waited he realised he shouldn't act in haste. That pillock Eric would merely add it to his list of pathetic complaints. And in any case, he'd not been suspended but he could be if he didn't stay away from Eric. They said they were going to call Julia as a witness as well. What if that got back to her dad? As the lift arrived, he decided to get out of the office altogether to buy some time.

Minutes later, as he collected himself over a pint of Kronenbourg in Mulligans, he took stock of the situation. There was no way he could be found guilty of harassment over these trivial incidents. Surely, they would conclude that Eric was an old woman who needed to grow a thicker skin? Would Julia put the boot in on him? Could he depend on her to back him? What a cock-up. They told him it could take a few weeks to investigate the claims. Why so long? Why not do it today and let him get on with making a few quid for the newspaper? He cursed the Didsbury dipshit who was trying to rain on his parade, motivated, no doubt, by pure jealously. Boy, was he going to get his own back on him. Then he'd know what a true wind-up was. But not in the office. Not there, under the watching eyes of HR and the sanctuary of contracts of employment. But where, and how? He took a deep draught of his lager. And then he had a brilliant idea.

PART TWO

PART TWO

CHAPTER SIXTEEN

It was time.

'Have you got your sandwiches?' Rosie asked.

'Yes,' snapped Con. 'I've got everything.'

'And your phone charger?'

'Yes,' he hissed. It was good of Rosie to come and see him off on his trip north this bright and sunny Friday morning but she didn't have to treat him like a five-year-old. 'I've checked everything, three times. I'm not a retard.'

Rosie, aware that Con's biggest strength wasn't personal organisation, decided he was ready. 'Well, this is it,' she said.

She gave him a hug and waited for him to reciprocate. He threw his rucksack across his shoulder and looked up at the departure board. 'I'd better get on board now. Bye.' With that he trudged up the stairs, only turning at the top to proffer an unconvincing wave. Rosie had been amazed when Con had decided to travel to Lancaster by coach instead of by train. It was almost seven hours by road but Con had stuck to his guns arguing that it made sound economic sense for him to make the journey in this way. Since Rosie was advancing the fees for the weekend conference he didn't want to appear profligate with her

143

hard-earned cash. Travelling by coach also provided the additional bonus of being dropped off at the campus rather than in the town, thus saving further money. A taxi from the railway station to the university cost around £10 according to the conference website. That was £10 each way. Of course, he wouldn't have got a taxi but there'd still be a few quid to shell out on bus fares so the coach made a lot of sense. The lengthy journey up the M1 and M6 would also give him plenty of time to review the conference programme and refine his pitch for his one-to-ones. More importantly, he calculated that the savings he'd make would fund around ten pints of Guinness – five on Friday and five on Saturday – allowing for university bar prices. He didn't want to look like a cheapskate.

He made his way to the rear of the coach and sat on the back seat, on the side opposite the on-board toilet. He hoped that if he spread out his bag and coat he could deter other passengers from sitting too close to him. He kept his head down, not looking to see if Rosie was hovering – he didn't want her waving him off like a war wife in a Pathé newsreel. At last the engine shuddered into life and the coach moved slowly off the stand. He had the back row all to himself – until Birmingham at least. Now he sought out Rosie one last time, only she'd gone. He felt slightly rejected, or maybe she'd just moved position and he'd missed her?

Clear of the station his thoughts returned to economics. He couldn't shake from his mind the cruel injustice of the organiser's last-minute offer to sell further one-to-one sessions at the conference. What he would have given to be able to do that – anything but the £50 a time they were actually asking. Con was incensed that less deserving writers could steal an advantage by dint of their deeper pockets. It riled him that the initial level playing field of two one-to-ones per delegate had been abandoned in order to crank out a few more quid for The Write Stuff – it was inequitable in his view. It was even more frustrating that he couldn't moan to Rosie about this discrimination as she would naturally interpret this as a request for extra money. He knew if she offered £50 – preferably £100 – for him to see another agent, he'd snap her hand off and that made it even harder for him to bellyache about it. He consoled himself that it would only take one agent to like his work and he would be on his way. One agent to recognise his potential and change his life. And he was seeing two – that was a 50/50 shot. He'd take that.

Selecting two agents to meet had been a challenge in itself as the list contained over 40 names. He had spent hours looking them all up online and whittling down his list of 'possibles'. Getting rid of book doctors was the easiest decision – he only wanted to see people who could give him a deal. Then he drilled down to get rid of those agents who were mainly interested in fantasy, children's, crime, historical and the like. He decided that he was very much 'literary fiction'. But that still left quite a few who claimed they were open to any genre of writing as long as it was great writing. Easy for them to say but harder to target in that case. At last he narrowed it down to a choice of five at which stage he started to look at the authors they represented, how many clients they had, and how big an agency they worked for – it was an exacting process to say the least.

More than anything he looked to see if they 'welcomed debut writers' – no point wasting his time on an agent who didn't. He looked at the available meeting slots still free on the one-to-ones calendar and up-weighted the agents who already had lots of appointments – surely the fact they were in demand indicated that they must be worth seeing more than the agents with only a few appointments? Then he mulled over whether a male or a female agent would be better for him given his writing style and his approach to things – who would be more empathetic? He studied the Twitter feeds of his shortlist and gawped at their photographs to see if he could find any clues there. Finally, he fine-tuned his 'probables' list down to three candidates. Unsure of whom to eliminate, he wrote the names on three pieces of paper, folded them up and asked Rosie to pick two out of his hand. Choices made and meetings confirmed online he told himself, 'no regrets'. Now, as he idled north, he was in the lap of the gods.

Travelling in the same direction at a rather faster pace than Con was the 10.43 train from Euston to Lancaster. Emily Chatterton and Hugo Lockwood sat in a rather deserted first-class carriage contemplating the complimentary sandwiches and beverages that had just been wheeled up to their table. Although the selections on offer looked rather unappetising at least there was a vegetarian option for Emily.

'I was dreading Reardon being on this train,' confessed Emily.

'Not much chance of that. I made sure he was on the

Saturday one. We'll only have to avoid him at tomorrow night's gala dinner. We should be able to manage that,' said Hugo. He pointed to a six-inch pile of paper in front of him. 'Do we really have to read all of these?'

'Apparently so,' giggled Emily. 'They seem to have put us on the slow train to make sure we do.'

'I'd noticed that – we seem to be stopping at every bloody station going. And they want us to fill in a form for each one?'

'"Sufficient to provide feedback" according to The Write Stuff.'

'I don't need a form to be able to do that.'

'I'm sure you don't, Hugo, but I've been warned some of the delegates can be rather tetchy when you don't give them good news. Best to at least demonstrate you've read their sample chapters.'

Hugo rolled his eyes, asking himself – not for the first time – how he'd ended up on this gig. 'I refuse to dress up criticism as praise. If it's crap I'm going to tell them.'

Emily couldn't help but smile at Hugo's dedication to forthright evaluation. God, he'd kill her if he ever found out how he'd come to be on that train with her. 'Go gently, Hugo, or some of the delegates might not repeat their booking next year. I'm sure that's not in the organiser's plans.'

'It sounds a good plan to me if I don't have to go again,' sneered Hugo, by now having dropped his mock enthusiasm for the trip. 'How many have you got, anyway?'

'Thirty in total. Today, tomorrow and Sunday morning.'

'Jesus – how did you cop for that? I'm doing 18 and thought I'd drawn the short straw.'

'If I'm going, I may as well do it properly. I'm on the lookout for new talent after all. Aren't you?'

Hugo checked himself. Yes, of course he was on the lookout for new talent – he had to remember to keep reminding himself of that. 'Yeah, it's just that I got added to the list later than you so don't have as many slots. Anyway, I'm doing a seminar session on "the perfect submission letter" as well as my one-to-ones. It's full on.'

'Well, you'd better make a start on that pile then, seeing you clearly haven't already,' said Emily.

'Have you done yours?'

'Yes – all 30. With notes.'

Hugo realised he was behind in this particular game. 'Anything that jumps up and bites?' he quizzed, indicating Emily's bulging briefcase.

Emily adopted a thoughtful demeanour. She'd decided some weeks before that returning to the office empty-handed after the conference would not find favour with Rocket. He would want to see evidence that his strategy for discovering new talent at source was bearing fruit for Franklin & Pope. She had to deliver. Her heart had sunk lower than the Mariana Trench on reading the sample chapters she'd received. Mostly they were awful but there were a couple in there that she could feasibly pass off as 'potentials', and she would only need one or two to justify this experiment. They did this winnowing technique all the time so what harm was there adding one or two more from the conference into the mix? At the next stage at least two or three colleagues would assess the work as well. If her recommendations got blown away in the wind at least she would have done her job; if one fell back into the basket, she'd be a hero. Granted, under normal circumstances, agents would normally have got rid of most of the chaff, but it was interesting that one or two examples did bear out Rocket's assertion that just because a writer didn't have an agent didn't make him or her a bad author. The two 'possibles' that had caught her eye so far could easily have been pitched to her via an agent. 'I have to say, Hugo, it's been an eye-opener. The quality threshold is far higher than I'd anticipated. There's definitely some potential there.'

Hugo concealed his alarm at this bombshell – after all, it was his livelihood that was at stake if publishers like Franklin & Pope felt they could cut him out of the equation. At first, he'd scoffed at Emily's news that they were considering going after unagented authors and found it hilarious that she was to attend a writers conference. His boss, however, had adopted a slightly different tack when he'd called him in and said they had to target more debut writers too. In Hugo's view he was wading through enough crap already without inviting more but, such was the zeal exhibited by his superior for this new approach, he'd taken it on the chin, if only to be proven right later that such a strategy was doomed to failure. Could his role as an agent be under threat? He seriously doubted it, but better to keep an eye on it rather than let it creep up behind. 'What if we both pick out the same writer?' he said mischievously. Had Emily thought that through yet?

Bloody hell, thought Emily. What would she do? 'Given the choice of picking between you or me, I don't think there would be much competition,' she blustered. 'I might have to sub my talent out to you, at a reduced rate of course.'

That's what Hugo had feared. Smiling, he pulled the pile of papers closer towards him and said, 'Right – I require a bit of studying time. May the best man win.'

Emily nodded and picked up her newspaper. *Or the best woman*, she thought.

As Hugo speed-read the opening chapters optimistically submitted by 18 expectant authors, the train pulled into Birmingham New Street. Six carriages down from first-class, Bronte Damson was about to close the door behind her when she saw a Marje Proops lookalike tearing down the platform trailing a giant Samsonite Spinner in her wake. Bronte stood aside as the woman hurled herself on to the train like it was the last one out of Paris in Casablanca.

As the woman bent over at the knees to collect her breath, the train set off. 'God, that was close,' she gasped.

Bronte, not wishing to abandon the tardy traveller until she knew she had recovered, asked, 'Can I help you with your bag?'

The woman, unused to such chivalry from the young, laughed. 'I'm all right, darling. I'm not ready for the knacker's yard just yet.'

The two made their way through into coach J and searched for their respective seat numbers. By chance they were seated on the same table, but an even greater coincidence occurred when they both pulled out their Write Stuff weekend conference packs.

'Ah,' said Alyson Hummer to her young companion, 'what are the odds on that?' Introductions made, now it was her turn to show deference as she insisted on sharing with Bronte the travel snacks she'd had the foresight to pack.

Bronte was beside herself that her conference weekend was starting earlier than she'd expected. 'Is this your first time?' she wanted to know.

'Yes, I'm a conference virgin,' confided Alyson.

'Me, too,' said Bronte. 'I'm so excited.'

Alyson innocently and logically pitched the question that was to be on everybody's lips all weekend. 'So what sort of stuff do you write?'

Bronte was only too happy to have an early opportunity to try out her carefully prepared rejoinder. 'Well, the simplest category would be fantasy, but I feel that's too limiting if I'm being honest. The Catacomb of Tongues – that's the title of the book I'm working on – is rooted in a medieval world of magic but owes a debt to the sci-fi tradition of Poul Anderson. Have you read any Poul Anderson?'

Alyson felt like she had just tuned into the Open University by accident. 'Pool Anderson? I can't quite place him, sorry.'

'Well, anyway, the first book of my trilogy is…'

'You've written a trilogy?' said a shell-shocked Alyson, feeling her spirits starting to sag in the face of such literary fecundity.

Bronte smiled. 'It's going to be a trilogy. It's not actually finished yet.'

Well, that's *something*, thought Alyson. 'So how much have you written to date?'

'I've not actually written –"written" – any of it yet, but that's going to be the easy part – it's all about getting the characters mapped out and chapter plan sorted. I'm pretty well on with that.'

This was news to Alyson, whose normal approach to writing was the same as her approach to sex – she just pounded away. 'So you don't just start off and see where it takes you?'

Now it was Bronte's turn to be taken aback. 'That was definitely frowned on at university,' she said, without the slightest hint of patronage towards her fellow traveller.

Alyson suppressed a rising sense of apprehension over the impending weekend. 'So what's the actual story going to be about?'

'It's set on the imaginary world of Altos, which is actually a cloud that floats from place to place although the inhabitants don't actually know that. The thing about a cloud is that it's always there; it's just that you don't always see it. The evil thaumaturge – that's like a warlock – Dinoween escapes eternal incarceration and decides he's going to destroy their world because it was the rulers of Altos, the Necergii, who'd imprisoned him for starting a civil war centuries before. The only person who can stop him is the heroine Belowyn who holds the sacred medallion of the moon, only she doesn't realise that at first…'

As Bronte paused for breath in her delivery, Alyson interjected. 'Gosh, Bronte, that sounds fascinating. Well done, you. Now, I'm going to have a coffee. How about you?'

As ViXen's most popular author negotiated her

way down the shuddering Pendolino towards the buffet car her thoughts verged on panic. Was it all going to be this academic? Was everybody going to be as full-on as Bronte? It would be like being back at school, and in her case, that wasn't a good metaphor.

One hundred miles further north Eric had already embarked on his relatively short drive to Lancaster. He had opted for two of his one-to-one sessions that afternoon and didn't want to be late. Eric had re-read the rules governing the ten-minute face-offs and realised that they were about as flexible as US immigration policy. As he joined the M6 at Bamber Bridge he was still wondering how to play it. In a way, it was just like speed dating – not that he'd had any experience of that either. Surely the author and agent would instinctively know? The recognition of common ground followed by subconscious attraction and a stirring of the passions? Where have you been all my life? A couple going over Viagara Falls in a barrel. But he really couldn't call himself an author, could he? Not yet. He'd authored a book, true, but you couldn't claim to be an author if you hadn't been published. Nor could you call yourself an author if you'd self-published – that was cheating wasn't it? Someone in Eric's position could say he'd written a novel. That didn't even make him a writer per se, just someone who aspired to be a writer and had given it a go. Everybody knew that just because someone had written a book, it didn't mean it was any good. Such a milestone, fulfilling as it was, certainly didn't earn the appellation of 'writer' or 'author' for the person who'd penned it. Still, if he wasn't a 'writer' or 'author' yet, what was he? An 'aspiring novelist', perhaps, or a 'would-be wordsmith'? God, both of those were twee. Best steer clear of epithets altogether or risk appearing presumptuous.

With the luxury of four agent meetings to reserve, Eric had wondered when to actually have them. Spread them over the weekend? Get them all over in one go? A lot of the names on the list were familiar, as Eric had already written to a number of them. And been rejected by them. No point in going over old ground? Eric decided to stick to agents to whom he'd not submitted Scrub Me Till I Shine in the Dark. But his resolve weakened when he saw Hugo Lockwood's name on the 'new agents added' list. Should he opt to see him or give him a wide berth? On one hand he'd been his number one choice of agent from the outset but on the other hand there was the inescapable fact that he'd already turned down his book, never mind the small matter of the Twitter exchange. In all probability Hugo wouldn't remember either. Would he? He could always apologise for the Twitter incident if it came up? No – what was he thinking? Why risk it? Eventually he'd left Hugo's name un-ticked, resolving instead to attend his 'perfect submission letter' session where he could hide in the crowd. Finally, he opted to see two of his four agents in the first afternoon, like putting half of his stake money on red or black five minutes after arriving at the casino.

As for the sessions themselves, should he lead the discussion, or let the agent hold court? All Eric had to tell them was he wanted an agent – he couldn't think of much else. What else was there for him to say? It was fairly self-evident, wasn't it? So that would leave nine minutes and fifty seconds of his ten minutes. They would have read the opening chapters of Scrub Me Till I Shine in the Dark – here, at last, was his opportunity to get feedback from the horse's mouth. Two chapters was quite a lot, certainly enough for them to start to form a view – this gave Eric profound hope. He had long harboured a deep suspicion that the faceless agents who sent him rejections never actually read his submission. Eric envisaged them spotting he was a first-time writer and deciding to read no further. Or maybe they'd passed it down to an underling for initial assessment and some illiterate Jocasta or Gideon on a gap year had not understood what they were reading. It was all down to chance – a roll of the dice, the toss of a coin, the spin of a wheel. His manuscript was the equivalent of Tess of the D'Urberville's letter to Angel, being slipped under the door of destiny.

Junction 33 came into view. He was almost there. A wave of excitement swept over him as he pushed the direction indicator down to the left. This was it. Which side of the carpet was his missive going to land?

CHAPTER SEVENTEEN

'That sign isn't straight. It needs to be re-hung.' Chapman was helping the team to set up the conference reception by pointing out where they were getting it wrong.

Suzie bit her lip and nodded to her assistant, Amy, to attend to the misalignment of the 'Welcome' panel stuck on the rear wall. 'Anything else, Chapman?' she said, with just the slightest hint of irony.

'Biscuits? Where's the biscuits?' said Chapman with consternation, as if he'd just realised they'd pitched up at Lancaster University on the wrong weekend. Suzie reached down behind the welcome desk and produced a large tin of Family Favourites. Chapman looked relieved, but only for a second. 'And the notices?' Suzie rummaged under the table once more and held up two signs. The first, an A4 piece of card, read 'Help yourself – you know you want to…' and the second A2 card read, 'There's no such thing as a stranger – only friends you haven't met yet.' Chapman nodded in approval. The last thing he wanted to see at one of his conferences was a delegate not having access to a sugar rush or, worse still, failing to break the ice with other delegates. 'Very good,' he said. 'Greet the unseen with a cheer!'

Suzie was used to Chapman 'fussing' as she called it. No matter how many times she told him to relax, that everything was in hand, he couldn't resist the temptation to stick his oar in. It wasn't nerves that made him like this – it was his unbending belief that there wasn't a single problem on the planet that couldn't be solved through applying his wisdom, experience and attention to detail. Chapman liked to think he was the ultimate team player, the midfield general through whom every ball was played. His staff on the other hand saw him as a despot who obsessively and unceasingly stuck his finger into every pie – they called him, behind his back of course, 'Louis', in honour of the Sun King. *'L'État, c'est moi'* would have constituted a fitting motto for Chapman. What the team couldn't understand was Suzie's apparent infatuation with her boss. Nobody was really sure if they'd ever been 'at it' together. Suzie was the only person in the office who could challenge Chapman but at the same time it was evident she was hopelessly devoted to him. Conversely, Suzie's was the only advice Chapman would ever take, not that he ever gave her credit for anything she came up with. New members of staff would quiz colleagues about Suzie and Chapman's relationship but nobody could say with any certainty how far the personal impinged on the professional. They were like an old married couple, which rather belied their personal situations. Suzie was 'unattached' and didn't appear to go out on dates while Chapman had been married for five years to Adele, a solicitor who had given up work the minute she had a ring on her finger. If Chapman was Louis XIV in the eyes of most of his staff, Adele made an excellent Marie

Antoinette. She constantly badgered her husband at work, spoke to the staff as if they were peasants and could drop the temperature of any room she entered within two minutes. While the workforce of The Write Stuff hated Adele with a passion, it nevertheless amused them to be on hand for the rare occasions when she and Suzie were in the same room, particularly as Chapman would perform a passable impression of a cat on a hot tin roof under such circumstances. While Adele treated The Write Stuff's offices as a convenient drop-in, she had never graced an annual conference. How Chapman had managed to keep her away was another source of wonder.

'We're behind,' said Chapman, looking at his watch. 'The first delegates will be arriving in an hour.'

Before Suzie had a chance to tell him to stop fussing again, three old-timers peered through the door. 'We're not too early, are we?'

Reception was still relatively quiet when Eric arrived, despite having wasted 20 minutes going to the wrong car park. He tut-tutted to himself at the inadequacy of the map – surely it wouldn't have been that difficult to make it a bit clearer? As he strode across the campus to the exhibition centre he realised how long had passed since his own carefree undergraduate days when life had been much simpler. No, Eric had to concede, he'd never been carefree at any age. In his Sheffield University days he'd always been the one prioritising study while his mates were out drinking, playing sport, chasing girls and generally enjoying a three-year holiday camp ahead of having to knuckle down for the rest of their lives. What advantage did missing out on all that earn him? Only that he adjusted more quickly to the conveyor belt of work, marriage and mortgage – nothing else. As for life having more to offer back then, well, that was true, but had he grasped a large handful or been at the back of the queue? He had a respectable, if slightly boring, job, and he was happy with Victoria and his two adorable offspring, Freya and Arthur. Why did he hanker for more? Why did he feel this compulsion to be an author? Well, whatever the reason, that's what he wanted and maybe this university trip could squeeze out one extra chance for him, an opportunity to move the monotony of his regimented life on to another plane.

As Eric took in the reception area he immediately felt like an outsider. He stood quietly in line as around him delegates exchanged air kisses and ecstatic welcomes – everybody seemed to know everybody else. He noticed the sign exclaiming 'There's no such thing as a stranger – only friends you haven't met yet' and immediately felt further excluded. He shuffled to the desk without exchanging words with anyone. Amy, on reception, and charged with processing over 200 souls that afternoon, greeted him with a punctilious, 'Name?'

'Blair. Eric Blair.'

Amy looked up from the desk as if she'd been expecting him. 'Ah, yes, I'd noticed that name on the list. We should have put you on the speaker's schedule – we could have sold more places.' Eric reddened at this cack-handed attempt at a welcome. Amy ploughed on. 'So, Eric, here's your badge, white for a first-time delegate. We advise that you keep it displayed at all times over the weekend.'

Eric took his badge, which he noticed was enormous, about three times larger than a normal lapel name holder. His name, in 36-point type, could probably be read from the next county. Perhaps he'd wandered into a convention for the partially sighted. Would there be audio assistance at the lectures? Could a partially sighted person actually write a book, or would they have to dictate it? 'It will be hard to get missed with this,' he said, attempting a stab at humour.

'Chapman thinks it's very important that the badges are as legible as possible – it helps to break down barriers,' replied Amy.

As Eric pinned his name to his shirt he surveyed the sea of badges still awaiting owners. Some were white, many were green, a smaller group were red, and there were a few random orange ones still lined up in alphabetical order. 'What are all the different colours for?' he asked.

Amy gave him a look that said she was coming to that. 'You're a first-timer – white. Returning delegates are green. Agents, authors, editors and book doctors are red, and organisers,' she pointed at her own lapel badge at this point, ' are orange.'

'I see. Very useful. Do I sign in here for my accommodation?'

Amy's reproving look indicated that she was coming to that also, if only he'd let her. 'The accommodation office is in the next building. Out of the doors, second on the right.'

'Is there free WIFI here?'

'The accommodation office will give you the code,' replied Amy in a clipped, 'OK – we're done' tone.

Eric was aware of a growing number of delegates joining the queue behind him. 'I've got one-to-ones this afternoon. Where do they take place?'

Amy pointed over her shoulder. 'Bowland Suite. Suzie will take care of you down there. Anything else?'

Eric still had a few points he'd like clarification on but deduced that this might not be the best time to ask. He shook his head.

'Welcome, then, and enjoy the conference,' intoned Amy. Then she remembered her manners. 'Would you like a biscuit?'

Twenty minutes later Eric opened the door to his room for the next two nights – more an ascetic cell suited to an Anchorite than a base camp for a newly sprung-from-home student hell-bent on scaling unclimbed peaks. It was sparse, bare and unwelcoming. A single bed, desk and wardrobe occupied most of the floor space and Eric had seen bigger bathrooms on a train. Notices warning against affixing items on the wall appeared to be affixed to every available surface. Had his room at Sheffield been as grim? Eric had to begrudgingly concede it probably was. Of course, back then, he'd have personalised his room with books, CDs and blue-tacked posters, but it would still have been clinical, tidy and unremarkable. Not for Eric the stolen traffic cones, accumulated dirty laundry, empty bottles and discarded takeaway wrappers of his fellow students. Even his posters spoke a different language, more Mike and The Mechanics than My Bloody Valentine, more Cambridge Folk Festival than Frequency Oblivion. He plonked himself down on the bed and his spine met the unyielding hardboard base providing support for the thin mattress. It jarred Eric out of his daydream. Good God, what was he doing here? Did he really think he could be discovered and become a *bona fide* author? Who was he kidding? He'd not lived an interesting enough life to spill his guts on the page – this room, staring back at him like a witness for the prosecution, was surely telling him that? Yes, he was competent, he could string words together, but that didn't make him a writer. Now he was about to be exposed to a level of scrutiny that would reveal him as the literary imposter and self-delusionist he clearly was. He'd received enough rejections to prove that already, so why was he paying a premium to have it told directly to his face?

Down in the Bowland Suite Suzie was briefing the agents and editors who were conducting that afternoon's one-to-ones. Hugo and Emily sat braced with a dozen other experts waiting for the onslaught. Suzie, who'd almost curtsied to her star attractions on being introduced, was determined to demonstrate that she ran a tight ship. 'Each session lasts precisely eight minutes so we advise delegates to cut to the chase. The same applies to you guys, as well.'

'I thought it was ten minutes?' interjected one of the experts.

'One minute to get them sat down, another minute to get rid of them – that's ten in total,' clarified Suzie. 'It may seem brusque but our advice is to dispense with the small talk. Every word counts so keep focused on the main issue – their writing.'

Hugo nodded in agreement. As if he was here for a nice, cosy chitchat.

Suzie continued. 'We've found that it works better if you let them have the first couple of minutes to get their pitch across. You'd think that they'd all come prepared but unfortunately that's not always our experience, no matter how many times we tell them how to prep.'

One of the other experts held up a hand. 'How candid should we be? I don't want to sound funny but some of the samples I've received are E-minus.'

On this particular question Suzie could quote Chapman verbatim. 'We're here to help, to inspire and to encourage the writers of tomorrow so we always suggest that the iron fist of criticism is clad in a velvet glove.' She omitted the concluding part of the quote: 'Because we want the buggers back again next year.' This time Emily nodded in agreement while Hugo looked sceptical. 'And remember,' said Suzie, 'while you're helping them, they're helping you. Each year many of our experts unearth new talent; discover new writers that go on to sell.' Hugo looked around quizzically – someone must have two in their pack as he certainly didn't have one. 'Now, a word about temperaments,' said Suzie. 'Some of the delegates are, shall we say, "sensitive" which, as I'm sure you'll agree, is only to be expected. For many of them this is a validation of their life's work, a make or break moment for them. For some, anything less than an offer on the spot is a rejection and we don't do rejection at The Write Stuff.' She slowly waved her right fist up and down. 'Remember that velvet glove.' Hugo couldn't believe what he was hearing – Christ, now he was being asked to act as a stress counsellor for ink addicts.

Another questioner raised a point. 'Suzie, last year we had a bit of a problem with certain delegates who wouldn't leave after their ten – eight – minutes. Is that something you're going to keep an eye on?'

Suzie, only too aware of the delegate 'extractions' required in earlier years, nodded. 'Yes. We've discussed this in great detail since the last conference, and you'll be glad to know that this year we're adopting a "zero-tolerance" approach. Anybody who hasn't left your table by the end of their allocated time slot will have me to deal with,' she said with great emphasis.

'An iron fist inside an iron glove, then?' said Hugo.

Suzie smiled. 'Yes, Hugo. I'll make sure that you are never perceived as anything less than the nice guy.' On that note, the briefing concluded.

The experts helped themselves to water and coffee ahead of the first appointments. Hugo found himself next to Lucy Nichols, a former intern at Motif who had moved on three years before. 'She's a barrel of laughs, isn't she?' said Hugo, referring to Suzie. 'Anybody would think we were about to invade France.'

Lucy, who had less than positive recollections of working for Hugo, nevertheless put the agent code first. 'You'll be glad of her later on, Hugo, believe me. Some of these delegates have to be dislodged with crowbars and buckets of water.'

'Really? You've done this before, then?'

'The last two years, yes. When she says some of them get "emotional", she's not exaggerating. They think the rules apply to everyone except them.' Hugo looked suspicious. Surely she was winding him up? 'But that's nothing compared to lunch and dinner times – there we're more out in the open and can be ambushed at any time.'

Hugo scoffed and beckoned Emily over. 'Have you heard this, Em? Apparently we need protection from the hordes.'

Emily introduced herself to Lucy as Hugo had failed to do so, and said, 'I'd heard that, yes. You must give us some tips, Lucy.'

'The key thing is, when we go for dinner we move into the dining area in a group so we can occupy a table by ourselves. That way we can avoid being stalked over our broccoli and carrots.'

'But that's preposterous, Lucy. Why don't they just allocate reserved tables for us?' Hugo said.

'Ah, Hugo, I see you still have a lot to learn about inclusivity,' said Lucy.

Before any more could be said on the matter Suzie proclaimed over everybody's heads. 'Five-minute warning, ladies and gentlemen. Incoming. And the very best of British to you all.'

CHAPTER EIGHTEEN

Eric pulled himself together as he made his way to the Bowland Suite for his first one-to-one. Now wasn't the time to succumb to self-doubt; this was his stage and he needed to perform on it. He made sure he was good and early for his 4.00pm slot with Brian Brooks, the boss of the boutique literary agency that bore the same name.

As Eric tried to enter the suite he discovered he couldn't go any further – there was a throng of people in front of him crammed between the inner and the outer doors. A bearded man bearing a clipboard and an orange name badge shouted out, '3.50 appointments. Who's got a 3.50?' and was met by a show of hands from all the people crammed into the tiny space. On some invisible signal the inner doors opened and a number of delegates added to the crush as they tried to pass through to the outer doors. It was like a hostage exchange in the airlock of the USS Enterprise. Eric noticed the shell-shocked look on the faces of the exchangees and deduced that their treatment at the hands of the Klingon captors must have been extreme. As they exited into the bright sunshine and freedom the new group marched forward to take their places. All except Eric who was told, as a

4 o'clocker, he had to remain in the airlock. Over the next ten minutes fellow 4 o'clockers slowly filled up the small atrium once more. The general atmosphere was subdued and apprehension hung in the fetid air. At last the inner doors swung open once more and the same circulatory process was repeated, allowing Eric to emerge into a large hall dotted with desks. The 3.50s were now taking their places at the individual stations while clipboard man was directing the 4 o'clockers to sit down on the row of seats positioned along the wall – it was like being a benefit claimant at the DSS. Clipboard checked each interviewee by name and pointed out to Eric where the curly-haired Brian Brooks was sitting in deep conversation with an arch-backed supplicant. 'Go only when I give the signal,' warned the man with the orange badge of authority.

Desperate for dialogue to break the tension before he was 'up', Eric turned to the middle-aged woman beside him who was wafting her face with a fan of papers in a bid to remain cool. 'It is rather hot, isn't it?' he said.

She, glad to have the conspiracy of silence broken, revealed a cut-glass accent to respond, 'The air conditioning mustn't be working – last year it poured with rain so it looks as if they've rather been caught out by this heatwave.'

'Oh, so you've done this before?' Eric asked, hoping to get some last-minute tips.

'Five times. It's one of my favourite weekends of the year.'

Eric didn't know whether to be appalled or impressed. Five times? Did that mean that she couldn't take 'no' for an answer or that she saw the conference purely in terms of a social get-together, an advanced form of residential book club? Glyndebourne, Wimbledon, Henley and The Write Stuff conference? 'So you must be an expert at these agent sessions, then? This is my first time.'

'Everybody's really lovely and very helpful. Nothing to worry about, I can assure you.'

'So how close have you come to gaining representation?' Eric asked, stretching for validation of his attendance.

Cut-glass peered at him over the top of her glasses. 'Oh, I'm not ready for that just yet. I'm still working on my first historical romance but everybody has been so supportive in helping me to make progress on it.'

Eric, who hadn't contemplated anybody attending conference without a finished manuscript under their belt, nodded as if it was obvious that all the delegates were in the same boat as she was. Before she could ask him about his work – surely she was going to? – Clipboard cut in. '4 o'clockers, please.' A mad scramble like the start of the Le Mans 24-hour race ensued as the next wave of writers ran to their marks. Eric, following Clipboard's instructions, started to walk over to where Brian Brooks sat but noticed that Arch-back was still very much in position and, by the looks of it, not planning to leave any time soon. He could see Brian looking around helplessly as his appointee tried to finish off cramming a quart into a pint pot. Should Eric wait? As the other 4 o'clockers eased into their sessions Eric gave a passable impression of a lamppost, too polite to intervene. Suddenly a manic voice hissed in his ear, 'She's stealing your time. Don't let her. Come on.' And with that he was frog-marched to Brian's desk where his intermediary virtually yanked the chair from beneath the guest who had overstayed her welcome. 'Ten – minutes – only,' she barked at the dilatory delegate. Even as she stood up and backed away from the table Arch-back was still summarising what she was going to send to the agent next week, until eventually she faded out of earshot.

'Thanks, Suzie,' said a relieved looking Brian as she pursued her quarry to the door. Turning to Eric: 'Who do we have here?'

'Eric Blair, Brian. Pleased to meet you.'

'Yes, yes. Eric Blair. Now you must tell me, I'm intrigued,' he chirruped, 'is that a *nom de plume*?'

'No. It's my real name,' said Eric flatly.

'Of course. Right, well, perhaps we could start by you telling me what you'd most like to get out of our session today, Eric?'

'It's quite simple, really. I've just written my first novel, I want to get an agent, and I want to get published,' replied Eric.

Realising that Eric had neatly dropped the ball back on his side of the net, Brian reached for his notes. 'Indeed. Well, let's take a look, shall we? Scrub Me Till I Shine in the Dark – that's quite a title.'

'You think the title is a problem?' Eric shot back. He'd known it was. Snookered in the first exchange.

'No, no, I didn't mean that,' said Brian hurriedly. 'It's just… unusual.'

'Do you think it would put readers off?' Eric wanted to know. This was an important issue that needed to be settled.

Brian ran his fingers through his curly locks and laughed off the question. 'The title isn't a problem, Eric, believe me. Just tell me about it – how would you describe the novel to someone you met in a bookshop?'

Eric had spent a considerable amount of time trying to encapsulate his opus into a few short, sharp soundbites but as soon as he started to deliver his lines they began to feel underwritten. 'Well, it's a coming of age, rites of passage story about a northern boy growing up in Thatcher's Britain. His life and escape from his grim surroundings are contrasted against the social disintegration of the period.'

'Do I take it that this is largely autobiographical?'

Eric, who had enjoyed the most feather-bedded of middle-class upbringings, shook his head. 'Not really.'

Brian tried to keep it light. 'And what is the message of the book? What does it say to the reader, where is its redemptive value, how does it change the reader's world?'

Eric was a bit taken aback at these questions, as they were things he'd not really considered when he was writing his novel. 'Well, it's predominantly naturalistic in style,' he volunteered. Realising that didn't sound like a good defence, he countered, 'Isn't that up to the reader to decide?'

Brian's expression indicated that Eric's response wasn't the answer he was looking for. 'So, tell me,' continued Brian, 'in what genre would you place this book?'

Eric pondered for a second. 'I guess it's literary fiction? General appeal?'

'You see what I'm getting at here, Eric? More specifically, *who* do you see reading this book?'

'I think it could appeal to lots of people, particularly of my generation?' said Eric, a question rather than a statement. His heart sank as he realised his focus had never shifted from the words he had been so determined to set down to consider what they had to say to people who weren't Eric Blair.

Brian had spotted another major flaw. 'I don't see this – I hope you don't mind me being candid here – as appealing to women. And if that's the case its sales potential is severely compromised.'

'My wife liked it. I think women would read it,' protested Eric.

'Enough of them? It's women who buy books these days, not men, so my view is that as concisely written as this is, it's just not commercial enough for me to consider taking it on. There it is.'

The pronouncement that Scrub Me Till I Shine in the Dark wasn't a particularly saleable piece of work would have been crushing in itself except Eric had stopped listening at 'concisely written'. What on earth did 'concisely written' mean?

Brian looked quickly at his watch to see how long they had left. 'You write very well, Eric, but – and this is only a personal view – maybe it's a little *too* precise? I liked the characters, the style, the pacing, all very good, but to me it felt more like a report than an engaging narrative. I'm looking to be emotionally engaged, I want to go on that journey with the characters; I want to see how their lives are transformed and I want to understand why. I don't see that here. Is that fair?'

As Eric took the left jab followed by the right hook,

a voice boomed out, 'One minute. Wind up now, if you please.' Eric pressed for a summary. 'So, in short, you think it's a pile of crap?'

Brian couldn't tell from Eric's glazed expression if he was joking but, remembering Suzie's advice, was determined to end on a positive note. 'I don't think that at all, of course not. All I'm saying is that there's a world of difference between a well-written story and a book that will sell. That's the game we're in, and if you want to get published that's the game you're going to have to be in, too.'

'So I've no chance of getting published?' Eric wanted him to say it.

Brian looked alarmed. Had he said that? 'All I'm saying is that this book isn't for me, for those reasons. Another agent may see it differently. I hope that's been helpful?'

Despite still having 30 seconds to play with, Eric stood up and offered his hand. 'Thank you,' he said and turned towards the airlock. Everything felt like it was in slow motion – it was as if he were on a space walk, struggling to maintain control over his limbs and hearing only a low ambient static through his helmet. As he resurfaced into the bright afternoon sunshine his hearing and senses cleared. Eric had a lot to think about. He also had to do it all over again in 50 minutes.

CHAPTER NINETEEN

Alyson, on her second gin and tonic, was feeling more relaxed now she had checked in to conference and, unlike some of the lost souls she could see wandering around the bar, at least she wasn't Billy no-mates. Her new buddy, Bronte, was quite sweet once she'd stopped auditioning for Front Row. The delegates were gathering for The Write Start, the event where writers who had been brave enough to submit their opening passage for scrutiny would find out after dinner whose had been deemed the best. As Chapman was fond of telling everyone, such an accolade could be the first step on the way to a publishing deal. Chapman was also wont to say, 'It's only a bit of fun,' but few of the entrants saw it that way; when it got going it was as competitive as the annual Ashbourne Shrovetide football match.

Signs of such determination weren't immediately evident as Alyson surveyed the room. Most of the people who had gathered for the weekend looked like they'd been hijacked en route to a flower show. 'Not many of these people look like writers,' opined Alyson. 'What do you think, Bronte?'

Bronte's experience of writers was limited. 'I don't

know. It's hard to tell. What does a writer look like, anyway?' she replied, not unreasonably.

'Like Melvyn Bragg or maybe that Fiona Bruce off the telly?' conjectured Alyson.

'The one who does Antiques Roadshow?' asked Bronte. 'My dad loves her. I didn't know she wrote books as well?'

'I don't think she does,' said Alyson. 'She just looks like she should.'

At that moment a wild-eyed, scruffy, greasy-haired man in his mid-30s attached himself to the two of them. 'Christ, I've had a nightmare getting here,' he announced in a broad Irish brogue. Bronte politely stepped back to allow him to join their circle. 'Frigging roadworks every mile of the way,' he continued. 'Thought I wasn't going to make it.'

'Did you drive far?' enquired Bronte.

'No,' replied the newcomer. 'I got the bus. From London. Took over eight bloody hours. Still, I'm here now.' He took a long draught of his pint of Guinness and then remembered his manners. 'Con,' he said, pointing at his badge.

Introductions out of the way, Con was interested to know who he was up against that evening. 'You entered in the Write Start competition tonight?' he asked them.

Alyson had thought long and hard about whether to expose her new literary direction to potential public evaluation while it was still in its infancy. 'I was going to, but to be honest I missed the deadline – I was away on holiday and it slipped by,' she lied.

Bronte hadn't actually written her opening chapter yet and saw nothing wrong in admitting this. 'I didn't bother with that but I hope to enter next year.'

Con drained his Guinness, cheered by the perceived boost the odds of his winning had just received if only on mathematical grounds. 'Well, it's just a bit of fun, isn't it? Probably won't get too far with it but thought it was worth having a go, just in case.'

Now Con realised he faced a predicament. After his harrowing journey the first pint hadn't touched the sides. He'd struck up a conversation with these two delegates – which was good as he didn't want to be standing there like a spare part – but now he wanted another drink and he only had a £20 note in his pocket to last the evening. He wasn't going to offer to buy them a drink but what was the protocol here? God forbid he got in a round with this woman and what appeared to be her daughter? He plonked his glass on the bar and announced, 'Just got to pay a visit'. Alyson eyed him suspiciously knowing that when he'd emptied his bladder he'd miraculously re-appear with a full pint. She wasn't wrong.

When the doors to the dining room opened an urgent press of people didn't waste much time in making their way inside – nobody wanted to be left behind. The reason for this soon became clear as small advance groups lay claim to empty tables, defying stragglers to occupy the vacant chairs. The unattached may as well have had a table in the corner with a sign reading 'Write Offs.' But Alyson and Bronte had each other, so opted for a table where four women had already planted their flag. The two new acquaintances were in turn joined by Con who considered himself an old friend by this stage. The final place, next to Alyson, was taken by a serious looking man in his mid-forties who had twigged that the Written Off table was the next resort if he didn't act decisively. All strapped in, the table relaxed as yet more introductions were made and conversation was pulverised to its smallest constituent parts. Eventually, though, the pilgrims who'd founded the table didn't bother to involve the other four delegates and thus they became 'group two' for social purposes. Alyson, having exhausted Bronte's youthful chatter and taken a dislike to the cocksure Irishman, found herself talking to the man who had been the last to board. At least the name Eric Blair meant nothing to her when he introduced himself.

So often were the same questions asked over the course of the weekend, delegates might as well have been issued with a set of flash cards on arrival. 'Is this your first conference?' followed by 'Have you got a finished book?' and 'What genre are you?' being the main three, until one could pitch 'Have you had any one-to-ones yet?' Similarly, the agents could have been equipped with the 'touch and go' cards beloved of lap dancing bars – most delegates knew not to make inappropriate contact with them, but there was always one…

As the table played 'spot the agent' Eric pointed out an unusual phenomenon he'd observed while cruising for landing space. 'Do you see those tables over there?' he asked, pointing stage right. 'Well, that's where the agents headed for straight away. Not many delegates made it past their drawbridge, I see.' The proliferation of red lapel badges on the tables pinpointed by Eric indicated his theory might hold water. 'Another thing,' Eric continued. 'Why that side of the stage? I'll tell you – it's so no one passes their tables on the way to the bar. They've got it all worked out.'

Con, noting the cynicism as well as the veracity of Eric's observation, was still of a mind to give the agents the benefit of the doubt. 'We'll be meeting them soon enough in the one-to-ones.'

'I've already seen two,' confessed Eric to the surprise of his fellow delegates.

'Already?' gasped Alyson on learning that Eric had achieved his mission before she'd even slipped into her LBD for the evening. 'You can go home now,' she said jokingly, not realising Eric had been thinking exactly the same for the past two hours.

Alyson, Con and Bronte proffered imaginary flash card five – 'What was it like?' – and eagerly awaited a first-hand account of an actual delegate-agent interface. It was as if Eric had returned from a scouting mission deep into enemy territory.

Eric was hesitant – after all, if he recounted the sessions truthfully wouldn't he be drawing attention to his own inadequacies? Eventually he said, 'The two sessions were very similar and very instructive but probably didn't tell me too much I didn't already know.'

Con wasn't interested in such weasel words. 'Did either of them offer you a deal?' he demanded.

Eric pretended such a thought had never crossed his mind. 'I don't think that's really going to happen to many people over the weekend if we're being realistic about it. My primary aim was to get quality feedback on my writing from agents, and in that sense it's been very useful.'

177

Alyson, who had two meetings lined up for Saturday, wanted details. 'And was it good feedback?'

Eric attempted to look casual as he shared the incisive critical insight that had been visited on his work. 'Apparently I write very well, with good pace and engaging characters.'

'Oh,' cooed Alyson, 'that's brilliant.'

Con, who held the belief that for every drop of goodwill bestowed on someone else's work there was less available for his, was less acclamatory. 'So they didn't offer you a deal, then?'

Eric shook his head. 'No. And for a very particular reason.' Three faces looked at him expectantly. 'I don't write for women, and as only women buy books these days apparently, I'm not commercial enough. There – that's it in a nutshell. Useful to know, isn't it?' Sarcasm may be the lowest form of wit but by this point Eric was past caring.

Alyson wasn't sure if this general rule of thumb could possibly be right but remained unperturbed as, whatever anyone might say about her writing, there was no doubt she was aiming at the right buying audience. Neither did Bronte have any reason to be alarmed at this bombshell, as she wrote for neither women nor men. Con, on the other hand, was flummoxed. Surely that was bullshit? 'Only women buy books? I don't believe that. That's cobblers.'

Eric had some sympathy with Con, but not a lot. 'Before today I would have agreed with you. But we have to face the facts as I have been told them, direct from the horse's mouth. Women buy considerably more books than men. So the agents are mainly looking for books that appeal to women. '

'What does sell, then?' asked Bronte.

'What are you writing?' asked Eric.

'Fantasy.'

Eric nodded and smiled. 'Bingo. Get those tills ringing. You have nothing to worry about. Fantasy sells as does crime, history and romance. Oh, and children's. All other genres need not apply.'

'What about erotica?' challenged Alyson. 'That sells millions.'

'Indeed it does,' said Eric, 'but that can effectively straddle all of the above, if you'll excuse my French.'

Con wasn't having this. 'I don't agree with that, *if* that's what they said. There's loads of exceptions to those rules.'

'Name some, then?' countered Eric. After five seconds of head scratching from the three of them he held out his hands and said, 'See? What these agents, this conference, is here to tell us is that we should forget writing about what interests us as writers and concentrate on feeding a machine that only accepts certain coins. I'm out of change; Bronte's got a pocketful. What do you write, Alyson?'

'Er… romance mainly.'

'Ker-ching. On the money, and you, Con? I hope to Christ it's not comedy.'

Con looked crestfallen. 'It's hard to explain.' Silence descended on their end of the table as the news of Eric's *reconnoitre* sank in. He realised he may have been a little carried away with his evaluation of the UK book trade. 'Of course, that's only the view of two agents so they might be talking rubbish.'

Suddenly the loudspeaker perched on a stand next to their table crackled into life. 'Ladies and gentlemen, please welcome the inspiration behind The Write Stuff, the man who puts the L into literature, Chapman Hall.'

A round of applause erupted as Chapman, for it was he, took up the microphone. 'Thank you, Suzie,' he said with all the modesty he could muster. 'A warm welcome to all of our friends, new and old, this evening. As Pasternak said, "Literature is the art of discovering something extraordinary about ordinary people, and saying with ordinary words something extraordinary".' A sea of heads bobbed up and down in awe at such well-chosen words. 'This weekend is all about extraordinary people who have an extraordinary ambition: to get published. Yes, I'm talking about you.'

Eric, an expert on well-crafted speeches as well as ones that fell short of that standard, leaned towards Alyson. 'Christ, he's going to be disappearing up his own backside with all of these "extraordinaries".'

Chapman was getting into his stride. 'No less an authority than Plato tells us, "The beginning is the most important part of the work." Without a compelling start to a novel why would anybody read further? Before conference many of you submitted the opening of your books for Write Start. I hesitate to call it a contest because we're not in competition with each other here – we're here to recognise the extraordinary talent gathered here in this room.' Con scowled as a ripple of applause met the reiteration of Chapman's non-aggression pact. 'So, remembering this is just a bit of fun, let me invite up to the stage the four brave writers who have been shortlisted from the scores of entries we received.'

Con caught Eric's eye. 'Did you enter?' he asked.

'I did, but got blown off at the pass,' said Eric as if it was a mere trifle. 'Got to say, I'm glad I didn't get selected now – wouldn't fancy going up there to read.'

'But how do you know you've not been selected?' said Con. 'They might call your name out?'

'No they won't. If you didn't hear from them by last Friday it meant that you weren't selected.'

Con, who had overlooked this rubric from the conference pack, felt a sense of deflation as his first victory of the weekend was dashed from his grasp. He'd practised reading his opening pages for the past three weeks and could almost recite the words without the text in front of him. The scene he'd imagined of his conquest, the bloody gladiator accepting the laurel wreath from Caesar, hit the cutting room floor.

Four delegates scaled the two steps to the raised dais and sat uncomfortably on the low-backed settees Suzie had ordered to create a 'South Bank Show feel'. The room hushed as Chapman explained that each writer would read the first 500 words from their opening chapter and then the delegates would decide the winner.

Eric, like everybody else in the room, was keen to hear the readings. In theory, this quartet represented the high water mark of unpublished writing and anyone wanting to get a deal needed to rise above it. The first reader, a strapping, sandy-haired man-mountain tented out in a plaid shirt, strode to the lectern. 'The Turning Of the Tide,' he said in a gruff Scottish accent, and then proceeded to read. 'He made his first mistake before they left the Quayside tavern. Playing spoof with Big Muldoon and Lennie Quinn was only going to end one way. Now, down to the emergency £20 note he kept in his boot, he was reduced to the cheapest deal in the whorehouse.'

'What genre is this?' whispered Bronte in Eric's direction.

Plaid shirt carried on, his broad accent punching the lights out of each word as if they were gatecrashers at a Hollywood wedding. 'In the dim light of the bordello she could have passed for 35 but close up he could see past the powder and paint to the cadaver that lurked beneath…'

Alyson paid especial attention at the mention of a bordello, while Con and Eric exchanged glances that said, 'This got shortlisted?'

As man-mountain's reading reached its premature climax he was met with polite applause and the second reader took to the lectern. Eric guessed from her appearance, a white-haired grandmother, that her extract might cover different ground to the first. 'The Sun Never Shines on the Poor,' she intoned in a flat Yorkshire accent that seemed out of kilter with her twin-set and pearls. 'Barely had the cord that connected us been cut, they took her away. Whatever life she was now destined for, the sense of loss would never leave me. They say when you lose a limb you can still feel the dismembered arm or leg tingling, itching and squeezing, protesting the denial of its existence. I wasn't even to be blessed with a phantom child.'

Alyson nodded towards Bronte as if to say, 'This is a bit more like it.'

Twin-set lowered her voice to gravel level and

continued, 'I'd never owned anything in my life, and now I owned even less…'

Eric started to feel his colour rise. If his work didn't possess literary merit, this did? But everybody seemed to be lapping it up so what did he know?

Next up was a young gamine who was so short it took about a minute to adjust the mic height. 'Dungeons For Eyes,' she eventually announced in Estuary English. 'There was no question of her paying the executioner to kill her any faster. Even if she possessed the means, the good burghers of Wilton liked their witches to suffer as they burned them to a crisp. "It was God's will," they said.' Bronte's ears pricked up – she liked where this was going. 'As they tied her to the stake she could see the crowd, whipped up into a frenzy, jeering her, taunting her. One face in the crowd stood out, passive against the seething backdrop of hate. Martha, whose life she had saved just twelve short months before…'

'That was my favourite so far,' pronounced Bronte.

'I think I preferred the second one myself,' countered Alyson.

The final speaker now readjusted the mic back to its original position and took a deep breath. Eric thought he looked like a professional man – middle-aged, smart and sophisticated in a casual sort of way. Not unlike how he viewed himself. He wanted him to win.

'My extract is from A Man Without a Shadow,' he began. 'Marvin Mitchell hadn't planned on a life on the run, but then he'd always been highly adaptable. It had all started when he was feeling peckish. That's not a crime in itself, of course, but even Marvin had to admit that finding the dismembered remains of his wife in the freezer when looking for a pork chop would arouse suspicion.'

'That's funny, and you said humour didn't sell,' said a smug Con.

'He couldn't remember putting her there,' continued the narrator, 'and in any event he'd only just restocked the freezer. This was going to ruin Christmas...'

'It's crime as well, and I said that did,' Eric hissed back.

'Shush,' said the four women in social group one, sat opposite.

The readings concluded, Chapman now returned to the mic to adjudicate on the winner. 'Four marvellous extracts, beautifully written and expertly delivered. But who will be the winner?'

Eric stared balefully at the stage. As far as he was concerned there wasn't anything he'd just heard that could hold a candle to Scrub Me Till I Shine in the Dark. Was this genre thing right? Was he writing the wrong stuff? But who could predict what would be selling next? Tastes change. What was the point of all these agents chasing after the sort of books that were selling now? He knew enough about business to understand that successful companies placed emphasis on innovation and trend setting – that concept didn't seem to apply in publishing, that was for sure.

Chapman was explaining how the best extract would be selected. 'Whichever author receives the loudest round of applause as I re-introduce them will be our victor. I know the Write Stuff clap-o-meter isn't exactly state of the art but it's served us well in the past,' he quipped, basking in the adoring warmth of his audience.

As the decibel levels rose and fell Eric felt very isolated indeed. Maybe he'd picked the wrong two agents to see that afternoon? Maybe he'd get a different view tomorrow?

CHAPTER TWENTY

Fifteen minutes later a bunch of diehards congregated in the bar while the sensible ones headed back to their spartan accommodation. Con, with £8 still jingling in his pocket, knew he'd paced himself perfectly. He slipped off to the end of the bar to buy another pint of Guinness for himself and, as the stout settled in the tulip glass, took stock of the evening so far. First: Eric was a knob. Just because he'd had two one-to-ones and got nowhere he was trying to spook everybody else. If any further evidence of Eric's general twattery was required surely it was the titbit he'd dropped into the conversation about seeing two additional agents tomorrow. Trying to buy his way to success. Two: all this talk about men not buying books and genres that sell – and by implication, those that don't sell. Con remembered his girlfriend's assessment of A Refugee From the Seraphim as 'dense'. Would his novel appeal to women? Tomorrow he needed to stress that it would. Three: that line – Eric again – about the conference not really being about getting signed up by an agent. Con knew what he was there for and feedback was bottom of his shopping list. If he didn't get a sniff tomorrow he might as well throw his manuscript in the bin. And four: he had nothing to worry about if those readings earlier represented the pinnacle of unpublished literary achievement (by now Con had convinced himself it had been an advantage not to have been shortlisted). His writing knocked spots off that hackneyed shite.

The agents had managed to once more circle their wagons in a corner of the bar. They might as well have brought their own velvet rope, bouncer and 'Private Members Club' sign. Alyson, Bronte and Eric studied them as they exchanged jokes and tried to score points off each other. Occasionally a renegade delegate would pluck up the courage to march over and try to engage them. Did they know them? Were they merely exchanging meaningless pleasantries in an effort to get on the agents' radar? Were they actually attempting a sly pitch? It was like watching riders on a bucking bronco – how long could they hold on before they were thrust skywards? Eric spotted Hugo Lockwood sitting among the agents and couldn't help but steal glances in his direction every so often. As he'd surmised from his tweets, Eric thought Hugo looked a bit too fond of himself. He was clearly holding court – he could tell that by the way everybody was laughing at what he was saying. Should he have had the courage to request a one-to-one with him? No, he'd definitely made the correct call.

As Con rejoined them Eric pointed at the agents. 'We're running a book on how long each delegate lasts talking to the agents. Do you fancy giving it a go, Con?'

Con, who'd spent a good deal of the evening working out how he could ingratiate himself with the red lapel badges, smiled and said, 'I'll take the turn after you, Eric.' It pained him to be still stuck with the three people he'd spent the past few hours with because he really wanted to be talking to the agents, editors and publishers whose presence was promoted so heavily in the Write Stuff's publicity material. He, too, had noticed that they didn't appear very approachable. Con reminded himself that this was the first night of conference and he'd find a way to buttonhole these people before he left, come what may. 'Anyway, it's all about the scheduled one-to-ones, isn't it? Our two shots at glory – or four in your case.'

Many of the delegates chatting at the bar were guessing they had better options elsewhere. They'd rather be hobnobbing with the experts, obviously, but they also harboured a suspicion that the other delegates would probably be more interesting than their current company. It was curious how groups thrown together, with the same randomness as the lifeboats on the Titanic, now appeared to be immutable. There was no getting off. Conversations were conducted with eyelines aimed over the shoulder of the person being talked to or listened to; the grass in the distance had never appeared as verdant and lush.

Alyson had graduated on to double gin and tonics. In her subconscious she'd already begun to give up hope that conference would produce anything worthwhile for her and her new literary direction in The Moon Pulls on The Tide. Everybody seemed to be taking it so seriously she was starting to think this was the sort of club she wouldn't want to join, even if invited. Talking to Eric didn't seem to help. 'So what do you do when you're not writing, Eric?' she asked to get him off publishing.

'Actually, I write when I'm not writing – I'm a journalist,' he said proudly.

'That's cheating. That's an unfair advantage over the rest of us,' said Alyson, further convinced that she was lacking the core ingredients for literary success.

Eric, mellowing as he enjoyed a whisky, remembered what Brian Brooks had said to him that afternoon – *it's a little too precise/more like a report than an engaging narrative.* 'I honestly don't feel being a journalist gives me any advantage at all. It could be a handicap.'

Alyson couldn't fathom why that would be the case. 'You know how to spell for a start, and the difference between stationary and stationery. I haven't a clue.'

'Ah, yes, but does grammar of itself guarantee that you can move the reader? That's the important thing.' Alyson was as impressed at Eric's modesty as she was at his unselfish observation – she could see the sense in that. 'If I'm being honest, that's what one of the agents said to me this afternoon,' Eric confessed. 'Maybe my writing is too rigid?'

Alyson was slightly surprised at Eric's change of mood – she thought he'd been quite chippy all evening. 'I'm dreading what the agents will say to me tomorrow,' confessed Alyson. 'I lashed mine together a bit quickly.'

'Is it finished?'

'No. I only started it when I knew I was coming here, so I'm about halfway through.'

'You must write quickly,' said Eric, knowing how long his own work had taken. 'Is it your first novel?'

Alyson hesitated. For the past few weeks she had been wrestling with the dilemma of whether to divulge her literary track record at conference or pretend it didn't exist. She feared mentioning her ViXen success would lessen her credibility as a writer in the eyes of the agents. Her conference experience to date had only reinforced that decision – she was feeling out of her depth. 'Well, yes and no,' she laughed, the gin dismantling any preconceived notions of strategy. 'This is my first mainstream book attempt, but not my first novel.'

'So you're switching genres?' said Eric, impressed. 'That takes some doing. What do you write normally?'

Alyson giggled. 'I write erotica.'

Eric suddenly saw Alyson in a whole new light. This unassuming, artless, middle-aged woman wrote erotica? He would never have guessed. His business-desk instincts immediately kicked in. 'Really? Can you make money doing that?'

Alyson's inner love light began to gleam. She felt on home turf for the first time since she'd arrived. 'I'm a long way off E L James in what I earn, but it pays the bills.'

Even Eric had heard of E L James and 'that book'. 'You write the same sort of stuff as her and you make money – what do you want to be a "proper" author for if you can do that?'

'I've been asking myself that all day,' said Alyson, feeling unburdened now she'd got it off her chest.

'Do you self-publish or do you have an agent? How does it all work in that game?'

'I don't have an agent but I do have a deal with a specialist online publisher – it's big business these days.'

Eric was starting to glow too – he'd never met anyone who wrote pornographic prose before. He was curious.

'Do you mind if I ask you something? How do you get your ideas? Isn't erotica supposed to be rather limited in its subject matter?'

Alyson laughed at his typical vanilla reaction. 'You'd be surprised, Eric. I find ideas wherever I look,' she teased.

Eric felt a stirring in his loins. 'And this website – how, er, racy is it?'

Alyson kept a straight face. 'Let's just say it starts where Amazon leaves off. Do you ever read or watch porn, Eric?'

The innocent scribe felt his face reddening at such a direct question. At the same time he was surprised at how the plain housewife he'd spent the majority of the evening with had now transformed into a seductive siren, beguiling him with her charms. It wasn't only his writing that felt rigid at this point in time. 'Catholic upbringing, so not really.'

'Oh, I've met some very randy Catholics in my time,' Alyson replied. 'There's something about being a left-footer that seems to heighten their pleasure.'

Eric sensed she was dangerous but was unable to tear himself away. Lacking a cold shower at that moment he tried to steer her back to why she was at the conference. 'Are you enjoying writing mainstream stuff?'

Alyson shrugged her shoulders. 'I don't know. It's a lot bloody harder, I can tell you.'

'Why bother then, if you're doing so well in your, er, stock-in-trade?'

'I want to prove to myself I can do it, and I want to gain recognition for being a proper writer. I know it sounds silly but I dream of winning an award and Richard and Judy recommending me. I could die a happy woman if that ever happened.'

Eric had no problem understanding such modest ambitions. 'Well, good for you, Alyson. I have to say if attitude counts you're halfway there already.'

Alyson's bosom swelled with pride at such encouraging words from this man of letters. She didn't meet too many professionals in her normal daily grind. 'Fancy a night cap?' she purred.

Across campus Suzie was getting ready for bed. She applied fresh lipstick and touched up her foundation before slipping into her new Victoria Beckham organza mini dress. She knew it was a bit young for her but it had been such a bargain in the Net-A-Porter summer sale. And it felt so right as it slid across the silky smoothness of her freshly waxed legs. In the bathroom a bottle of champagne stood chilling in the sink while two glass flutes she'd carefully wrapped in her luggage sat expectantly by the bed. She turned off the overhead light to allow the reading lamp to cast long, dramatic shadows across the wall. In the league table of love nests it was hardly a suite at The Langham, yet Suzie had thought of little else all day. As she awaited Chapman's hesitant knock on the door she was still nervous – what if he didn't turn up? Such uncertainty was understandable as their previous trysts had all occurred without any specific arrangements actually being discussed, starting with the first ever Write Stuff conference when a triumphant Chapman had shown his gratitude to her in the most intimate of ways. Afterwards, and throughout the intervening year, neither Chapman nor Suzie mentioned their night of passion to each other but at the second conference Chapman once more stole to her room 'to discuss arrangements for Saturday'. And so it had continued year after year. When Chapman had married, Suzie feared that their tacit 'tradition' would cease yet once again she heard his soft footsteps outside her door. If anything, that night she felt she had won an even greater victory. Deep down, though, Suzie knew she had no hold over Chapman. She wondered whether he was merely indulging himself, or worse still, indulging her? But she looked forward to this night more than any other in the calendar, when she and Chapman became one and the rest of the world didn't matter. She never divulged their secret to anyone – friends or family, and certainly not to work colleagues.

They were nothing if not creatures of habit. It was always the first night of conference on which their clandestine coupling took place and Chapman never returned for the second night. As nothing was ever discussed between them she never really found out why this was the case. It just was – these were the unspoken rules. Chapman would wait until all was still, quietly knock on her door and innocently say he wanted to discuss a few things for tomorrow. Suzie would invite him in and ask if he would like a drink. They'd talk shop for ten or fifteen minutes pretending nothing was going to happen and then he would reach forward and take her in his arms. Their lovemaking was surprisingly varied, enthusiastic and agile, as if they were fitting a whole year's shagging into one night – which is exactly what they *were* doing. Despite putting on a lot of weight over the years Chapman still insisted on a bewildering variety of sexual positions, as if he was on a Rotary Club sponsored campaign to re-enact every page in the Kama Sutra. There was very little conversation – all of their efforts were focused on the physical. Their lovemaking lasted as long as it took to drink the by-now traditional bottle of champagne, and Chapman would then sneak off as if staying the night was somehow an act of infidelity to his wife. The next day, and over the successive 364 days after that, nothing would be said but Suzie knew that Chapman had endorsed, once more, that they were an item despite all the outward signs to the contrary.

Suzie selected a new playlist on her iPhone, generated especially for this evening, and adjusted the volume on the travel speakers to low. Where was he? A look at her watch told her what she already knew – he'd never been this late before. Had he given her any signs earlier today? Yes and no – he'd given her no signs but that was normally the sign that the usual arrangements were in place. Should she text him? No – she'd never done that before and she didn't want to look presumptive, or desperate. But the prospect of him letting her down filled her with woe and longing; how could she endure the rejection if he broke their trust of seven years? As the hands of the clock climbed to one o'clock the feeling of abandonment sharpened, matched only by a deep sense of shame for being such a fool and then a rising tide of anger. She decided to open the champagne and to give him until the end of the playlist before capitulating. As each song on 'Book-Ends' shuffled forward she took swigs straight from the bottle. Finally the only sound from the speakers was a low hum. She was all played out.

CHAPTER TWENTY-ONE

The next morning at breakfast Emily and Hugo were comparing notes. To help inject some added value into the weekend the agent had invented a game of 'conference bingo' on the journey north. He was keen to see if he was ahead of Emily. 'To be honest, Em, I should have made it harder. I cleared half of my card with just one delegate, and that was within the first half-hour.'

Emily suspected Hugo was showing off as usual but agreed they should have thought longer and harder over the rules. 'We should have weighted the comments for degrees of difficulty, not just given a point to each one.'

'Next time, not that there will be one, we will. Go on then, let's see what you've got so far.'

Most of the delegates had already eaten in order to be at the guest lecture kicking off Saturday's programme. 'OK,' she said. 'I got "it would make great TV", "my partner read it and thought it was brilliant" and "how much can I expect to earn?" in double-quick time.'

'Check. They're the easy ones. How did you do on "look-a-likeys"?'

'Two Harry Potters, two Twilights, one A Song of Fire and Ice, one Bridget Jones and one Da Vinci Code.'

'A good haul. You did better than me there,' Hugo conceded. 'But if we had weighted the scores surely I'd have got more for the Wolf Hall and Captain Corelli's Mandolin ones I had?'

'I don't disagree, but would remind you that you set the goalposts.'

Hugo couldn't argue with that. 'Free scoring section: I had one cover design, one "can I have my photo taken with you?" and a Kendal Mint Cake gift set.'

'That's not really trying, Hugo. I had two people who came along with book covers they'd designed, three who gave me new mug shots they'd had done especially for the jacket and I got asked out on a date back in London.'

'Impressive. It's looking pretty even at the moment but we've a long way to go,' said Hugo who had quickly worked out that he was behind in the scoring.

'Pretty even? I don't think so,' said Emily. 'And what about unsolicited pitches? How many of those did you get?'

Hugo thought for a second – should he overegg the number a bit? 'Two in the bar before dinner, three afterwards, and one on the way into breakfast just now.'

'Pathetic, Lockwood. I see you and I raise you – I can match that and throw in a pitch through the cubicle door when I was having a pee before last night's readings.'

'Male or female?' queried Hugo.

'Woman, of course.'

'Shame – I would have given you extra points for a bloke.'

Over in the main auditorium Alyson Hummer was listening to guest author, Melanie McCardle, delivering

196

the opening lecture. With ten novels and over two million sales to her name Alyson was keen to derive inspiration from an acknowledged queen of women's fiction. In Alyson's preparation for conference she'd read two of Melanie's bestsellers, Mascara Tears and Cold Kisses. She was delighted to see that sex – albeit pretty tame sex – was a vital ingredient of the novels and her hopes soared momentarily. When she'd finished reading the two books, however, she experienced an overriding sense of woe. It wasn't the writing (which was pretty formulaic and repetitive) and it wasn't the plots (which she had to concede were paper-thin) that caused her dismay. It wasn't even the boring sex (which was tediously dull). What really unsettled Alyson was how the settings and the characters portrayed a world she had never experienced and in which she knew she could never feel comfortable. Melanie's books were chock full of first-world problems like not being able to get a suitable nanny, husbands who couldn't get it up (with their wives, at least), ageing, dieting, holidays and fashion. Her women were either career wives spending their husbands' money or young professionals working their way up to that status. They called each other 'Darling' and 'Sweets', as if anybody in real life spoke like that. Alyson reasoned that if this was the kind of stuff that was selling it was outside her terms of reference and she would be wasting her time in trying to emulate it. If, on the other hand, she stuck to what she knew then she'd be back to what she was already writing. Of course, Alyson was sensible enough to know that self-doubt was a monkey that sat on every writer's back – could Melanie's talk help remove hers?

The lecture started well, for Alyson at least, in that Melanie had a distinct northeast accent – she hadn't been expecting that. Perhaps she'd misjudged the author and she was as down to earth and normal as Alyson was? Maybe, like a modern-day Catherine Cookson, she wrote about ordinary people as well? But Alyson soon found her class barometer to be incorrectly calibrated as Melanie, not an author given to coyness, regaled the audience with tales of her privileged upbringing, university education, blessed marriage, supportive family and her blossoming career as a lawyer before 'fate' intervened. Some 'fate' thought Alyson enviously. Around her, scores of delegates were busily writing notes to capture such gems as 'never give up', 'if I can do it so can you', and 'make time to write'. The crowd broke out in spontaneous applause as Melanie told them that henceforth the word 'chick-lit' was never to pass their lips again. All around Alyson people were scribbling these words of wisdom in their notepads, or tapping them into their phones. *Why?* wondered Alyson. Would they ever look at them again? What did the words actually mean? It was like the draft syllabus for a 'statement-of-the-bleedin'-obvious' GCSE – sitting the exam proved the pupils had attended class but they would gain no practical use from the so-called knowledge they'd ingested. If Melanie was supposed to be inspiring the eager delegates to write women's fiction then she was having the opposite effect on Alyson. She not only found herself begrudging the author's success, she found herself wanting to stand up and tell her she was talking bollocks. Was it the gin last night that had put her in such a foul mood? She couldn't be sure. When, mercifully, the lecture ended, Alyson crept out of the auditorium with two monkeys clinging to her back.

Eric had skipped the lecture and opted for one of the work groups on how to write a perfect pitch. He was finding it hard to concentrate. It wasn't only his whisky hangover making him feel unfocused – he couldn't get Alyson out of his mind. In his strictly ordered life Eric had come across few women like her. Once she relaxed she exuded such sensuality, fun, daring and a sense of danger that he'd felt entranced; there was an allure there, a promise of the forbidden that would cause many men to abandon normal constraints. Many men, but not Eric. He was the mouse who could resist an appetising piece of cheese while others threw themselves on to the Little Nipper. When the bar closed a terrified Eric had scurried back to the protection of his bedroom, aghast that such thoughts, however fleetingly, had entered his mind. He was so steamed up he Googled Alyson and within minutes found himself on the ViXen site.

'The pitch is the single most critical means of getting an agent. It has to be honed to perfection…' said the workshop leader. Eric wasn't listening.

The staid journalist's eyes were on stalks as he'd surfed the erotica site. It was all very professional and as Alyson had said it was aimed squarely at women. He'd never imagined. Did Victoria ever access sites like this? He doubted it. He searched for Alyson's name and found a dozen works listed. The titles and the taglines alone were enough to raise his blood pressure another notch. At first he hesitated to download anything from the site in case he was bombarded with dirty junk emails for the rest of his life but the temptation to read Alyson's work proved too strong. He joined up to buy Backlash Love Affair and No Price on Love.

'A pitch is not a description of what happens in the book. It's the bait to hook you a deal.' Eric's notepad remained blank.

As Eric devoured Alyson's graphic prose, outlining acts he didn't know existed or if they were even legal, he marvelled at how she had come up with these ideas, never mind actually setting them down in print. And there was a consistent theme running through the pages – it was all about the pleasure the woman was feeling in the highly imaginative sexual scenarios dreamt up by the author. About how the woman was in control of her passions. If Victoria ever read this she'd want Eric to up his act, that was for sure.

'The ideal length should be no longer than a tweet.' Eric was still deep in thought, staring out of the window.

And she must have sold thousands of her books looking at the bestsellers list. And if what she said about her deal was true, then she was more than making a living; she must be very comfortable indeed. She was probably earning more a year than Eric and yet she wanted to cross over to so-called serious writing?

'If I say, "In space no one can hear you scream" we all know what movie I'm talking about. This is your benchmark.' Eric unconsciously scratched his balls.

There was definitely a formula to Alyson's erotic structure. She never went more than two pages without a sex act or a description of how the heroine was feeling about sex. It was a lascivious equivalent of the Atkins diet – you can have meat, meat, meat or meat. Eric recognised that to be able to write like this took enormous discipline.

'A very simple way to get started is to use the "x meets y" approach. If I say my new novel is Wuthering Heights meets The Shining I've immediately got you interested.'

Eric devoured Alyson's steamy shenanigans in a state of intense arousal, tossing and turning under the sheets until 3am before falling into a dream where he and Alyson were making love in a bath of baked beans.

He was trying to recapture this image as he stared out of the window but his reverie was suddenly and rudely interrupted. There, crossing the car park and making its way to reception, was a giant monobrow and underneath it the smug visage of Dylan Dylan. If Eric had been paying attention he may have summed up his puzzlement at this sight as The Visitor meets Revenge of the Werewolf.

Dylan had completed his registration when Eric burst into reception and marched menacingly in his direction. 'What do you think you're playing at?' was the business editor's less than friendly welcome.

Dylan couldn't believe he'd scored so early after his arrival. 'Eric, what are you doing here? What a coincidence.'

'Coincidence? You've deliberately come here to wind me up, you cretin.'

Dylan tried his best to look offended at the very suggestion. 'I'm just finding out how to get published, that's all. You must take some of the credit for that, Eric. You've inspired me.'

'You need to write a book first if you want to get published. In your case it would help if you'd actually read one.'

Dylan was unfazed. 'How do you know I haven't written a book?'

Such a possibility didn't hold water for Eric. 'Don't be ridiculous. Look, this is all very amusing but you need to go – now.'

'Why would I leave, Eric? It's a free country. I've paid my money and I'm looking forward to the conference.'

A tired, disoriented and angry Eric clenched his fists in frustration. 'Are you seriously telling me that you've booked in as a delegate?'

Dylan pointed at his white lapel badge. 'Yes – Saturday and Sunday. What time does the gala dinner start tonight? That should be really good.'

'As jokes go, Dylan, it's a very expensive one. But you still need to leave.'

'I'm not going anywhere. I've got the next 24-hours all lined up. Maybe we can go to some of the sessions together?'

Other delegates passing through reception were now looking at Eric who was clearly upset over something despite the pleasant, smiling young man talking to him. Conscious he was creating a scene an exasperated Eric stomped off as briskly as he'd arrived, cursing and muttering under his breath. Dylan watched him go and allowed himself a twisted smile of victory. If he could get Eric so pissed off within five minutes of arriving, what would he be like by tomorrow? Time to explore, thought Dylan, and see what's going down in conference-land.

CHAPTER TWENTY-TWO

Reardon had the whole first class carriage to himself as he made his way to Lancaster. He'd completed The Guardian crossword and flicked through the conference agenda and now he turned his attention to preparing some notes for his speech later that evening. He was feeling good. In fact he couldn't remember the last time he'd felt so relaxed. He and Belinda had recently returned from two weeks in Tuscany where, in between taking in the sights of Florence, Siena and San Gimignano, they'd enjoyed tranquil evenings listening to Puccini and restful days lolling by the pool of their rented farmhouse. As Reardon brushed up on his Ghibbelines, Guelphs and Grimaldis Belinda busied herself with a daily ritual of preparing authentic Tuscan cuisine for the two of them using only local, simple ingredients. It was the most serene vacation they'd ever shared. Belinda, too, was considerably more relaxed now that Reardon's demons appeared to have been subdued. He was no longer ranting over the lack of a publishing contract and almost seemed to be looking forward to starting the university posting. Calm had descended, so much so that when Belinda dropped Reardon off at the station she gently chided herself that only a few weeks back she'd been offering to chaperone him on this Lancaster trip. Well, that wouldn't be necessary now – the medication was working wonders. She had nothing to worry about.

Just before Birmingham the steward parked his trolley next to Reardon's seat to offer him refreshment. 'Would you like a snack box with that, sir?' he enquired as he handed him his tea.

'There's no food?'

'Saturday, I'm afraid. Only hot beverages, soft drinks and snack boxes today on the complimentary service.'

Not so long ago this denial of a traveller's basic rights would have led to an eruption from the crotchety author. But not today. 'That's a shame. I was feeling peckish, too.'

The steward looked sympathetic. 'Have two snack boxes,' he suggested. 'It's dead on here today.'

'Why, that's very kind of you. Thank you,' said the grateful passenger.

The steward smiled and pointed at the bottom of the trolley. 'Would you like a proper drink, sir? I'll just pretend it's a weekday.'

Reardon was impressed at the flexibility and discretion Virgin allowed its staff in their pursuit of customer satisfaction. 'Why not? I'll have a gin and tonic in that case. Nobody need know.' By 'nobody' Reardon had Belinda in mind rather than Richard Branson.

The attentive steward filled a glass with ice and lemon and handed a miniature bottle of gin and a can of tonic to Reardon. Then, with a wink, he placed a further bottle and can on the table. 'Have a pleasant journey, sir,' he said as he set off up the aisle. Reardon raised his glass to the back of the departing steward. The West Coast service had certainly picked up since the last time he had taken it.

By the time he was on his second gin Reardon had completed a page of notes for his speech. In a self-deprecating device he planned to open by recounting his reaction on being offered the creative writing professorship at Edward VIII university: 'creative writing can't be taught'. His conversion from this credo would mirror that of St Paul on the road to Damascus and provide a rich vein for his address. Yes, that would do very nicely.

Chapman noticed, much later than the rest of his team, that Suzie had been avoiding him all morning. She had skipped breakfast, which wasn't like her, and put Amy in charge of Melanie's book-signing session, a responsibility she wouldn't have parted with lightly under normal circumstances. Shortly after the mid-morning coffee break Chapman spotted Suzie in the conference office, printing documents. He slipped in and closed the door behind him. The rest of the Write Stuff team gave each other knowing looks. Suzie, standing by the open window on another stiflingly hot day, gave him a stare that would have frozen helium.

Chapman started to walk over to her, then caught her look and hesitated. As casually as he could he flopped into the office chair. 'Suze? Is there anything the matter?' he asked innocently.

Suzie had agonised over how she should confront Chapman on his no-show the night before. The bottom line was that she couldn't. As there was no arrangement in place, he'd not officially broken it. As there were no promises made, there was no letdown. She knew how he'd squirm his way out of it anyway, like a barrister who'd given up the law for politics. All she could do, she reasoned, was to give him the cold-shoulder treatment and never let herself be treated like a sex slave again. 'I'm fine, thank you. Busy,' she said tersely.

'You don't look fine, Suze. Has somebody upset you?'

She shook her head in disbelief at his brass neck. Now she looked directly into his piggy little eyes and saw him anew. Not as a Capability Brown reshaping the literary landscape, nor an alchemist turning leaden scribblers into gold bullion. What she saw in front of her now was a fat, arrogant, conceited, pathetic excuse of a man over whom she'd been deluded enough to put her life on hold for a decade in the hope of, what? The cold-shoulder plan bit the dust. 'Has somebody upset me? Let me think,' she mused. 'Oh, wait a minute. How about the glutton of a boss who takes what he wants, when he wants, but suddenly put himself on a diet last night?'

Chapman sat up straight in his chair. He didn't expect her to kick off like this. 'Listen Suze, if you're referring to what I think you are, I can explain everything.'

'Go on, then,' she urged. 'This will be interesting.'

Chapman groaned. 'Look, I know we've had a bit of a thing at conference in the past, but it's difficult. I'm married now.'

'You were married last year, and the year before that, and the…'

'Yes, I know. We should have stopped it then,' he said before adding, rather inadvisably: 'But I didn't want to let you down.'

'Let me down? So you were doing me a favour, were you? Shagging me senseless instead of giving me a company bonus – was that the idea? Is it a benefit in kind? Taxable? I'll have to check with Accounts.'

Chapman could feel the hole he was in getting deeper. 'It wasn't like that. You know it wasn't. I'd have said something but what was there to say? I thought it would be best to quietly draw a line under it.'

Suzie looked at him with contempt. 'Quietly draw a line under it? By which you mean don't mention it at all. You know what? You're a coward and a shit. Adele is welcome to you – you deserve each other.'

Chapman chivalrously defended his wife's honour. 'It's not fair to drag Adele into this, Suze.'

'Fair? You talk about fair? What do you think she'd say if she knew what we'd been up to?'

Was this a threat? Surely she wouldn't tell her? Chapman couldn't be sure. 'Please, Suze. Let's not go there. You have to see it from my point of view?'

'You know what, Chapman, I'll tell you how I see it. I'm a mug. Always have been. Ever since I let you pretend you'd written A Poisoned Heart and A Twisted Memory. How prophetic a title that was, wasn't it?'

'You know I was grateful for that. It's not helpful to bring that up.'

'No? It only made you and your poxy company. You've said so yourself. Go on – admit it. You only came on to me to get my book because you were incapable of writing one yourself.'

'You know that's not true. It was just, well, it just happened, didn't it?'

207

'With you begging me, you mean. *I* could have been published. *I* could have written more books by now if I hadn't sacrificed myself to you and your frigging business.'

Chapman knew he was losing control of the situation. The last thing he needed was a scene, or worse still, his number two not doing her job properly this weekend – the whole conference depended on her organisational prowess. 'Suzie, keep your voice down. Someone will hear,' he pleaded. 'Why don't we meet up next week and *calmly* talk it all through?'

'Forget it, Chapman,' said Suzie as she made her way to the door. 'I don't ever want to talk to you again.'

Chapman put his head in his hands as she slammed the door behind her. No, he'd not been expecting an outburst like that. Maybe she was overstressed with the conference planning? He hoped to God none of the staff had overheard any of their exchange.

Below the window Dylan Dylan was congratulating himself on having picked such a great spot for a fag break. He thought his ruse to haunt Eric at conference might lose its sparkle after a few hours but then he'd not counted on the free theatre that was included in the price of admission.

'"Every time I thought I was being rejected from something good, I was actually being re-directed to something better". These sage words from lifestyle coach and empowerment guru Steve Maraboli hold particular meaning for the aspiring writer.' Bronte was busily speed typing on her laptop, almost verbatim, the work group presentation on 'Handling Rejection'. She was learning so much and finding so much inspiration she'd hardly paused for breath as she rushed from session to session all morning. Bronte was looking forward to prioritising her notes when she returned home – it was like learning for an exam, but one she knew would stand her in good stead for her future writing career. The self-help and lifestyle philosophy continued. 'You need to know you are not alone when you receive a rejection slip. Many famous authors have been in your shoes. J K Rowling, Dan Brown, Paulo Coelho, J D Salinger, Margaret Mitchell, Stephenie Meyer, Yann Martel, John Grisham – I could go on – were all rejected.' Bronte was struggling with some of the spellings as she'd not heard of many of these authors, but she got the general drift. 'Were they upset? You bet. Did they give up? No. But what they didn't do is blame the agent for rejecting their work – they set out to improve and raise their standards so the next time they would do better.' Bronte dutifully wrote this down too, not realising that the observation wasn't strictly accurate, as many of the authors mentioned had work taken on by one agent after dozens had rejected the same submission. But the presenter knew delegates had not paid hundreds of pounds to hear advice along the lines of W C Fields' famous dictum, 'If at first you don't succeed, try, try again. Then quit. There's no point in being a damn fool about it.'

If Bronte had one regret about the weekend it was that she wasn't yet in a position to have any one-to-ones as her work was still at the planning stage. A quote on rejection more applicable to her might have been, 'Rejected pieces aren't failures; unwritten pieces are.' As well as the fabulous insights and tips she was gleaning she was pleased to have met so many interesting characters at conference – this was the real world, not at all like university. Alyson reminded her of a school dinner lady but she was funny and didn't give a toss about anything. She wondered if Alyson could actually write as she didn't give the impression she could, but it was great that she was trying at her age. Con, admittedly, was super intense and scary, but his keening desire to make it as a writer was stirring. In all probability James Joyce and Samuel Beckett had been like that, so maybe that's what it took? Eric – she was sure she'd heard his name somewhere before – was uptight in a different sort of way to Con. He seemed very intelligent, but in a schoolmasterly or priestly kind of way. Did he have the passion to make it as a writer? She couldn't see that he did. But then it was so hard to tell who did have what it took to be a success, there was so much to it. Back to rejection: 'You may think that once you have an agent and an editor you'll never have to accept rejection again.' The presenter was wearing his sincere face. 'But you'd be wrong. Because that's when you'll be told that your novel would benefit from restructuring, tweaking the characters, refining the dialogue and changing the ending. What do you do then?' Bronte didn't like the sound of this. Really? 'You have to trust the agent and the editor in those cases – they know what they're talking about. Where your work is good they will make it great; where your work may sell thousands, they will help you sell millions.' As an unelected official for the agents and editors union the presenter was doing a fine job. Bronte typed the next inevitable quote illustrating this point into her laptop. 'If you want the rainbow, you've got to put up with the rain.' Another author she'd not heard of – she made a mental note to look up what books Dolly Parton had written when she found a minute.

CHAPTER TWENTY-THREE

As Eric left the buffet counter his eye caught Con frantically waving at him from the large settee he was sharing with Alyson and Bronte. Eric, hesitantly, took his lunch tray over to join them. Con couldn't wait to tell him his news. 'Guess who's just had a request for a full manuscript?' He paused for dramatic effect, pointed at himself and then flamboyantly pulled on an imaginary cigar.

Eric was dumbstruck. This brash Celtic bullshitter, this fairground roustabout, had received interest from an agent? There really was no justice in the world. And as for those pathetic mime gestures – how bloody puerile. 'Really? That's fantastic, Con. Well done,' he said, trying to sound pleased for him.

'I couldn't believe it. My first session – boom! She actually said she'd been waiting to meet me as my intro was so intriguing.' Con had already recounted the timeline of his triumph to Alyson and Bronte but he was minded to make sure Eric didn't miss out on the details. 'She said my manuscript was fascinating, dark, different and definitely had potential.' Con was so excited Eric had no doubt that by midnight there wouldn't be a single soul left on the campus, kitchen staff included, who wouldn't know that he had thrown a six at the start of the get-an-agent game.

Eric, quickly losing his appetite for lunch, had no option but to keep teeing up the Irish braggart. Besides, despite his envy, he was keen to know exactly what Con's work possessed that his was so clearly lacking. 'What genre are you? You never said last night.'

'I was being a wee bit superstitious last night – you know how it is. What genre? Well, it's genre-bending to tell the truth – maybe that's what appeals to her so much.'

'Which agent is it?' asked Eric, thinking maybe he could buttonhole her later.

'She's over there, blonde hair, black glasses, but don't all look at once,' said Con, gesticulating in Emily Chatterton's direction. Three pairs of eyes followed his glance. 'But get this. She's not an agent. She's the top editorial director at Franklin & Pope.

Eric refused to believe that someone like Con could land on his feet like this. 'But you're not supposed to submit to publishers; you have to get an agent first.'

Con couldn't contain his glee. 'Usually, yes. But they've got this new initiative to discover original, unagented talent – I picked up on it online. It pays to research, you see. I could be their first signing.'

How on earth had Eric missed seeing that? Adopting his best investigative journalist demeanour he asked, 'What was it she liked so much about your book?'

Con, no longer hampered by the need to maintain an aura of secrecy around his work, unloaded. 'The best way to describe it is as a "psychoactive" novel – it transcends normal genre rules,' he said loftily. 'She described it as "high-concept" – that's what they're all looking for these days.' Eric, Alyson and Bronte looked stupified so Con elaborated further. 'The central character, Coyne, works in a hospital and ends up taking MDMA to get through the night shifts. When he's really spaced out he spends time in the mortuary and starts up a relationship with a baby boy who's died a horrible, violent death. So Coyne decides he has to live this baby's life for him.'

'That sounds really spooky,' gushed Bronte. 'What's it called?'

'A Refugee From The Seraphim,' said Con, proudly.

Eric's eyes widened. *What pretentious crap.*

Alyson was curious. 'How did you come up with a story like that? That's really unusual.'

Con was enjoying the interrogation. 'Let's just say it came to me in a vision.'

Eric couldn't believe his ears. So junkie Con gets off his tits on Ecstasy in order to put up with his crappy job, starts hallucinating and decides to write a bestseller as a result? He should have been sacked from the hospital for a start. What if you had a relative in that morgue with the likes of Con and his Phenethylamine-preoccupied pals in charge? And Franklin & Pope were interested in shit like this? Incredible. How was that going to appeal to women anyway? Did they think they'd found the next Irvine Welsh? 'You need to keep your feet on the ground, though, Con. There's still a high rejection rate even when they ask for a full manuscript.'

Despite herself, Alyson chided him. 'Don't be so negative, Eric. It's wonderful news for Con.'

Con was feeling magnanimous. 'No, Alyson, Eric's right. But I dreamed that this would happen, and

213

nothing, absolutely nothing on earth is going to stop me now.'

Not to mention anything in the underworld either, thought Eric.

'Well you're definitely one up on all of us,' said Bronte sweetly.

'Thanks, Bronte.' Con looked at his watch and stood up abruptly. 'Could be two up on you in half an hour – got my second one-to-one now. If you don't mind, places to be.'

Eric wanted to strangle the pill-popping porter on the spot. If Con got a second request for a full manuscript that afternoon he thought he probably would. 'Don't waste a lucky streak. You should buy a lottery ticket while you're at it.'

Con wasn't listening and certainly wasn't bothered by Eric's comments. He had a destiny to fulfil.

As Con vacated his seat a fellow delegate took advantage of the space. Eric's lunch hour took an even more unhappy turn as Dylan Dylan plonked himself down.

'Eric – what a surprise,' said Dylan breezily. His work colleague froze. 'Aren't you going to introduce me?' Alyson and Bronte looked at Eric expectantly: who was this? As Eric appeared to have lost the power of speech the newcomer saved him the bother. 'I'm Dylan. I work with Eric. It's great here, isn't it?'

Eric knew he was outmanoeuvred. If he refused to join in the conversation he would appear rude and cantankerous in front of his new friends. He grunted 'Alyson' and 'Bronte' as he introduced his acquaintances to Dylan.

Alyson took an immediate interest in the Liam

Gallagher *doppelganger* who certainly looked a bit more stimulating than the rest of the fusty male delegates. 'Are you a journalist too?'

Dylan smiled. 'I run the sales team. But we both share a love of the printed word, don't we, Eric?'

Eric didn't look at him. 'It's fair to say you've always been a fan of fiction, yes, Dylan.'

Bronte, who had missed Eric's occupation the previous evening, was intrigued. 'What newspaper do you work on?'

'The Manchester Chronicle,' breezed Dylan.

Bronte was beside herself. What were the odds of that? 'That's amazing. My friend's working there as an intern at the moment. She's on the business desk.'

Eric and Dylan were taken aback in equal measure. 'Julia?' asked Dylan.

Bronte almost bounced up and down on the settee. 'Yes. Yes it is. Do you know her?'

Both men instinctively recognised that Julia being known to Bronte compromised their ability to carry off a conference persona that couldn't be challenged. What was going to get back to Manchester about their respective visits to Lancaster?

Eric piped up first. 'She's working for me – I'm the business editor.'

Bronte shrieked. 'Incredible. She told me all about you. I hadn't realised it was you.'

Eric shifted uncomfortably. 'Well, I hope it was all good. She's a remarkable young lady.'

'Jules is great. She loves working at The Chronicle,' said Bronte.

Eric took the absence of any implied criticism as an endorsement. 'Well, we do our best.'

'I tried to persuade her to come here with me since she's finished her book. How cool would that have been?' Bronte said.

Eric wasn't sure he'd caught that last bit right. 'Julia's written a book? She never mentioned that.' Dylan said nothing.

'God, she's such a talented writer I could kill her,' confessed Bronte. 'I'm surprised she didn't mention it to you when she knew you two were coming.'

'Yes, I'm surprised too,' admitted Eric, sincerely.

'She was probably just being modest. She is, I find,' added Dylan.

Alyson detected something was being left unsaid and changed the direction of conversation. 'So what do you write, Dylan?'

'Yes, Dylan. You must fill everybody in on that,' echoed Eric.

'I'm doing a book on my Uncle Danny – he was a big wheel in the music scene in Madchester and I reckon it's a story people will want to read about.'

On hearing this dubious announcement Eric decided to press his colleague further. 'Tell them the title, Dylan.'

Dylan didn't miss a beat. 'Crash The Party,' he smirked. He looked at Eric inviting him to have another go.

Alyson recognised two feuding schoolboys when she saw them. She tried to distract them once more. 'You know I heard a terrible story this morning in one of the groups I was in. Apparently, there was this bloke who was getting divorced, and he'd just finished his novel after two years of work on it. Guess what the wife did? She deleted the file on his computer.'

Bronte gasped in horror at the prospect. Eric was rather more circumspect. 'Didn't he have it backed up? Surely the only file wasn't sat on his hard disk?'

'No, it wasn't,' said Alyson. 'But she cleared all of his files and back up as well – beats cutting someone's clothes up, doesn't it?'

Bronte thought she could top this tall tale. 'Well, at university, a girl lent a story she'd written to another student, and it ended up appearing in the university newspaper under the name of the girl who'd borrowed it – she just stole it completely.'

Eric nodded sagely. 'That's why I haven't let anybody see my work except my wife.'

'Let's hope you're not going to get divorced anytime soon, then,' Dylan quipped.

Eric sighed – he was finding it difficult to control his irritation.

'You should tweet that story on the conference hashtag, Alyson,' Bronte suggested. 'Delegates would love it.'

'Oh I don't do that Twitter stuff, love. And what's a hashtag when it's at home?' Alyson said.

'It's a tag that groups messages together – there's one for this conference. Everyone here is posting on it,' Bronte announced, surprised that they didn't know simple stuff like this.

Eric had already spotted the conference hashtag. 'Let's just say if Twitter is a show-off medium,' he said, 'then a hashtag is the equivalent of streaking at Lord's during the crucial last over of an Ashes test.'

This wasn't exactly how Bronte would define this most useful of metadata signposts. 'Well, I find it interesting,' she said petulantly.

'Seriously,' said Eric, more to Alyson than anyone else, 'that hashtag is populated by creeps trying to suck up to agents and the organisers. They re-tweet every post an agent puts out and add their own "witty" comments and agreement. Worse, they "share" what they're learning here by replicating their conference "notes" to all and sundry. But it's not about being helpful – they're just blowing smoke up the backsides of the speakers and shouting out to anyone who'll listen, "look at me".'

Nobody said anything, but they all wondered the same thing: what had got into Eric?

Alyson broke the awkward silence with another digression. 'So, who's got any one-to-ones this afternoon?'

Eric seized upon the question. 'Yes, Dylan, you must have some lined up, surely?'

Dylan looked back at him coolly. 'Yes. Two. In fact I'd better get going – got one in ten minutes.' He unhurriedly stood up and sauntered out of the dining room with a cheery 'laters'.

Lying bastard, thought Eric, resisting the temptation to follow him to see where he went.

Bronte also took her departure to attend the 'Fantastic Fantasy' workshop that was top of her agenda for the day.

'You didn't mention you had a friend coming?' said Alyson. 'He was nice.'

'How remiss of me,' said Eric. Then, realising he was acting like a tart again, 'Have you got any one-to-ones this afternoon?'

'I'm all done,' said Alyson. 'They might as well have told me not to bother.'

Eric realised her news had been overlooked in all the excitement with Con and Dylan. 'I'm sorry to hear that. Surely they didn't say that?'

'As good as. They tried to be nice about The Moon Pulls on the Tide but that was the bottom line. Apparently my writing is "one-dimensional", "lacking in action" and "over-emotive". I felt humiliated.'

Eric, remembering his treatment from the day before, felt for his new friend. He tried to be encouraging. 'We have to remember that they don't know everything. Just because they're the so-called experts doesn't mean they're not guessing as much as we are. It's a common professional failing – I see it all the time.'

'Thanks, Eric. But I have to be realistic – I don't think my plan to go mainstream is going to work. They both sort of suggested the same – re-do everything, come at it from a different angle, change the tense, change the point of view and stuff like that. Christ, it would take years to write a book doing all of that. I don't have the luxury of time – I've a living to make.'

'Did you tell them about your writing experience?'

Alyson shook her head. 'To be honest, it never came up. They clearly thought I was some deranged housewife with an itch to scratch – they didn't ask, and I didn't tell them. What would have been the point?'

Eric didn't have an answer to that. What would have been the point? About the same as for the two one-to-ones he had scheduled that afternoon.

CHAPTER TWENTY-FOUR

'Have you heard from Eric yet?' Geraldine was being nosey about how the birthday gift was working out. She and Victoria were demolishing a bottle of white Rioja while the kids rampaged around the Blairs' Didsbury garden. Eric's absence had created the bonus of weekend chill time – something that wouldn't normally have been the case if he'd been present.

'He just called and, to be honest, he sounded a bit fraught,' reported Victoria.

Eric seemed to be fraught all of the time in Geraldine's view. 'Oh dear. That doesn't sound good.'

'Where do I start? Well, his one-to-ones were a letdown. He said he had no chance of getting published if the agents he saw were representative.'

'I thought they were paid to be all supportive and encouraging. I didn't realise they'd be so tough.'

'It seems that they were quite direct. In a nutshell, Eric's book is uncommercial – not enough people would buy it, so they wouldn't take it on.'

Geraldine could see the sense in that. 'Well, it's probably a good thing to know that. You can see their point – if it's not going to make money then it's not going to get signed.'

Victoria bristled at this curt, capitalist computation. 'Possibly, but he's clearly disappointed. And he said that an absolute toe-rag he'd met had been asked for a full manuscript, so he was very put out over that.'

'Well, it must have been a more saleable proposition. You know, Eric shouldn't resent other people's success.'

Victoria thought this a little harsh, too. 'He doesn't really – I think he just took a dislike to this particular guy.'

'So how's he enjoying the lectures and the workshop thingies?'

'Well, you know how Eric is. Thinks it's like being back at school where the teachers are only one page ahead of the pupils. He wasn't very complimentary.'

Geraldine tried to remember the last time she'd heard Eric pour praise on anything. 'I'm sure he's picking some good tips up. And meeting people in the same boat. It sounds highly useful to me.'

Victoria had retained the most important part of her conversation with Eric until last. 'But the worst thing is that one of his work colleagues – one who Eric's having a bit of trouble with – has turned up at the conference. Eric's going spare.'

Geraldine couldn't immediately see why that would be a problem. 'Well, it's the only writing festival in these parts so bumping into someone he knows isn't that implausible. What do you mean by "having trouble with" anyway?'

'Eric's convinced he's turned up on purpose just to harass him. Eric reported him at work for bullying and he thinks he's trying to get his own back.'

That Eric should be so paranoid didn't come as a shock

to Victoria's best friend. 'Come on, Vic, nobody's going to spend all that money and waste a weekend just to annoy Eric. He's obviously there for the same reason as Eric.'

'I thought that, but when I said so to Eric he said this guy couldn't write his own name and couldn't possibly have written a book.'

'Someone who works on a newspaper can't write? Hardly likely, Vic.'

'No – he's in sales. That's why Eric is suspicious.'

Geraldine thought it typical of Eric to report someone for bullying. 'Well, that sounds like the least of Eric's problems to me. He should stop being so sensitive and make the best use of the rest of the conference.'

'I know. You're right.'

Geraldine was bored talking about Eric so attempted to draw a line under this particular topic. 'Tell you what though, Vic, his Christmas present this year should be easy. You can get him a book on self-publishing.'

'I thought I'd be pleased. I know I should be. But I'm not.' Rosie was sharing Con's news with Grace as they strolled over Paddington Recreation Ground looking for a picnic spot on this blazingly hot Saturday afternoon.

Grace, whose expectations for Con at the conference had been low to say the least, sought clarification. 'Did they actually say they'd take it on, or what?'

'They've asked to see the rest of the manuscript, so Con's cock-a-hoop. Says it's as good as an offer.'

'Well it sounds a long way off an offer to me, Rosie. Just the next step.'

'I agree, but you know what Con's like.'

Grace didn't comment – she knew full well what Con was like. The two sisters laid out their rug on the grass and began to unpack cheeses, homemade salads and lemon drizzle cake from their basket.

Rosie continued to wrestle with her conscience. 'I should be ecstatic for him, for us, but all I can think of is that he'll use it as an excuse not to go back to work.'

Grace could sympathise with that fear. However, now that Rosie was entertaining such doubts she didn't want to attack Con too hard in case her sister felt the need to defend him. 'Say he did get a deal, then that would make him a proper author, right? So he wouldn't need to go back to the hospital in that case?'

Rosie had considered this already. 'Yes, but what if he's not telling the truth about this offer – how would I know?'

While it wouldn't surprise Grace for Con to pull such a stunt she was taken aback that Rosie should consider the possibility. 'I don't think even Con would stoop that low, surely?'

'When he got the bus to go up there yesterday, I just thought, don't come back. He's so self-absorbed I might as well not be here. Except I have to pay for everything.' The penny's dropped at last, thought Grace. She didn't stem her sister's flow. 'I know it sounds horrible but it made me think how he's taken me for granted and treated me like a mug ever since we started going out. I hate to admit it but I was actually clinging to the hope that he'd get nowhere in Lancaster and have to drop this book-writing idea once and for all. I thought we could get back to a normal relationship. Now he's going to be even harder to live with.'

'Won't he go back to work until he gets an actual deal?

Rosie tugged absent-mindedly at the grass. 'There's no way he'll go back if he thinks he'll be signed. He'll come up with a million reasons why it's not the right time and how he needs to keep working on the book. I know it.'

An obvious consideration struck Grace. 'But say, and you never know, Con did get a deal, he could become a famous author. It could happen.'

Rosie looked miserable. 'No. It won't happen, Grace. I've read it, remember? And even if it did, I've had enough.'

Grace suppressed the urge to cheer. 'So what are you going to do?'

Rosie grabbed a large handful of grass and tore it from the ground. 'I'm going to finish with him. I'm kicking him out. This is the end.'

Grace nodded her head softly at this pronouncement and reached into the basket. 'Wine or beer?' was all she had to say.

'Hi Jules. Conf is gr8. Just met your boss Eric and Dylan from Mcr Chron! They think ur brill. XXX B'

'Wondered if you'd bump into E. Treat him gently. Dylan? Confused. Dylan not at conf. J. X'

'He is – looks like Oasis? XXX'

'JFC – that is Dylan. Him and Eric hate each other. WTFIGO? X'

'They seemed OK. See what u mean about E being a bit grumpy tho … XX'

'He can be, but if D there, not surprised. What did D say he there for?'

'D sez he's written a book about Madchester. XX PS – What's Madchester?'

'Oldsters music scene. No way!'

'That's what he sez. X'

'Seriously – were E and D actually together?'

'Yeah – at lunch. Sat with us. D came this morning – E here lst nite'

'Long story, but v surprised at that. Deffo keep an eye on them'

'How do u mean? X'

'They might end up killing each other'

'OOhhh! Brill. Fight! XXX'

'OMG – just twigged!!!! BSTD!'

'WOT???'

'TYL. J. XX'

'Have you been drinking? Belinda could sniff alcohol on her husband's breath even though he was over 200 miles away.

'No, of course not,' Reardon replied.

'You're awfully cheerful,' came back the damning accusation.

'I don't need to have a drink to be in high spirits, my love. I'm just enjoying my day out. I feel like St Patrick setting forth to convert the pagans,' he said with a guffaw.

Yes, thought Belinda, he's had a drink. 'Reardon, now listen to me, you have to be very, very careful about alcohol – we've been through this a hundred times.'

Despite the fact his wife couldn't see him, Reardon held up his hand to quieten her. 'Darling, you have nothing to worry about.'

'Where are you now?'

'Lancaster Station. Journey's end beckons.'

'Promise me you'll call me later?'

'Of course, my lamb.'

Reardon rang off and picked up his overnight bag from the station bench. Two minutes later he was in a taxi heading south to the campus. Belinda could be such a worrier at times – he was quite capable of looking after himself. There was no doubt about it – he was ready for the evening. His speech was fashioned now and, if he said so himself, it was a jolly good effort. He was back in the public eye – admittedly not a book launch but at least an audience who were keen to see and hear him. He was getting paid – the first pay cheque had arrived earlier in the week from Edward VIII and compared to his recent royalty cheques wasn't too shabby at all. Life could be a lot worse. And who knows? Maybe his ineffectual agent might land him a new contract soon – why not? Reardon felt a warm glow as he thought of his representative – not out of fondness but amusement at the prospect of Hugo attending the conference. Hugo had tried to bullshit him that he'd always intended to be there but the author knew better – he was under orders. As long as he didn't have to sit with Hugo, Reardon thought he could definitely enjoy the evening that lay ahead. As the ugly stone terraces on the A6 gave way to meadows and hedgerows Reardon saw a road sign announcing that the university campus was a quarter of a mile away on the left. On his right a charming-looking hostelry called The Boot and Shoe hoved into view. On a whim Reardon called to the taxi driver to pull into the pub. He had plenty of time – a pint of local cask ale would be just the ticket.

CHAPTER TWENTY-FIVE

Not for the first time in the past 24 hours Eric was beginning to question why he'd signed up for this weekend of despair and disappointment. He felt further away from a publishing deal than at any other time since he'd first put pen to paper. His two one-to-ones after lunch only confirmed what he had already learned – Scrub Me Till I Shine in the Dark was destined to linger in the shadows a bit longer as far as the book industry was concerned. Now Eric had lost hope his one-to-one meetings took on the aspect of counselling sessions. His expectations well and truly lowered, he treated the ten-minute slots as light-hearted exchanges, taking consolation from the observation that at least his work was well-written even if it wasn't the sort of thing anybody was looking to publish. And now Eric sat in the largest lecture theatre Lancaster had to offer waiting to listen to Hugo Lockwood tell him and other delegates how to compose a killer submission letter. Would he even need such information in the future? It didn't matter – he had a compulsion to see Hugo Lockwood up close.

As the heralded agent walked in to begin his address a man wearing a large black caterpillar across his forehead followed him through the door – Dylan had tracked him down. Worse still, he made a beeline towards Eric and jumped into the empty seat next to him. 'Wouldn't want to miss your Twitter mate, eh?'

Eric was trapped. 'Can't you just bugger off and annoy somebody else? This is ridiculous,' he spat.

'Be quiet,' came the admonition from the people sitting behind them.

Hugo began by dumping a huge sheaf of papers on the desk in front of him. 'This, on average, is how many submissions I receive every single week – about 100. That's 5000 a year. How many make it through?' He paused for effect. 'About five. Now you know what you're up against.' What a charmless, smug tosser thought Eric as those around him scribbled these vital statistics down. 'I, of course, have to read these efforts while actually managing my roster of established authors. It's no mean feat.' *Spare us the bloody martyr act,* Eric spluttered under his breath. 'So as part of my talk today I thought I'd give you a live demonstration of how a typical reading session goes. Bear in mind that for me this may be at midnight after a long day, or on a Sunday morning when you're all doing something interesting with your lives.' Eric shook his head in disbelief at such arrogance. Even Dylan, the natural salesman, was finding such pomposity hard to fathom – he wouldn't get far selling space at The Chron acting like that. 'These examples are purely random, and apologies in advance in case one of your submissions is in here.' Eric stiffened. Christ, he wasn't joking. Hugo took the top document off the pile. 'First one. Hugh Lockwood. Wrong.' He threw it into the bin at his feet. 'If you can't get my name right, don't bother.' He picked up the next one from the pile. 'She Sang Angels to Rest – does that title grab me? No.' Into the bin it went. 'Now you'll have noticed I've not even started to read the accompanying letters yet. Let's try this one.' He picked up a further submission and scanned it. 'This author is telling me all about how she started to write at the age of five and would read her stories to her teddy bears. Charming.' He smiled, and then he hurled it into the bin. 'What does that tell me? That she probably still can't write for a grown-up, book-buying audience.' Muffled gasps mixed with uncertain laughter as Hugo continued his diatribe. 'Next one – 'Dear Mr Lockwood, blah, blah, blah… always wanted to write, blah, blah, blah… interesting life, blah, blah, blah.' He tossed it over his shoulder. 'Dull, dull, dull. I don't care about his interesting life unless he's David Beckham. Print it up and give copies to your friends and family if it means that much to you.' Hugo selected another submission. 'My novel weighs in at 49,000 words… Well, does it really? Forget it. That's not a novel. It's a premature birth. Bin.' Eric was so tense by now he felt almost delirious. 'This one has possibilities,' said the agent as he held up a submission for all to see. '"The novel is set in a mental institution where the patients are saner than the staff".' Hugo paused for effect, then struck. 'On one level an interesting premise but in my experience most likely the work of someone who's actually spent too long in a loony bin. Whether as an inmate or an orderly is immaterial but my verdict is still…'

'Bin,' came the shout from around a quarter of the delegates.

Hugo read the next submission for a few seconds. '"My novel is a fantasy adventure young adults will adore…" Great, but I don't do YA, which would have been easy enough for the author to establish before submitting to me. Bin.' Eric wondered how much longer was this going to go on for? Pray God Scrub Me Till I Shine in the Dark wasn't in that pile? 'Now this is interesting. Opinions Are Coffins. I like that title.' He read on momentarily. 'But it's another "No". Why? Because while the letter tells me everything I could ever want to know about the writer, he omits to tell me what the story is all about. Double fail. Hook me, get me interested, or don't bother.' Within what seemed like minutes the heap of submissions had been pulverised, razed and wracked into thin air. Eric's knuckles turned white at the disregard and utter contempt the callous agent was displaying towards work people had poured their hearts and souls into. As Hugo stood knee deep in a pile of unstapled 90gsm A4 pages he reminded Eric of a cowardly hunter, a smoking rifle in his hand, posing for the camera over the carcass of a once-proud lion he'd just blasted to death.

Next to Eric, Dylan was struck dumb, something that didn't happen very often. It had never crossed his mind that people would actually pay to be insulted in this manner. And by a jumped-up public schoolboy who, like Dylan, had probably failed his English GCSE. The interloper looked sideways at Eric and could see he was ready to burst. Now, for the first time, it dawned on Dylan just how cruel his Golden Fleece prank had been. It would have devastated Julia, too. Books *were* like babies – ugly or not, they were yours. And all this beautiful baby judge had to offer was bananas.

Hugo now opened the session out to a Q and A. A succession of banal questions were proffered up for Hugo to heave over the boundary rope. 'Did the work have to be finished before it was submitted?' 'Was it OK to chase after an agent if you hadn't heard back within a week?' 'Was a friendly, humorous enquiry letter a good idea?' Hugo could have patiently clarified the due protocols on these points but couldn't resist the opportunity to continue his 'this is what I have to contend with on a daily basis' riff instead. Then one of the delegates asked, 'Would you say it's important to follow agents like you on Twitter?'

Hugo's eyes lit up. 'Now that is a good question. I've found Twitter is a double-edged sword. On the one hand it allows me to keep followers updated on what I'm doing, new deals, what I'm looking for in a submission; on the other hand it's like asking people to stand in line so they can fling custard-pies in your face. You wouldn't believe the abuse I receive. Or maybe you would.'

The audience tittered on cue. Then Eric's voice boomed out. 'They wouldn't believe the amount of abuse you dish out either. *Or maybe they would.*'

Hugo was taken aback. 'I'm sure I've never abused anybody on Twitter. Corrected a few people, possibly.' A few delegates laughed, but hesitantly this time.

'I follow you on Twitter,' said Eric. 'You're a nasty piece of work in my opinion.'

Hugo was suddenly back in the playground – he could dish it out but he couldn't take it. 'If I've offended anyone I'd be the first to apologise, I assure you. But sometimes unlooked-for exchanges occur – normally aimed at me, not the other way round.'

'You didn't sound like a victim five minutes ago when you were trashing everybody's work, did you?' said Eric looking around for support. Half the audience looked shocked at his intervention; the other half nodded in agreement.

'I was simply employing a dramatic device to get my message across,' struggled Hugo in defence. 'I think you're confusing the message with the messenger.'

A new voice joined the debate. One with a flat, sneering, Salford accent. 'I think you're confusing yourself with someone whose shit doesn't stink. You're a tosser, mate.'

Eric could hardly believe he was the recipient of support from such an unlikely quarter. He looked at Dylan, who simply sat back in his seat, crossed his arms and nodded back at him. A stunned silence descended on the room. Nobody had ever witnessed an encounter quite like this at a Write Stuff conference.

Hugo was at a loss. A few more seconds elapsed and he said, 'Well, that just about takes us up to our scheduled finish time. Thank you.'

'Yeah, mate. You up and run,' Dylan taunted as Hugo made a quick exit.

As the room emptied Dylan and Eric remained in their places, facing out the accusatory stares of the blue rinse brigade and the under-25s and not daring to acknowledge the jovial winks and nods from everybody else.

Once the room had cleared, Eric spoke. 'You didn't need to come to my aid, but thank you.'

'He's a pillock. Deserved everything he got. I enjoyed it.'

Eric wasn't sure what to say or do next. Then he knew what he had to ask. 'Dylan, why have you come here, really?'

'You know why, Eric. To wind you up. To irritate you. You've got me in the shit at work and I'm majorly hacked off. I knew you'd hate me turning up here so that's why I came.'

'Well, you were right about that. But why did you have a go at Hugo in that case? Why support me?'

Dylan spoke slowly. 'I get now why you were so upset about my spoof asking for the rest of your book. People here are all so desperate – no offence – to get published, it hurts.' Eric couldn't believe his ears. Dylan had discovered sensitivity? His nemesis continued. 'Crawling to wankers like him to get a deal must be the hardest thing in the world. I hit a rawer nerve than I thought when I pulled that stunt. I guess I owe you an apology.'

Eric didn't recognise the co-worker sitting next to him. He'd never heard Dylan express regret over anything. And he was apparently sincere. 'You did upset me, Dylan. But I overreacted reporting you to HR. That was probably unnecessary.'

'I won't disagree with you there,' Dylan said.

Eric made a decision. 'I'm going to tell HR I'm dropping my complaint when I get back to work on Monday.'

Dylan hadn't been expecting such an outcome when he'd set off for Lancaster. In fact, it had been the furthest thing from his mind. 'Really? That would be great. Thanks.'

'I think it's me that owes you thanks. By the way, you're right about getting agents to accept work. It's impossible.'

'"Impossible is nothing" as they say. Keep going, Eric. They're not all like him, believe me. Some new books will get across the line – it's just that you don't have to be treated like shit while you're trying.'

Eric was impressed at these wise words from Dylan. 'Let's just say I'll be taking stock of my future publishing prospects after this conference.'

Dylan nodded. 'Don't waste it, that's all.' Then, 'Listen, I'll get off, Eric, and stop bugging you.'

Eric shook his head. 'You've paid for the gala dinner, haven't you? Why waste it?'

Having already noted the potential for fun at the pinnacle event of the Write Stuff conference, Dylan was only too happy to stick around. 'OK – deal. Fancy a pint while we wait? There's a boozer outside the main gates.'

It was the best suggestion Eric had heard all weekend.

CHAPTER TWENTY-SIX

Despite her renunciation of all things Chapman, Suzie still refused to let herself or the team down by being anything less than professional in her duties. That's why she found herself anxiously calling Reardon Boyle's mobile number for the sixth time in an hour. 'He should be here by now,' she said to Amy, who was helping herself to coffee and biscuits now that most of the delegates were mid-session.

'Maybe his train is late? There's plenty of time yet,' replied the unconcerned assistant. She had her own list of jobs to worry about.

'His train was on time, if he was on it. I checked.' Suzie bit her lip. 'I don't like hassling him with all these calls but I wish he'd bloody well pick up.'

Amy rolled her eyes. 'Honestly, Suzie, he's an author – he's bound to be a drama queen. He'll just be wanting to keep us all waiting so he can make an entrance.'

Suzie recognised that this very probably was the case.

'Does Chapman know he's not here?' Amy asked. 'I suppose that's the biggest problem – not that this guy is late, but the blue funk Louis will be in if he knows.'

Suzie pondered. Yes, Amy was bang on there. If Chapman got wind of Reardon's non-arrival he'd go into meltdown. Good. 'Actually Amy, I was putting off telling him but he really does need to know, just in case he has to make any contingency plans. Could you go find him and tell him while I try Reardon again?'

Leaving the afternoon sessions behind to more industrious delegates the two Manchester Chronicle companions crossed the A6 and entered the car park of The Boot and Shoe. As Dylan went to the bar Eric looked around for a table in the beer garden and was surprised to see another conference asylum seeker, this time in the shape of famous author Reardon Boyle, sitting under a giant parasol and taking the top off a pint of Cross Bay Nightfall. Eric had long been an admirer of this iconoclastic literary giant. When Dylan returned with two pints of ice-cold lager Eric whispered to him, 'See him, over there? He's the guest speaker tonight. Can we go say hello?' As Dylan had never met a famous author before he was only too happy to expand his cultural horizons.

Eric led the way over to where the flannel-suited writer sat perusing the local CAMRA bulletin. 'Mr Boyle? I'd just like to say how much I'm looking forward to hearing you speak tonight. I've been a massive fan of yours ever since The Wrong Heartbeat.'

Reardon looked up and squinted in the sunshine. 'Ah – an early convert in that case.' Gesturing to the two empty seats next to him he invited them to sit down. 'Please.'

Eric couldn't believe his luck. 'If you're sure,' he said, but only after he was safely seated. For Dylan's benefit he brought him up to speed on whom they were sharing a pew with. 'Reardon – may I call you Reardon? – is *the* pre-eminent figure of the British literary scene over the past quarter of a century.' He turned to Reardon. 'I've grown up with your books, and would go as far as to say I've been inspired to write by you. It truly is an honour to meet you.'

Reardon was tickled pink. He still counted. Dylan, recognising this guy must be a big-hitter, looked suitably impressed. Eric, dazzled at this chance meeting, now remembered his manners. 'Oh, and this is Dylan. Dylan Dylan to be exact.'

Reardon's eyes lit up. 'Ah, so good they named you twice. Well, with a name like that you must be possessed of the muse. Most Likely You Go Your Way And I'll Go Mine.'

Dylan's face broke into a grin. He was, not surprisingly, somewhat of a Dylanologist himself. 'More a case of Mixed Up Confusion,' he replied, self-effacingly. 'I missed out on the whole writing thing – I work in sales.'

'Ah, but doesn't His Bobness describe himself as a song and dance man?' Reardon shot back. 'In my estimation that equips you perfectly for your current craft.'

Dylan beamed. He liked this author guy they'd bumped into. Reardon peered at Eric, inviting him to introduce himself. Even more self-consciously than usual the aspiring author said, 'I'm Eric. Eric Blair.' He grimaced slightly, almost inviting derision.

Reardon's eyes widened at the announcement. 'Really?' Eric nodded. 'Well, in that case, you are blessed. Honoured, in fact, to bear the torch. What better motivation to write than to be swaddled in the blanket of genius?'

Eric was taken aback. 'Oh, thank you. Sometimes

people, well, they take the mick about my name.' He looked sideways at Dylan.

'Nonsense,' boomed Reardon. 'He that has an ill-name is half-hanged – you don't have that problem. Wear it, bear it like a trophy, and follow its path.'

Eric's breast swelled with pride. Dylan, recognising the grounds of another charge against him, nodded enthusiastically at these stirring words. He'd have to apologise about that later, too.

Reardon looked at his phone, which had been buzzing intermittently during the past few minutes, and thrust it back inside his jacket pocket. 'I deduce from your presence here that the magnetism of the conference has somewhat lost its attraction?'

Eric didn't answer immediately. He knew he was truanting but didn't want to admit that school wasn't all it was cracked up to be.

In the end it was Dylan who explained their absence from the afternoon programme. 'To be honest, we had a bit of a run-in with one of the speakers, so thought we'd lie low for an hour.'

Reardon was bemused. 'Is that so? It appears I've misjudged the passion of these conferences. You're not going to heckle me are you? I'll have to prepare some rebuttals in that case.'

Eric jumped in. 'Oh, no. It was just that this particular agent basically trashed everybody's work and made us feel about two inches tall. There was an exchange of views shall we say.'

'You have my sympathy, gentlemen,' Reardon said. 'Agents are like wasps. It's hard to fathom what possible practical use these parasites serve but we are told that without them our problems will only multiply. Did this pest have a name?'

Eric hesitated again. He was uncomfortable naming and shaming any member of the publishing fraternity; surely these people all stuck together and it might rebound on him and Dylan if they were loose-lipped and indiscreet?

'Hugo Lockwood,' said Dylan. 'A right pillock.'

Reardon spat his beer out as he was struck with a coughing fit. As his faced turned red and tears welled in his eyes an alarmed Eric and Dylan looked at each other in panic, unsure what to do. Reardon clutched at his chest as his airways gave the impression they had ceased to function. Just as Eric was looking round to see if the pub was equipped with a defibrillator he realised that the award-winning writer was actually laughing.

It took Reardon a good minute to regain his composure. 'Hugo Lockwood? Excoriating people's work and diminishing them? That's not the most surprising news I've heard today but it's certainly the funniest.' He started to cackle again.

'So you know him?' Eric ventured.

'Know him? He's my agent,' stuttered the convulsed author. He composed himself temporarily. 'Yes, "a right pillock" just about sums him up. I couldn't have put it any better myself.'

Relieved that they'd not traduced anyone's reputation without justification, Eric felt emboldened. 'If I may say so, Reardon, I wouldn't have paired you with him.'

'Lesson One for a writing conference – misery

acquaints a man with strange bedfellows,' Reardon said as he downed his pint. 'Now, have we time for another before we join the flock? I'd quite like to try the Sunset Blonde, purely for medicinal purposes, of course.'

Dylan jumped up to stand the next round. He couldn't believe that the day was turning out to be so eventful.

The thought struck Eric that perhaps he shouldn't be drinking during the afternoon, what with the gala dinner that evening. Then he pinched himself – what was he thinking? He was sharing the company of one of the most important authors in living memory. And Reardon was giving a speech later and he was having another drink. Of course he wasn't going to skip. 'Just a half for me, Dylan, please.'

Amy found Chapman hidden away in a side office, busily putting the finishing touches to his gala dinner speech. He understood how important it was to get the tone right for his announcement about The Write Stuff's foray into self-publishing territory. Tonight he would be traversing a tightrope suspended between two asymmetric clouds – the cirrus of traditional publishing and the stratocumulus of DIY publication – and there was a long way to fall if he made even the smallest slip. He instinctively knew that his fortunes depended on how well this evening's announcement was received. If he could engender enthusiasm for the new venture he had effectively created a second income stream. If he'd misjudged, then his current cashflow might start to reduce to a trickle. Normally Chapman would have relished drafting and practising this exercise in obfuscation but today he was finding it hard to concentrate – the spectre of Suzie kept breaking his train of thought. He couldn't fathom what had got into her. It was obvious that she was being unreasonable and, worse still, trying to back him into a corner. If he didn't continue to indulge her he feared consequences. But that was tantamount to blackmail – coitus or calamity? OK, they'd had a bit of grown-up fun once or twice – it was hardly an invitation to join the board, was it? They both knew the score so why was she being so bloody-minded now? He'd not liked the way her mood had turned ugly – who knew what a woman in that frame of mind was capable of? If news of their dalliance – yes, dalliance, it was nothing more – became known it would tarnish his reputation and reflect badly on his business – never mind Adele finding out. No, it was just too bloody inconvenient to have this thrown back in his face like this now; inconvenient and unfair.

'Suzie's asked me to tell you that Reardon Boyle hasn't turned up yet,' said Amy.

Chapman threw up his hands in frustration. Did he have to do everything around here? 'Well, tell her to call him. I'm sure he won't be far away.'

'She has, and he's not answering. She said you might need to make some contingency plans.'

Chapman stared coldly at his assistant's assistant. 'Can you please advise Suzie that I expect her to make contingency plans; that is her job, is it not? Can't you see that I'm exceptionally busy?'

Amy shrugged, turned on her heel and left him to it. Not her place to proffer an opinion. She was, however, looking forward to making the rest of the team laugh later that evening when she would recount her role as a shuttle diplomat between the two warring factions.

Chapman wearily lay down his pen on the desk. Surely Reardon Boyle would turn up? Suzie was playing games. He was very probably already here. But then the image of a packed gala dinner crowd flashed into his mind, hundreds of eager faces all anticipating The Write Stuff's greatest speaker coup ever. How could he tell them the maestro wasn't going to be appearing? How could he replace the speaker at this late stage? There was no Plan B. It was sure to lead to disappointment and reflect badly on him, no matter what the reason was for the author's absence. Well if Reardon wasn't going to turn out he hoped it was something bloody serious so the delegates wouldn't bad-mouth the organisers. He sighed and stood up. *Come on, Chapman, pull yourself together*, he whispered to himself. *You've faced bigger odds than this growing the business.*

Suzie and Reardon were not going to rain on his parade, not tonight of all nights. His biggest triumph in the history of The Write Stuff. Did Suzie expect him to stop drafting his crucial speech so he could join in a hue and cry over Reardon's whereabouts? Yes, that was her game. Well, he wasn't going to rise to the bait. He sat down again and picked up his pen. He had a speech to write. Suzie could bloody well do the job he paid her for.

CHAPTER TWENTY-SEVEN

Emily and Hugo raised their glasses of Sparkling Blanc de Blancs to each other and braced themselves for the evening ahead. Having realised that being sedentary made them sitting ducks for delegate attention they had positioned themselves in the corner of the bar and determined to remain on their feet. 'It's a good time-management technique,' Hugo theorised. 'Insist on having meetings in someone else's office and then you can always leave when you want to.'

The conference pack had helpfully suggested a dress code of 'glam and gorgeous' for the gala evening. As the delegates filed in for the complimentary drinks reception the smell of mothballs battled for domination over the fetid air and the deepening scent of *eau de perspiration*. To combat the stifling heat the catering staff had thrown all the windows open and even positioned fans down the side of one wall. Despite this the room's thermostat remained firmly stuck on 'sixth circle of hell'.

Emily had heard the gossip about Hugo's altercation that afternoon. 'How did your talk go, Hugo?' she asked innocently, fanning her face with her hand.

Hugo twitched in a self-righteous way. She bloody

well knew. 'It went very well, I'd say. I engaged them from the outset.'

'Worth the effort, then,' Emily said. 'Get any sort of feedback?'

'Yes, as it happens. I had a number of people tell me how much they had learned from my talk.' Hugo wasn't giving anything away.

'I heard a malicious rumour you'd had a *contretemps* with some of the delegates,' Emily countered. 'Your troll friends?'

Hugo blushed, and this time the suffocating heat wasn't the cause. 'Rubbish,' he snorted. 'Two louts tried to ruin it for everybody but it wasn't anything I couldn't manage. I know how to handle that sort.' He crashed his gears. 'More importantly, Emily, have you discovered any gold nuggets yet? The primary reason we're here?'

The editor looked him firmly in the eye, as if to say 'we'll return to that topic later'. She answered his question. 'As it happens, I have. I could almost take tomorrow off – my mission is accomplished. And you?'

Hugo beckoned to the waitress carrying a tray of drinks and swapped his empty glass for a full one. Surely Emily was bullshitting? 'Are you sure it's not fool's gold, Em? It's hard to tell the difference. My pan remains deposit free.'

Emily knew the agent was rattled, and didn't know whether to believe her or not, but the truth was she was rather excited at her day's haul. At the outset of this experiment she had been totally opposed to the idea of unagented writers and highly sceptical about the chance of anything positive turning up. Now she was genuinely looking forward to reporting to Rocket come Monday. Most of what she'd read and seen over the weekend had not been of publishable standard, that was true, but that wasn't to say there was a shortage of good writing. Far from it. It had been sobering to talk to a succession of aspiring writers, some self-deprecating, some bullish, all of them bursting with desire and hope. It wasn't their characters, plots, structure or genre that let most of them down – it was just that their books wouldn't sell commercially, at least not in the quantities required by her behemoth of an employer. Being so close to the chalkface had been humbling for Emily and she was perfectly sincere in her exhortations to delegates not to give up and to think more about who would want to read their books. 'The book itself is half the battle,' as she told the majority of those with whom she shared her carefully regulated face-to-face sessions. Being a missionary for the publishing industry wouldn't have been half as satisfying if she'd not glimpsed some flashes of glitter amid the silt. She'd requested full manuscripts of two books during the day. One she was particularly excited about and couldn't wait to read; the other she knew was a flier, but offered enough to justify a closer look and would also provide contrast to her top choice. Both novels would, she felt confident, demonstrate to Rocket and her colleagues that she hadn't lost her touch. She also knew who the eventual winner would be – she, the fielder, had the choice of who to run out and whose wicket to spare. Yes, she was energised and the pleasure she felt at her day's work was only heightened by Hugo's steadfast refusal to shed the carefully contrived straitjacket of conservatism he slipped into each morning.

'Well, Hugo,' she said, 'you'll have to call at Mappin & Webb on the way home. You wouldn't want to go back empty-handed after all of this, would you?'

Hugo grimaced. At that moment, a mild hubbub erupted at the other side of the room. As he looked over he saw the unmistakeable lean and lanky frame of Reardon Boyle being escorted through the reception by the indomitable Suzie. As she steered him through the crowd towards the dining room he noticed his client appeared to have acquired the protection of two bodyguards – the two cretins from this afternoon's talk. What the hell was going on?

On reaching the empty dining room Suzie turned to Eric and Dylan. 'Do you mind? Delegates aren't allowed in for another 15 minutes and I need to brief Mr Boyle.'

Reardon threw his arms around the shoulders of his new friends and boomed, 'No, no, young lady.' He gestured at the troops nobly mustered this St Crispin's Day. 'We few, we happy few, we band of brothers, shall not be parted.'

Suzie bit back her annoyance. Time was short. 'All right. But I do need to tell you the plan for the evening.'

'By all means,' said Reardon, swaying slightly.

'The delegates will be let through at seven. You're sitting on the top table with Chapman, and we've also put your agent and editor on there. It's not a top table as such, it's round, but it's next to the stage. The rest of the seating is unreserved,' said Suzie, as if she was on a Ryanair flight pointing out where the exits were and how to don a life jacket. 'There's a three-course dinner and then there's a presentation to Chapman to celebrate ten years of The Write Stuff. He knows that's coming but he doesn't know about the surprise video we're going to show at that point. Then he'll say a few words, and then you're on. Chapman will introduce you. We'd like you to keep it to 15 minutes if possible?' Reardon sat down heavily as if they'd just hit turbulence. 'Or ten minutes if that's better for you,' she added. 'Anyway, whatever you think. OK. That's it. Any questions?'

'Is there a bar in here or do we have to go back out there?' asked Dylan.

'The bar in here opens in ten minutes,' replied Suzie, just pulling herself back from adding 'if you can wait that long.'

When, earlier, Amy had reported back to camp following her mission to Chapman, she hadn't exactly softened the tone or thrust of the self-help supremo's words. Suzie simply said, 'very well,' and then spent the next hour and a half playing Scrabble on her iPad. She'd make sure Chapman crumbled first. When, much to her surprise, Reardon did turn up at conference she'd been slightly disappointed that Chapman had somehow prevailed in the argument that they weren't really having. Now, however, she couldn't help but notice that the august author, this leviathan of literary luminescence, was acting rather strangely. Was he pissed? He certainly gave that impression. Slowly, the implications of this inferred intemperance began to dawn on her. So Chapman thought he'd won, did he? It would be interesting to see how he handled this. She flashed her brightest smile at Reardon and his accomplices. 'I do apologise. Now the briefing is out of the way can I get any of you gentlemen a drink from the bar? I'll make them open up early for you.'

As Alyson and Bronte sprang from the starting blocks on the starter's pistol to be first into the dining room they were surprised to see Eric and Dylan already seated dead centre of the room. Dylan beckoned them over.

Alyson squealed with delight as she raced over. 'Good work, boys. How did you manage to sneak in?'

'Friends in high places, Alyson. It's all a question of who you know.'

At that moment a tall, grey-haired gentleman clad in a crumpled beige suit appeared. 'The Americanisation of our language continues unabated,' he said as he sat down next to Eric. 'I have just been directed to the rest room.'

Eric looked slightly taken aback. 'I thought you had to sit up front, Reardon? Won't you get in trouble sitting with us?'

The newcomer laughed. 'Just let them try. I have no desire to grace their self-appointed Mount Olympus, especially with my agent up there. I'm perfectly happy here,' he said. 'As long as you are?'

Eric couldn't believe their luck. 'Happy? We're delighted.'

Dylan nodded enthusiastically. 'Introductions. Alyson, Bronte – Reardon Boyle, our guest speaker for tonight.'

'Charmed, ladies,' oozed Reardon, with a gracious bow in their direction. Alyson and Bronte giggled in their bewilderment. Was this really happening?

In the controlled explosion of table selection that was taking place around them Bronte spotted Con weighing up his options. Now he was elevated to author class he had promised himself a different set of tablemates for the evening. At least an agent, a publisher or one of the organisers. He didn't want to sit with the same people as yesterday – they weren't going anywhere, certainly not on the journey he was now embarked upon. Caught in the headlights of Bronte's smile and summoning wave, he froze. Around him, options were disappearing as seats were sequestered faster than jurors at the OJ Simpson trial. With a resigned shrug and an unconvincing smirk Con trudged forward to take his place.

At the business end of the room The Write Stuff table found itself in some disarray. Chapman had arrived late having just finished drafting his speech while Hugo and Emily were quizzing Suzie as to Reardon's whereabouts. She pointed out the author and said loudly, for her boss's benefit, 'It looks like he prefers to sit with the delegates. That's very democratic of him, isn't it?'

Chapman, torn between being denied a VIP tablemate and having to address Suzie directly, harrumphed his irritation. She called her assistant over. 'Amy, would you go and sit on that table over there and make sure Mr Boyle has everything he needs? It's rather sweet of him to want to sit with the normal people, isn't it?' Amy filed away this development to add to her grand anecdote for later, which she could see was getting better by the minute.

Just before dinner Suzie had deftly switched the place cards on their table, the only one with a 'reserved' sign on it, removing Reardon and Amy's names. She now sat three to the left of Chapman instead of on his right-hand side leaving her boss with an empty seat on each side of him. To fill the gaps Suzie flagged down two dilatory delegates and invited them to complete their table. Chapman's expression at this liberty suggested that when it came to egalitarian gestures he tended more towards General Pinochet than Mother Teresa.

The tidal wave now having reached the extent of its bore, the crowd settled. Everybody was seated and they peered around wondering how they'd come to be washed up with whatever flotsam and jetsam surrounded them. The dinner could begin.

'I don't know whether to be pleased or insulted,' moaned Hugo to Emily under his breath. He was staring at Reardon, sitting some 20 yards away, surrounded by a welter of wannabes. 'I don't get why he's down there with them. He hates mingling with his readership, even at signings.' Emily followed Hugo's stare and had to admit that the author's behaviour was atypical. The agent continued to be nonplussed. 'I mean, he even looks like he's enjoying himself. What's got into him?'

Even at this distance it was clear that Reardon was animated, smiling and giving every impression of being at one with the world. 'Well, good for him,' said Emily. 'He's certainly lightened up since the last time I saw him.'

Hugo looked dubious. 'Can't say that's been my experience.'

'Well, there you go,' said Emily, the target too big to miss. 'Obviously, you're the problem then.'

Hugo shook his head. 'Look,' he pointed. 'Look there.

He's drinking wine. Before a speech? That's not Reardon.'

'Well, it's hot, isn't it? One glass won't kill him.'

'No, but he's never done that before. He's very disciplined usually.'

'God, Hugo, you almost sound as if you care,' said Emily. 'Has the heat got to you or have you had a compassion injection you didn't tell me about?'

'I'm just saying, that's all. Very odd. Very odd indeed.'

Dylan had assumed the role of master of ceremonies on the usurpers' table. Everybody was now introduced, a warm welcome had been extended to their VIP guest, and four bottles of benumbed Muscadet nestled in the ice bucket in the centre of the table. Dylan was as naturally hospitable as only a man on expenses can be but even he couldn't spot a more expensive wine on the *carte du vin*. Con, who minutes earlier thought he'd contracted an STD now discovered the doctor had made a mistake – it was somebody else's sample. He'd never read any Reardon Boyle and had airily criticised the author's inclusion in the programme to Rosie – 'a has-been and a never-was'; now he was a convert. Even better as far as Con was concerned was the presence on the table of Amy and her sidekick, Paula, who had pushed two land-grabbing grannies off the table with a quick flash of their organisers lapel badges so they could take their places. Well, this was certainly a bit more open and inclusive than Friday night, he thought.

The salmon mousse starters, set at table an hour before, curled before them in the stultifying heat, challenging the diners to a game of E-Coli roulette. The guests pushed the plates aside in favour of the wine, the chilled melon grape providing marginal comfort against the rising room temperature.

Eric was keen to ensure that the level of conversation at their table was pitched at an intellectual level befitting their esteemed guest. With all the clockwork clunk of a chat show host he wound himself up. 'I read somewhere that Dan Brown likes to hang upside down in gravity boots when he's writing. Do you have any particular habits you adhere to when you're working, Reardon?'

The author pondered for a moment. 'Are you sure that wasn't Bram Stoker?' Nobody got his little joke, so he continued. 'I was unaware of Mr Brown's writing quirk but the revelation does explain quite a lot. Perhaps his books should be read in the same manner? I myself am a creature of habit. I like to be at my desk for 9am and write until 1pm. I take lunch for an hour and then write from 2pm until 5pm. I take weekends off.'

Seven heads around the table bobbed in acknowledgement. 'So you subscribe to Auden's diktat that routine, in an intelligent man, is a sign of ambition?' Eric said, taking his interviewer duties rather too seriously.

Con chipped in. 'Victor Hugo wrote in the nude apparently. And Lewis Carroll and Ernest Hemingway standing up.'

'And Truman Capote wrote lying down,' Reardon said. 'Each to their own.'

'Do you turn your email and internet off when you're writing?' asked Bronte. 'It's very distracting, I find.'

'I never turn it on, so it's hardly a problem,' said Reardon. 'I do, however, wear earplugs. No music, just earplugs to eliminate extraneous sound.'

Con, who normally listened to drone ambient while writing, had a further question. 'And how do you break writer's block, Reardon? That must be the biggest challenge facing an author?'

Reardon pulled a face. 'Writer's block is a psychosomatic affliction. Pullman nails this very neatly, I think, when he asks if plumbers get plumber's block? Of course they don't.'

Con tossed a half-recollected factoid into the conversation. 'I read somewhere about an author who masturbated to get rid of writer's block.'

Alyson looked from face to face trying to gauge their reaction. At least she shared one authorial habit with the great and the good.

'Are you sure that wasn't a reference to Will Self?' said Reardon. 'He has been called an onanist by many people, but they may not necessarily have been referring to his techniques for summoning the muse.'

Eric coughed and tried to change tack. 'I believe you've just taken up a post at Edward VIII, Reardon?'

The creative writing professor held up a finger. 'Ah, very true. But you mustn't prefigure my speech, Eric.'

Eric held up his hands in apology. Mariella Frostrup might be able to make artful conversation sound effortless but this interlocutory stuff was a lot more difficult than it first appeared.

CHAPTER TWENTY-EIGHT

Chapman Hall was not a happy man. As he gnawed his tasteless, stringy lamb he felt the appetite for everything he held dear slipping away. This conference, taking place in The Write Stuff's tenth year, was supposed to be his crowning glory yet he divined it was coming apart at the seams. He could hardly bear to look at Suzie; she'd not only deserted him, she'd mutinied too, drawing her Fletcher Christian up against his Captain Bligh. *Betrayal is the only truth that sticks* he muttered to himself as he mopped up the last of his gravy with his mashed potatoes. As mad as he was at Suzie, at the same time he felt angry and frustrated that there was no one on hand to do his bidding, especially with Amy having been despatched to the farthest post of the empire. And as for Reardon Boyle, well he'd not even paid him the common courtesy of a greeting, never mind his refusal to sit with them. Who did the author think he was?

The entrepreneur's mood was hardly improved by the intentness of the two delegates seated next to him. Would they ever stop going on about how wonderful it was to be invited to join his table? Well, welcome to the captain's table. On board HMS Bounty. As he attacked his

Strawberry Pavlova, Chapman caught Suzie giving him a furtive look. He bristled. He didn't need her. He didn't need anybody. Had he not built up his business singlehandedly through his own efforts? He wasn't going to be derailed now. He felt in his breast pocket for the reassuring shape of the cue cards bearing his speech to conference. Yes, this is what it was all about. Dazzling the delegates with the possibilities of the future, the turnkey services that only he could provide. Reinforcing everything The Write Stuff stood for, and now with added extras. Nothing would spoil his flow tonight. He was invincible. He smiled broadly at the two delegates between whom he was seated. 'Do tell me,' he gushed, 'is this your first conference?'

Suzie was keeping a careful eye on proceedings in between exchanging pleasantries with Hugo and Emily. The table occupied by Reardon and his chums was buzzing with merriment (in marked contrast to the rest of the tables, it must be said). She noted that Reardon had already drunk two glasses of chilled white wine. It was hard to tell if they were full measures as the man with the Etch-a-Sketch eyebrows kept topping up everyone's glasses; whatever, it was hardly the best preparation for addressing an audience of 300 people. She stole occasional glances in Chapman's direction – he looked as happy as Paul McCartney after four years of marriage to Heather Mills. She had the perfect grandstand position to monitor Chapman's face when Reardon took to the lectern – surely the addled author would only add to her boss's woes?

She turned to Hugo. 'I wonder if I could ask you a big

favour?' The agent looked at her suspiciously. 'We have a small presentation for Chapman to mark ten years of The Write Stuff and I though it would be really lovely if you could do the honours?' Suzie had planned to undertake this task herself but wasn't going to give her boss the satisfaction after the way he'd treated her.

Hugo flashed her his 'Do I have to?' look. Suzie ignored this and took his grimace as an acceptance. 'That's brilliant, thanks. You don't really have to say anything except that you're pleased to mark the anniversary by presenting the founder with a few well-chosen items.'

'What am I giving him?'

'It's all gift-wrapped in a box under the table. It's a number of book-themed presents we've picked out. There's a personalised library embosser, a scented candle that smells like old books, an iPad case with the cover of The Book Thief screened on it. Stuff like that.'

'The Book Thief?'

'Yes – it was top of the bestsellers charts the month he launched.'

Hugo blinked back his distaste at the type of tat you'd normally find being doled out in the office Secret Santa. 'OK, I'll do it,' he said, non too graciously.

Suzie hadn't finished. 'Oh – and then it's just a question of introducing the special anniversary video, which Chapman doesn't know anything about.'

Hugo wondered if he should scribble this brief down on a piece of paper. How many other things was she going to land on him? 'Right,' he grunted.

Suzie had thought long and hard over the film clip during the past two hours. She'd been foolish to lavish so much care and attention on it – he didn't bloody deserve it. But there was no way she could sabotage it at this late hour. She'd thought of excuses for canning it – after all, he didn't know about it – but the rest of the staff were aware the surprise was going to be sprung and it would be just too obvious to pull it now. No, it would have to run, which was a bloody shame.

Dylan declared, unilaterally, that another four bottles of Muscadet were in order for the heat-deprived corps gagging around their table. This time Reardon placed a hand over his glass as Dylan attempted to pour. 'Better not. I'll sit this one out.' He patted his jacket pocket to denote the speech he still had to deliver.

'Sorry,' said the good-humoured Dylan. 'Force of habit. Let me pour you some water.'

Reardon gratefully accepted the tumbler of ice-cold water proffered by Dylan and drank it down in one. All of a sudden he was feeling decidedly odd. Must be the damn heat. He wished they'd hurry up so he could do his speech and go and lie down in his room.

Eric had noticed that Reardon had gone quiet over the past ten minutes. 'Are you alright, Reardon? You look a little pale.'

Reardon held up his hand in acknowledgement of Eric's concern. 'Fine, fine, thank you. It's just a little stuffy in here.'

'It's as hot as a docker's armpit,' echoed Dylan. 'I've never known it as clammy. A Hard Rain's Gonna Fall.'

Reardon poured himself another tumbler of water and rallied. 'Rolling Thunder, or Hurricane do you think?'

'Don't care as long as there's Shelter from the Storm,' Dylan shot back.

As Alyson and Bronte didn't have the faintest clue what they were talking about, Eric helped them out: 'Bob Dylan songs'. They were still none the wiser. Con smirked like he'd been in on the exchange all along despite thinking the Voice of a Generation was overrated and not a patch on Jake Bugg.

The coffees were now being poured. Reardon blew his cheeks out. He didn't know why, but he was starting to feel apprehensive. The thought, '*Come on, come on, get on with it,*' was streaming through his mind. '*Concentrate. Keep it together for another half an hour.*'

After more food than had been consumed was returned to the kitchen, the room's expectations rose as the lights were dimmed. At the spotlit lectern Hugo shuffled through his presentation to Chapman, who at least managed to look suitably overcome with emotion as he accepted what appeared to be a bumper gift pack from Etsy. As the applause rang out he managed a full death stare at Suzie for abandoning him. The cow. Then his ears pricked up – Hugo hadn't finished. A surprise video to mark ten years of The Write Stuff? He didn't know anything about this. He turned his chair so he was facing the screen.

It started. A celesta picked out a slow and unmistakeable musical signature as an owl flew across the black night to alight on a lamppost.

There were already a few muffled titters of recognition from some members of the audience.

A gravelly voiceover intoned. 'It takes someone special

to make special things happen.' A distant object on the screen now hurtled towards the viewer while a familiar stolen voice asked, 'Did you ever make anything happen, anything you couldn't explain?' As the far-off image zoomed closer the audience could see it was a boy riding a broomstick. As the frame froze, high above an instantly recognisable, silhouetted building, the audience cackled in delight – the schoolboy's face, neatly photoshopped, bore the unmistakeable features of Chapman Hall.

Bronte nudged Alyson in the ribs. 'It's Harry Potter,' she squealed with unconcealed joy. Alyson rolled her eyes.

Now the camera was soaring down Diagon Alley, stopping at a sign that read 'Flourish and Blotts'.

'That's the bookshop,' said Bronte excitedly.

Con sneered. 'They're going to get into trouble ripping off the actual films,' he said. 'Haven't they ever heard of copyright infringement?'

Dylan corrected him. 'No, perfectly OK. Private use – we do it all the time in our presentations.'

The voiceover continued. 'Back in the old, old days, the book industry was as traditional as goose for Christmas dinner.' A lightning bolt split the screen. 'Then one visionary changed it forever.' A picture of Chapman beneath The Write Stuff logo filled the screen. 'This man decided that anybody could write a book; he also pledged to help aspiring authors to realise their dreams.' As the gleeful delegates broke out into spontaneous ovation, another purloined audio clip was heard. 'You're a wizard'.

Chapman was dumbfounded. He hadn't expected this. Instinctively, he grinned and nodded in the right places as he tried to take it all in. He knew Suzie must have arranged the video and as he watched it he wrestled to separate the 'then' from the 'now' in his relationship with her.

A huge photo album looking like a tome from the Hogwarts library unfolded on-screen; the pages turned of their own volition to 'Year 1' and a multitude of images floated out of the album, including the first ever Write Stuff team shot.

'He's been at the chip pan since then,' commented Alyson on the entrepreneur's all too evident weight gain over the years.

Dylan spotted the young woman stood to Chapman's right in the picture. 'That's Suzie?' And the penny that should have dropped earlier now tumbled from his consciousness and rolled across the floor. He turned to Eric and said, 'She and him are shagging, you know.'

Eric tutted. 'Really, Dylan, you shouldn't make baseless accusations.'

'No – honestly,' he said as both Alyson and Reardon tuned in to this tasty titbit. He put his finger to his lips. 'I'll tell you in a minute.'

As the tribute plundered yet more of the Harry Potter soundtrack the story unfolded further. Now a picture of Chapman behind a huge book display appeared. The screen cut to a close-up of A Poisoned Heart and A Twisted Memory. 'A man who could not only talk the talk, but walk the walk…' boomed the voiceover.

Dylan's eyes mirrored those of the owl's last seen sitting on the lamppost while his mouth gaped opened like the entrance to the Mersey Tunnel. Slowly, the penny he'd just parted company with completed a full 360-degree arc and rolled back to him. 'Well, the conniving old bastard,' he whooped as he slapped the table.

Seven pairs of eyes tore themselves away from the screen and locked on Dylan. Years four to ten could take care of themselves. What was Dylan on about?

As the video concluded, with the legend 'The magic continues...' Chapman stood to receive the audience's adulation. The clip had lasted only two-and-a-half minutes but in that brief passage of time he had found himself experiencing a rapid softening towards his inestimable number two. She had done this for him. Had he possibly been too harsh with her, unfeeling even? He tried to catch her eye, to signal to her that they could be friends again. This time she didn't evade his gaze but stared straight back at him with steely defiance.

One thing at a time, he thought. Now he gestured with downward palms to still the audience. He was once more a giant among men, the visionary. And he still had a vital speech to deliver. 'What can I say?' he began. 'I didn't know that was coming. Believe me, I'm as surprised as you are.' He placed his right hand on his heart to demonstrate his deep-felt gratitude and humility. 'The film, of course, celebrates the past ten years. Tonight, I want to talk to you briefly about the *next* ten years.'

Hugo looked at his watch and then across at Emily as if to say, 'We're going to be here all night.'

Chapman glanced at his cue cards and began. 'We have always had a very simple business philosophy here at The Write Stuff. We love – we live – to innovate.'

Suzie dug her nails into her palms. It really irritated

her that he always used 'we' when he really meant 'I'. He was as big a team player as Cristiano Ronaldo.

'Our mission is to see our clients, our friends, achieve publication. And we have been most fortunate to have ushered a number of first-time authors towards that particular achievement.' He paused for acknowledgement, but apparently nobody in the audience had a deal or knew anybody who did. Undaunted, he continued. 'Earlier this year I had a rather interesting conversation with some aspiring authors. One said he would probably self-publish, and the other said that he would consider that a defeat. When I ventured the opinion that self-publishing was a very valid option, a tremendous opportunity for an author to get work out there, I was accused of being "contradictory". Why? Because The Write Stuff was all about getting people "properly published " according to this particular writer.'

'I was there when they had that conversation,' Bronte whispered to Alyson. 'The guy who said it isn't here this weekend.'

Chapman was reaching full flow. 'But what is being "properly published"? The discussion got me thinking. I re-read all of our promotional material; I even went back to my original business plan – I couldn't find it set down anywhere that The Write Stuff was *against* self-publishing. Our message was consistent and clear.' He punched his fist into his palm for emphasis. 'We were pro-publishing, full-stop.'

In the audience, Eric slowly shook his head. He'd heard all of these weasel words a thousand times before, the sincere tone, the phased delivery, the re-writing of history presented as fact. He knew exactly where this was heading as Chapman raised the cover of the memory hole.

'We've just seen on-screen an image of my book, A Poisoned Heart and a Twisted Memory. I'm very proud of it. I was delighted to get a deal for it. But, as I said to that self-publishing naysayer earlier this year, if I hadn't been fortunate enough to acquire a publishing deal would I just have abandoned my work? Thrown the manuscript, into which I'd poured my very soul, into a drawer to gather dust?' The answer to his rhetorical question surprised nobody. 'No. I would have self-published. In an instant.'

Eight faces on Eric's table exchanged incredulous looks.

'I enjoyed our whistle-stop journey down memory lane.' Chapman could busk as well as anyone when he needed to. 'Ten years, but more like light years so much has changed in the world of publishing.'

'Here we go,' thought Eric.

'We've helped many writers to find agents and publishers, and we'll continue to do so.' Chapman's hand covered his heart again. 'But not everybody finds a deal – we know that. Does that mean that these authors should give up? Abandon their work? Feel that they've failed in some way? No, it does not.'

Hugo turned to Emily. 'Jesus, he's launching a self-publishing arm…'

'Which is why, today, I'm exceptionally proud to announce that The Write Stuff is forming a strategic partnership with Wellington, a new self-publishing business. In the future, if your particular journey doesn't end with a traditional publisher, we'll be there to show you another way.' He made a chopping action with his right hand as he punched home the message. 'We won't abandon you at the crossroads.'

Chapman stepped back half a pace in order to invite the audience to show their appreciation, and it was clear that his words had impressed more people than they had offended.

Suzie watched her boss milk the applause. Not all wizards were good. He was no Harry Potter; he was Lord Voldemort. She returned his death stare from earlier and under the cover of her napkin pointed an imaginary wand in his direction while muttering a muted incantation. *Expelliarmus.*

CHAPTER TWENTY-NINE

A volley of disconnected words boomed over the speakers – *pleasure, award-winning, literary giant, Wrong Heartbeat, welcome* – informing Reardon it was time. He was on. As he slowly raised himself from his seat, a voice – he didn't know whose – bade him 'break a leg'. As his lower limbs already appeared to be struggling to bear his weight he wasn't sure he hadn't. He gripped the edge of the table, took a deep breath and launched himself in the direction of the stage, hugging an imaginary straight line strung between his seat and the illuminated lectern. He was aware of applause as he urged himself forward. *Come on, come on; let's get this over with.*

Eric's gaze followed the author as he manouvered towards the raised dais – he imagined people had skipped to the gallows with more brio. He tried to attract Dylan's attention to see if he, too, had noticed Reardon's sudden torpor, but the sales supremo was busily engaged in making Alyson and Bronte laugh at one of his jokes. Eric turned back to the stage, a sense of foreboding descending on his hitherto jolly mood.

Reardon appeared to have aged ten years from the afternoon, from an hour ago even, when he'd been so light-hearted and engaging. As the author gingerly ascended the low platform he turned to face the audience but instead found himself looking straight into a blinding spotlight levelled at his eye line. He raised his hand to shield his eyes. Suzie, noting his discomfiture, remained firmly fixed in her seat. The author looked down at the lectern to avoid the glare and his hand moved to his pocket for his speech. A comic dumb show now ensued as Reardon tried each pocket of his suit for the five A4 sheets bearing his succession of bullet points, all carefully written in large, bold, black capital letters so he would be able to read them without difficulty. Chapman, taking in Reardon's abstraction from his ringside seat, forced himself to catch his assistant's eye and gesticulated urgently in the speaker's direction with an unmistakeable 'do something' appeal. Suzie guessed immediately that Reardon's speech was in his overnight bag. The one she'd locked in the office when Reardon had turned up with 20 minutes to go. She smiled back at her employer and calmly raised her coffee cup to her lips.

A hush of anticipation fell on the audience as they realised that Reardon and his notes had somehow parted. All eyes were fixed on the brightly-lit spot insulating this hesitant figure from the encircling void of darkness. A trickle of sweat rolled down Reardon's forehead. God, it was hot. He looked for a glass of water and saw that there wasn't any to hand – the small side table next to the lectern remained empty. Suzie knew immediately what he was searching for and felt a momentary twinge of guilt over her wilful neglect. Some of the delegates were now beginning to feel uneasy at the extended hiatus. Others, more worldly, wondered if Reardon was employing a bold oratorical device to ensure everybody in the room was fixed on his opening words.

Thoughts raced through the author's mind. He felt unwell. Feverish. Disorientated. He'd not eaten. He'd been drinking, but surely not enough to feel this bad? Belinda's words – are you sure you should be? – echoed deep within his consciousness. Why was that, again? He didn't want to be here. His notes – gone. Think. *St Paul. Damascus.* Yes, that was it.

He placed a hand on each side of the lectern and drew himself up. 'Writing cannot be taught,' he said finally with slow deliberation. 'That may come as news to some of you here.' Unencumbered with notes and the need to read them, Reardon was now peering down at the front row tables to avoid the glare of the spotlight. His furrowed brows lent him a sinister aspect as his head shot maniacally from side to side. 'I have been offered a lot of money to pretend it can. To tell *you* it can. Be taught, that is. But do you know what?' The audience held their breath. 'That's bollocks.' Laughter erupted in small pockets across the room.

Now Dylan picked up on Eric's sense of apprehension. 'What's wrong with him?' he said in a low, urgent, voice. 'He was all right before he went on.' Eric slowly shook his head. What *was* wrong with him? He'd been drinking but not enough to make him appear as if he'd just ingested a horse tranquiliser.

'So how come I'm now the Professor of Creative Writing at Edward VIII University? I'll tell you.' Like a newly-launched ship whose bows had been smacked with a bottle of champagne, Reardon gathered speed as he slipped down the runway. 'When I told my agent – that's him over there, by the way, the shifty-looking one with the glasses – that writing couldn't be taught, he said "nonsense".' Hugo squirmed as 300 pairs of eyes switched to his side of the net before swinging back to Reardon's end of the court. '*He* pointed out something that *I'd* overlooked in all of this.' He uncertainly held up a finger in front of his face. 'One. I've just been dropped by my publisher – that's my ex-editor sitting next to my agent by the way.' He waved over in their general direction.

A gasp escaped from the floor at Reardon's revelation. His publisher had dropped him? Chapman clenched his fists under the table to mask his fury. His assistant had booked this busted flush? Suzie wore an expression of genuine surprise – she'd not known that. It was getting better as it went along.

'So, I was a beggar, not a chooser.' Now Reardon shot two fingers into the air, Agincourt style. 'Secondly, being surplus to requirements, I still had to find a new publisher. Or rather, my agent had to find one, but as he's about as much use as an Elastoplast on cancer I had to assume that I might be in between engagements for some time.'

Hugo closed his eyes and bent his head, but it was no use – he was still visible to everybody in the room. At the same time, Emily experienced a baleful sense of regret – not for herself, but for her former client.

'So, three.' Now Reardon waggled three digits in the spotlight. 'And this was – what was the expression? – the *no-brainer*, the clincher. If *I* didn't sell myself out and take it, somebody else would. So what would *you* have done?'

The feeling of unease in the room could have been cut into slices, wrapped in Icarus-themed napkins and placed in party bags to be transported home. As Reardon's eyes slid from left to right looking for an answer to his rhetorical question an enormous crack of thunder broke the silence. 'Exactly,' said Reardon. 'Exactly.' Strangely, despite his drowsiness, he experienced a compelling compulsion to say more. It struck him as being important to say more, vital to address what he had been suppressing for months. 'I have been bought. I'm not proud of that, I confess.' He held up his hands in surrender. 'I can't make any one of you here a better writer. Sorry if you thought I could.'

Chapman had had enough of this. He nodded violently in Suzie's direction, pointed at Reardon and then drew his finger across his throat in a slitting motion. She continued to study the light fitting on the wall behind him.

'But what about this lot?' Reardon continued, gesturing to the organiser's table. 'Can *they* make you a better writer?' At this, Dylan turned to Eric. 'He seems to be perking up a bit now.' Eric didn't disagree.

'Do you know what The California Dream is? I'll give you a clue – it's nothing to do with the Beach Boys. It comes from the gold rushes of the 19th century when many speculators headed west, thinking that hard work and good luck could be rewarded with a new beginning. All they had to do was strike gold. Few did of course, but that didn't stop the dreamers.' Reardon seemed to grow as he uttered his words. The bumbling, shrunken figure of a few minutes ago had been replaced by an authoritative, magisterial presence the audience couldn't tear their eyes from. 'And who, do you think, made the most money from these speculators? Let me tell you. The men selling the shovels, pans and pickaxes to these dreamers with the cheery exhortation that, "tomorrow, my friend, *you* will strike it rich". Not unlike, of course, this very writing weekend that you have all paid so handsomely to attend.'

At this, Chapman stood up. This had to stop, and if it fell to him then so be it. But he didn't get very far. Alerted by the movement, Reardon pointed directly at Chapman. 'You, sit down. I'm coming to you.' Chapman meekly did as he was instructed. A dazzling flash of lightning outside the open windows momentarily illuminated the room and cast an eerie aura around Reardon. 'This mountebank, this hustler, is the man selling you the tools – everything you've ever dreamed of to get you an agent and get you published. *He* can't lose. If you strike gold, he'll claim the credit. If you don't, then you were looking in the wrong place.' Suzie had to stop herself breaking into spontaneous applause. 'And of course, he's not the only one looking to make a fast buck out of your dreams. What about our publisher over there? Diamond Lil, running the local saloon. As for him, my so-called agent, he's just pimping the best talent for the cathouse.' This time there was more laughter, particularly from Dylan and Eric's table. Emily and Hugo remained looking at each other, mainly so they didn't have to look at anyone else.

'And have you ever really considered what this dream of being published entails? To have an agent, and a publisher, and to make a living out of writing? So you can end up, what? Like me? Well, be careful what you wish for is my advice.'

271

Reardon imagined that he'd left his body and was viewing the speaker with as much scrutiny as the audience. While he continued to bear the extremities of the confusion, exhaustion and anguish weighing down on the author, his proxy was making a good fist of taking the listeners into his confidence.

'Now, I said I'd return to you,' he said as he pointed menacingly at Chapman. The entrepreneur remained rooted to the spot, unable to resist the onslaught, incapable of flight. '*He* would contend that one of the most compelling arguments for buying *his* shovels and picks is that he's already struck gold himself. He's had a book published so it follows that, if you buy from him, you'll get lucky, too.' On Eric's table seven people guessed simultaneously where Reardon was heading. 'Well, you know what? It turns out that our Mr Hall has been somewhat economical with the truth. Remember his book, A Poisoned Memory and a Twisted Heart?' A terror-struck Chapman, anticipating the axe that was about to fall, didn't bother to correct him on the mispronounced title. 'Turns out he didn't even write it.' An exclamation of disbelief swept up from the floor. Chapman could only look at Suzie in horror. Suzie, as dumbstruck as her boss at the revelation, wondered how the hell Reardon had unearthed this most classified of secrets. But casting doubt on Chapman's penmanship could only be validated by naming the real author. Reardon swung his finger in Suzie's direction. 'There's the real author. He only stole her gold nugget, didn't he?'

Eric thought Reardon might be stretching this particular metaphor by now but nevertheless felt a surge of pride in his new friend's denunciation of this literary hijack. Dylan started to boo as if he was at a pantomime and a few of the other delegates began to join in. On the top table Suzie weighed up the unintended consequences of letting Reardon run wild and came up with a snap verdict that it couldn't possibly have gone any better. Not only was Chapman disgraced, her creation, at last, had been rightfully recognised. But, again, how did Reardon know? The man at the lectern wasn't finished though. He held up his hand for silence. 'Why would an author, having written a novel, give it up and let someone else pretend they'd written it?' It's a question this particular audience had never really considered before. 'We shouldn't be surprised what an infatuated woman will do to ingratiate herself with the object of her affections, especially if that man is a self-centred, domineering, user. This woman deserves our sympathy on a number of levels.' Then, as if he'd just remembered something important, he added, 'Oh, but don't mention any of this to Mr Hall's wife – I wouldn't want to get him into trouble.' A number of heads in the audience could be seen shaking their heads in disapproval, accompanied by a low murmur of condemnation for their host.

Chapman had to do something. He made to stand up and address the audience, to implement an impromptu rescue plan. A voice rang from the crowd, 'Sit down. He's not finished yet.' Dylan could always be counted upon to put the boot in when someone was on the floor.

But Reardon was almost finished, in every way. He felt his out of body version rejoin its twin with a shudder and a jolt. He buckled slightly, only the lectern momentarily bearing his weight. But he was determined to share one last thought with the audience. 'You want some advice? I'll give you some advice.' With all the effort his voice had reduced to a rasp, but he persevered. 'You can't move for literary quotes in this place, but I'll pass on the only one you'll ever need.' He was struggling for breath, but he wasn't going to quit now. 'This author published only one book in her life. But what a book. This is what Harper Lee has to say on writing.' He raised his face to the audience, closed his eyes against the blinding spotlight, and recited from memory as if his life depended on it: '"Any writer worth his salt writes to please himself. It's a self-exploratory operation that is endless. An exorcism of not necessarily his demon, but of his divine discontent." There. It's that simple,' he said. 'Please yourself.'

A vacuum of silence gripped the room. No one knew whether to applaud or not. Then Eric stood, and put his hands together as enthusiastically as if he were at a school play. The rest of the table rose to join him. And then the rest of the tables rose to join them. Reardon released his grasp from the lectern and staggered back, just managing to stay on his feet. He stood forlornly in the middle of the podium, a lonely, frail and lost figure. On seeing his distress, Alyson made a beeline for the stage and gently wrapped her arm around his shoulders, ushering him on to a chair. Dylan rushed up behind her carrying a glass of water.

On cue, the charged air outside finally cracked and the rain began to fall to earth as surely as if Noah had just hammered the final nail into the Ark.

274

In the confusion, Chapman picked up the microphone. 'Thank you, everybody, for joining us tonight. If you'd like to make your way through to the bar, it will be open for another hour.' It was as if he'd just finished calling the bingo. With that, he quickly scuttled out of the door.

Hugo suggested to Emily they exited the room as quickly as their host. Emily had other ideas. 'We can't leave, Hugo. Reardon doesn't look at all well. We should make sure he's all right.'

Generosity of spirit was the last thing on Hugo's mind. 'Make sure he's all right? If I go over there I'll kick his head in for him.'

'Don't be ridiculous, Hugo. He's over-wrought. He's clearly been through a lot.'

'He's been through a lot of wine, more likely. He's as pissed as a penguin.'

Emily, a better student of the human condition than Hugo, knew he was wrong. 'No. He was having some kind of breakdown. We have to help.'

'After a car crash like that I'm not going anywhere near him. I'm finished with him.'

'Don't be horrible. You can't abandon him.'

'If I recall, Emily, it was you that abandoned him first. I'm just catching up.' And with that, Hugo strode off, pushing his way through the crowd of delegates blocking his way to the exit.

Suzie was still seated, picking through the wreckage of the past half-hour. She knew Reardon hadn't looked in shape to present a speech and she should have stopped him. However, her primary motive – to embarrass Chapman and The Write Stuff – had been too strong. She'd guessed that Reardon was tipsy and would be a poor speaker, a bumbler who'd irritate the hell out of her perfectionist boss, but in her wildest imagination she couldn't have prefigured what actually took place. How had Reardon even known about the book and their affair? She was, of course, red-faced over the second of those revelations, but at least she was now free of the vice of secrecy Chapman had clamped around her. It had been ugly, yes, but now everybody knew what an imposter and a bastard Chapman Hall was. As satisfying as that was she realised the truth had come at a cost and that their guest speaker had been forced to foot the bill. She went over to assist the makeshift medical detail attending him.

'How is he?' she asked, as if he wasn't there.

Reardon had a cold-compress draped over his forehead, fashioned by Alyson from a napkin dunked in an ice bucket. 'Poor man,' she replied, 'He's all done in. Too much excitement.'

'Has he been drinking?' Suzie said, *sotto voce*. Then realising that the question sounded like an accusation, quickly added, 'It's very hot, that's all.'

'He'd had a couple of drinks, but not enough to fell him like that,' said Dylan, who was fanning the author with a towel. 'He was on great form one minute, and then the next … whoosh.' He rotated his finger over his head like a helicopter. Reardon was oblivious.

'Could he be on meds?' Alyson said. 'He went very quickly.'

'Well I didn't like to say anything, but I thought he looked a bit, you know, when he arrived,' ventured Suzie.

Dylan wasn't having that. '"A bit you know"? Rubbish. He was in high spirits, that's all. Anyway, I bet you've not had a speech like that before at one of these conferences.'

Suzie's expression didn't suggest she was going to contradict him. 'Look, do you think we should get him to bed?'

'Good idea,' Dylan agreed. 'Can you two give me a hand?'

'I'll get his bag and key and show you where his room is,' said Suzie.

'He'll be right as rain after a good night's kip,' Alyson ventured – she considered herself somewhat of an authority on sleeping it off. 'Come on Reardon, love. You've got an appointment with the land of nod.'

As they helped him to stand up, Reardon was trying to speak. 'Please yourself,' he mumbled.

CHAPTER THIRTY

The bar was fuller than on the Friday evening – delegates didn't want to go to bed while there was so much excitement to discuss. However, there were few agents, editors or organisers to be seen. Eric found himself alone, propping up the bar, wondering when Dylan and Alyson were coming back. He sipped his whisky and tried to make sense of the day. So much had taken place in such a short time.

Two women of a certain age, finally giving up on seeing Chapman in the bar, passed Eric on their way to the exit. 'Disgraceful. Should be strung up. No wonder he's been dropped by his publisher if that's how he carries on.'

Had it all been a waste of time? Not only the conference, but writing a book? What was he going to tell Victoria about it all? The upshot was that he wasn't going to get a publishing deal. That much was clear – with Scrub Me at least. He clinked the ice around the bottom of his glass. Well, he'd laid that ghost if nothing else. That was something. No, that was a very big thing.

He'd also made peace, of sorts, with Dylan, and could drop his ill-advised Human Resources complaint. That was an unexpected bonus of coming to Lancaster. And

Dylan had been brilliant, sticking up for him with Hugo Lockwood. He smiled. Yes, that had been a highlight.

Best of all though was spending the afternoon and evening with his literary hero – how incredible had that been? He hoped Reardon would be OK – he was very concerned about him. Maybe he shouldn't have been drinking before his speech but they could hardly have told him to stop, could they? Besides, he'd not drunk that much. What had made him go off like that? It was like somebody flicked a switch – one minute he was having a ball, the next it was like his batteries had run out.

He tuned in on two men, about his age, queuing for drinks lower down the bar. 'The dirty old bastard,' one guffawed to the other. 'You wouldn't have thought he had it in him. You would though, wouldn't you?'

The other nodded enthusiastically. 'You'd have thought if that was the deal he should have been writing a book for *her* to put her name on.' They went back to their table carrying a tray of drinks, trailing dirty laughs in their wake.

What a speech though, Eric thought. He'd been convinced Reardon was going to dry, or worse, be hauled off. It had been touch and go. God, he'd given it to them with both barrels when he'd got going. Chapman being outed – all of that was down to Dylan. Bloody hell, Dylan, how do you do it? Hugo would remember the conference too, that was for sure. Good – he deserved everything he got.

No, all told, he'd learned an awful lot over the weekend, if he thought about it. Only not what he'd expected to discover.

There was still no sign of Dylan or Alyson, and he had no inclination whatsoever to seek out Bronte or Con. 'Sod this' he thought, and drained his whisky. Sod the rest of the conference, too. Tomorrow he'd make his goodbyes and get off home early. Maybe he could take Victoria and the kids out to Mobberley for a pub lunch. That would be nice.

'Proper stair rods. We're all gonna drown.' Dylan was eyeing the torrential downpour as he and Alyson emerged from the student block where they'd just put Reardon to bed. Rather, they'd helped him on to the bed, removing his shoes, jacket and tie, and placed a glass of water on his bedside table. At Alyson's suggestion Dylan had turned the author on to his side – 'just in case' – and left the bathroom light on so he wouldn't be confused if he woke in the night. On letting them into Reardon's room Suzie had disappeared, taking the large golf umbrella she'd held over the heads on the way over – now they faced a drenching as the downpour showed no signs of abating.

'It's bouncing,' said Alyson with delight as the torrents of water overwhelmed the swollen storm drains and backed up to flood the concrete quad.

'Make a run for it?'

'I've got a better idea,' she said and tore off towards the ornamental lake on the other side of the campus square, squealing at the top of her voice.

Abandoning himself to the elements, Dylan launched after her. As he neared the small rotunda on the edge of the lake he threw himself feet first into a huge puddle and hydroplaned the last five yards towards her. The resulting huge sheet of water almost knocked her off her feet. Alyson screamed with laughter. They were both soaked to the skin. 'I'm going to get you back for that,' she warned.

'Come on then,' said Dylan, playfully squaring up.

'When you least expect it,' she teased, and ran off into the square again. As she windmilled through the rain she looked like a young girl on her first Club 18-30 holiday. She turned to face Dylan and started to gyrate as if she were auditioning for a low-budget pop video. Then, in a tuneless voice she started chuntering on about him coming under her umbrella-la-la-la-la, topped off with what he took to be a chorus of eh, eh, eh, eh. Her singing was so tuneless it took Dylan some seconds to recognise she was channelling her inner-Rihanna. He ran to join her in the bump and grind choreography – any stragglers from the bar would have been most taken aback at the unexpected sight, even on this night of surprises. As Dylan accompanied her eh, eh, eh, ehs he couldn't help but notice how different Alyson looked from earlier in the day. Then she'd looked old and frumpish – nothing special at all. Now her hair was plastered all over her face and she should have looked like a drowned rat but, to Dylan, it was as if Salome had opted to enter a wet t-shirt competition. He stopped dancing to take in the glorious and wondrously beguiling sight. Spotting her opportunity, Alyson kicked out furiously sending cascades of water into his face. Before he could retaliate she took off again, back towards the rotunda. Wiping the water from his eyes, Dylan pursued her, bringing her to the ground with a deft rugby tackle. They rolled on the surface like escaped submariners, clutching at each other to stay afloat.

Dylan spoke first. 'I needed that to cool down.'

'Me too' replied Alyson. 'I'm all wet now though.'

'We'll have to do something about that,' said Dylan, with a glint in his eye.

Alyson innocently cocked her head to one side. 'I've got plenty of towels in my room,' she said.

'As long as they're fluffy,' replied Dylan. 'Sounds like just the job.'

All around him, there was darkness. He extended his hand in front of his face, but came into contact with… nothing. He was smouldering like the Vietnamese jungle after a napalm attack. He ripped his clothes off, but it made no difference. His body seemed to be burning at a temperature that would have tested the Space Shuttle's heat shield on re-entry. He needed to douse the flames and find respite; he had to quell the inferno and alleviate the pain. Haphazardly, he drove forward, nothing to bar his way. But where was he going? He didn't know but that wasn't important – it was what he was getting away from that counted.

Now he became aware of a barely perceptible balm promising a hint of reprieve to his body and mind – moisture and, gloriously, cool air. He was outside. But it still wasn't enough to extinguish the flames licking away at his tired and weary bones. He needed an ocean to stem this fever; all of the rivers in the world to conjoin and pour down on his suffering. Blindly, he pressed on. A succession of thoughts flashed into his mind, each struggling for domination over the others.

Then, salvation. An abatement of the storm. He felt as if he'd been pulled from the furnace by a master blacksmith and plunged into a tub of cooling water. So violent was the contrast of elements he imagined there must be column of steam rising a mile above him. Only now could he let go and allow himself to drift within this healing haven of peace. The competing images in his head now took on a clearer, if somewhat chaotic, form: A woman asking him if he was all right. A wild west prospector panning for gold. A schoolmaster in mortar and gown flexing his bamboo cane. The government front bench laughing, laughing, laughing. A serious young man writing, writing, writing.

Slowly, but surely, he could feel the heat leaving him; now he could abandon himself without any further anxiety or fear. A smile played on his lips as he recalled a line – 'Those are pearls that were his eyes'. Yes, now he remembered.

Alyson Hummer glanced at the bedside clock as she manoeuvred on to all fours. She and Dylan had been sharing each other's intimate company and bodily fluids for over three hours now. He certainly had some stamina, she thought. She was exhausted. He was funny too – he'd sung She's Electric to her when she'd roused him for the third time, and he was a most considerate lover, not at all like some of the young men she'd had before. At 3.30am, as he shuddered to a climax for the fourth time, she thought it was probably about time they knocked it on the head. She had to catch her morning train back to Bristol and pick up the kids – she daren't leave them with Alison any longer than they'd agreed.

'Time to go, lover,' she said to Dylan after he'd got his

breath back. 'Isn't there a rule about not bringing fellow students back to your room, anyway?'

'Too late to expel us now,' replied Dylan. 'Speaking of rules, are you sure I can't have a fag?'

Dylan was gasping, but Alyson had been steadfast in stopping him lighting up in her room. She had some standards after all. 'You can have one when you get outside,' she said. 'You've earned one, I reckon, but not in here.'

Dylan smiled. He wasn't complaining. It had been a long day. Never mind the conference and all his adventures, he'd just completed the equivalent of the Ironman course, plus his hangover wasn't going to wait until morning to remind him he had company on his trip back to Manchester.

He started to pull on his clothes. 'Might see you at breakfast,' he said.

'Yes – that would be good,' Alyson replied. Both knew that wasn't going to happen.

Dressed, he gave her a chaste peck on the cheek and casually offered his hand up in a goodbye wave.

As the door clicked behind him, Alyson lay on the bed and gleefully waved her little fists in the air. A very unexpected bonus and a great way of rounding off her conference. She should write about her escapade – there was plenty of material there. She thought back to what she'd told Alison – how she wanted to go mainstream and become a 'serious' author. Well, bugger that. If she'd learned anything this weekend it was 'stick to your knitting'. She reached over for her iPhone and began to tap some bulletpoints into her notes app while they were still fresh in her mind: *Ad man and Eve. Column inches. Multiple insertions. Double spread. Male order.* She could definitely do something with that. She put the phone down to go to sleep, but 30 seconds later picked it up again. She'd had another idea: *Rock 'n' Roll Star. Roll With It. Cigarettes & Alcohol. Acquiesce. Definitely Maybe.* Then it struck her. Yes, *Wonderball* would do very nicely.

At the bottom of the stairwell Dylan was drawing on his first nicotine for some hours. It tasted divine. It had been some night. He thought of Alyson's face illuminated in the bedside lamp as he bade her farewell. How, once the heat of passion had diminished, she'd looked plain and ordinary again. He took another deep pull on his cigarette. Funny how that always happens, he mused. For the past three hours he'd been locked in a fight to the finish with Kylie Minogue and then Dame Edna had somehow reappeared and taken her place. Still, Alyson could teach some of the younger girls he knew a thing or two. She might not know her Christian Louboutins from her Manolo Blahniks, but she could shag for England. Yes, he was very glad he'd joined the ranks of the literary elite. It had been well worth it. He flicked his cigarette end into the bushes and set off across the square to find his room for an all too short sleep.

The rain had long stopped and the air was cool. Large puddles from the storm still dotted the piazza and he took care to step around them. As he neared the rotunda he caught sight of a dark shape floating in the water on the edge of the ornamental lake. The flickering overhead sodium light made it difficult to pick out the silhouette and he stepped closer for a better look. As he peered at the unmoving form the buzzing of the damaged light fitting seemed to get louder, as if he was being attacked by a swarm of hornets. Finally, his focus adjusted sufficiently to discern a naked corpse floating face-down in the water.

SIXTEEN MONTHS LATER

Eric was nervous – as anybody would be at their first-ever book launch. Around him there was a whirligig of excitement as glasses were chinked, air kisses mwah'ed, and hugs exchanged. So this was what it felt like. He clutched his paperback copy of Scrub Me Till I Shine in the Dark and wondered at what time the official business would start.

Julia spotted him and came straight over. 'Eric, it's brilliant to see you.'

'There's a couple of us down from Manchester – safety in numbers, eh?' he replied jovially. He hesitated. Should he? 'This probably isn't the best time but I've got a present for you.' He sheepishly offered up to her the copy of his novel.

'Oh, you got it published after all? How brilliant.'

'Well, no point in leaving it in a drawer, so I bit the bullet.'

'I hope you've signed it for me,' said Julia as she flicked through the pages to the front of the book.

'I did, yes. I hope you're going to do the same for me?'

'Promise. You'll be first,' said Julia.

'I really like the cover and the displays for it,' Eric

ventured. 'That "Dr Who meets Shirley Holmes" is a really good line.'

'It was Dylan who came up with that, you know. Once it lodged in my brain I just couldn't shake it.'

'Really? He told me he had but I didn't believe him.'

'I'm glad you two are friends now. I didn't think that was on the cards. Or you self-publishing your book for that matter.'

'Well, never say never and all that.'

Emily Chatterton rushed over to join them. 'Five minutes, Julia, and then we'll start. Oh, hello…' She couldn't remember Eric's name but knew she'd seen his face somewhere before.

'Eric. Blair. I was at The Write Stuff Conference the year before last.'

'Oh, yes. Hard to forget,' Emily said, pulling a slight face. 'Still, I'll be eternally grateful for that weekend or I would never have discovered The Pendulum Swings – or Julia of course.'

Dylan appeared carrying four glasses of wine. He'd got himself and Eric two each, and now offered one to Julia and Emily as if that had been the order all along. Both declined.

'Ah, your unofficial agent, Julia,' joked the editor. 'It really was kind of him to bring Pendulum to Lancaster for you when you were ill.'

Dylan, Eric and Julia all exchanged conspiratorial glances.

'Did you go again, for last year's conference?' Eric asked Emily.

'Oh, yes. Having found Julia there we wouldn't dare miss another.'

Surprised that the conference was still being held, Dylan enquired, 'Was it as busy as the year before?'

'Busy? It was heaving. They had their best attendance ever according to Chapman Hall.'

'And did Hugo Lockwood turn out again?' Eric wanted to know.

'Oh – he's far too important these days,' Emily replied. 'Reardon's books have been doing a bomb since his unfortunate drowning and Hugo has been mad busy as a result. Still, he's not complaining – he won the literary agent of the year award on the back of it.' Emily didn't think it appropriate to inform them that sales of Reardon's back catalogue had also spiked Franklin & Pope's profits in the past year. For the same reason, she didn't think to mention the killing they'd made on releasing Original Motion after she'd hastily re-signed her former client in a pre-emptive handshake deal with Hugo on the train back from Lancaster.

She looked at her watch. 'Well, this is it, Julia. Time to unleash your literary masterpiece on the book-buying public.'

As the two women made their way to the front of the bookstore Dylan looked at his friend. 'It could be you up there next time, Eric. Are you going to write any more?'

Eric smiled. 'Remember that piece of advice Reardon passed on? "Any writer worth his salt writes to please himself". Well, if I do ever write another, next time I'll know who I'm doing it for.'

ACKNOWLEDGEMENTS

I'd like to thank the following people for their help and support in easing Written Off to publication: Mark Beaumont of Dinosaur for cover design and marketing support; Chris Stamp for illustrations; Glenn Jones of Home Design for the www.paulcarrollink.co.uk website; Gio di Cosmo of Brazen PR for social media expertise; Nathalie Bagnall, Catherine Barrett, Patrick Carroll, Liam Ferguson, Brendan Gore, David Hargreaves, Peter Jones, John Kelly, David Lomax, Gerry McLaughlin, Charles Rose and Nina Webb for first draft feedback and comments. Especial thanks to David Lomax and Patrick Carroll for their eagle-eyed assistance at, respectively, MS and proof stages.

ABOUT THE AUTHOR

Paul Carroll has been drawn to ink and the written word for as long as he can remember. Born and raised in Leeds, Paul studied English at the University of Manchester and went on to form his own PR consultancy, Communique, which he ran for many years. Nowadays Paul concentrates on his writing. His first novel, A Matter of Life and Death, was published by Matador in 2012.